LOSING LADD

Dianne Venetta

LOSING LADD
Book #5

Ladd Springs Series:

LADD SPRINGS ~ #1
LADD FORTUNE ~ #2
HOTEL LADD ~ #3
LADD HAVEN ~ #4
LOSING LADD ~ #5

Other novels by Dianne Venetta

Romantic Women's Fiction
The Gables Trilogy:
JENNIFER'S GARDEN
LUST ON THE ROCKS
WHISPER PRIVILEGES

Women's Fiction
CONDEMN ME NOT

Losing Ladd
Copyright 2013 by Dianne Venetta
ISBN: 978-0-9911182-1-2
Publisher: BloominThyme Press
Editor: Best Foot Forward
Cover Design: Jaxadora Design

Acknowledgements

For a writer, research is critical. Not only because your imagination can take you to some amazing places and spin some wild tales, but because your readers might have been there, done that, actually experienced some of the crazy stuff you come up with! You don't want them reading a scene only to say, *that couldn't happen*. Hospital scenes are a prime example. Doctors and nurses understand the procedures. Life and death situations are nothing new to them. But explosives? Who knows anything about those details?

My nephew, for one. Ex-Navy, he worked as an EOD technician and is well-versed in the mechanics of how bombs are made, what makes them tick—and how to disable them. EOD is short for Explosive Ordinance Disposal, which means it was his job to locate the device, assess its capability and neutralize the threat, protecting your fellow men and women. It's a tough job, especially considering much of his duties were performed underwater. Without his help, I wouldn't have been able to create authentic scenes for this book.

Dedication

This book is dedicated to my family. Without their support, I wouldn't be able to spend hours upon hours playing with my imaginary friends. It's a great life!

Meet the cast of characters of Losing Ladd...

Ernie & Albert Ladd – Brothers of Ladd Springs
Susannah Ladd Wilkins – Sister to Ernie & Albert
Delaney Wilkins – Ernie's niece, married to Nick Harris
Nick Harris – Founder, Harris Hotels
Felicity Wilkins - Delaney's daughter
Travis Parker – Boyfriend to Felicity, twin to Troy
Troy and Casey Parker – Newly married
Cal and Annie Owens – Son of Gerald &
Victoria…Annie is mother to Casey
Jeremiah Ladd - Ernie's forsaken son, father to Casey
Jillian Devane – Hotel developer,
competitor to Nick Harris
Malcolm Ward – Hotel developer, partner to Nick Harris
Lacy Owens Ward – Wife to Malcolm, sister to Annie
Jack Foster – Brother to Cal, Delaney's ex-husband
Beau and Clint Foster – Cal's brothers
Gerald & Victoria Foster – Cal's parents
Hank Dakota – Town lawyer working with Jack
Fran Jones - Owner of Fran's Diner,
aunt to Annie & Lacy
Candi Sweeney - Annie's best friend
Jimmy Sweeney – Candi's nephew, Assistant Mgr.
Fran's Diner

Chapter One

Felicity Wilkins took the sharp turn with a death grip on the steering wheel. Negotiating the rural mountain road as fast as she could, she had to get to the hotel fast. Someone unlocked the gates at the hotel stables, setting the animals loose. Some were gone. Her horse, Blue, was one of them. Visions of what could happen to her black mare inundated her mind.

Felicity's mother had called, her deadpan tone sinking in deeper with every mile. Blue was missing. Gone. Tightening her two-fisted grip, Felicity focused on the way ahead. There'd been a string of horse disappearances in the last month. Properties along the forest were being targeted due to the ease of escape. If anything happened to Blue, Felicity would die. She would die!

With a tap to the brakes, she veered hard to the left, then lurched right, taking the snake turn at high speed. As she barreled down the final stretch of pavement, she prayed no one pulled out of their driveway. She wouldn't be able to stop. The road was heavily lined with forest, nothing but trees and bushes as far as the eye could see, save a few tin mailboxes poking out. A route ingrained in her memory, a road traveled many times with Blue.

Blue. Felicity's heart caught in her throat. The mare had to be okay.

Driving past a wall of rock, Felicity faintly registered the stream of spring water spurting from its façade. The neighbors had inserted a makeshift pipe for easy collection of the water, water that belonged to Ladd Springs. Her family's property. As she passed a rusty old house trailer parked twenty feet off the road, memories of Clem Sweeney flushed through her mind. Not only did he try to steal their water, but he tried to steal their gold. Gold that had been discovered deep in the forest of her family's property little over a year ago. *Her property*. Last year, Uncle Ernie had signed it over to her before he died. Muscles jumped in her jaw. It had been a sore spot between him and her mother, Ernie refusing to give in and sign the deed as promised, but in the end he did. Ernie had signed it over and died weeks later.

At the time, Harris Hotels had been vying for the land to build a hotel. They specialized in luxury eco-resort hotels around the world and wanted to incorporate the Tennessee landscape into their portfolio. At first, her mother resisted. But once she and the chain owner became romantically involved, her position flipped. Felicity leased the land to Harris Hotels, and they transformed the property into a beautiful mountain resort, complete with spa, restaurant and stables. Stables someone had deliberately opened and forced the animals to flee.

Felicity's car reverberated over the wooden planks of the creek bridge, skidding in a cloud of dust as she floored the gas pedal and headed uphill. The staff parking area would be closest to the stables. Spying an open space near a clump of trees, she spun the wheel and braked to a hard stop, pitching her body forward. Pushing out her door, she slammed it closed, startled by the thunder of noise behind her.

She whirled, calling out breathlessly, "Troy!"

Troy Parker's truck rocked back and forth as it too took the gravelly terrain at high speed, mirroring her arrival. He parked haphazardly, jumped out and headed straight for her, his muscular swagger reassuring in her time of need. Relief swept through Felicity. Her mom must have called him to come help. As Troy closed the distance with determined jean-legged strides, she saw concern digging through the brown of his eyes. "Your mom told you?" he asked.

Felicity nodded. "Blue—" she sputtered, words choking away.

"She told me someone unhooked the gates," Troy said. "Is that true? Do you know what this is all about?"

She shook her head, overwhelmed by a horrible help-lessness.

The brown of Troy's gaze darkened, underscored by the black of his T-shirt and cowboy hat. He was not a man to contend with lightly. Not with that matchstick temper of his. "Whoever did this is going to pay, Felicity."

She nodded, suddenly grateful for Troy's brash, bull-headed nature. She wanted whoever did this to pay, to suf-fer—especially if her horse had suffered. Felicity began to shake. "We need to find her."

"We will." Troy grasped Felicity by the arm and directed her toward the stables of Hotel Ladd, a place he loved as dearly as she loved it, marching them onward. Troy and Fe-licity had been friends for as long as she could remember, along with his twin brother, Travis. The three were a trio. They rode together, played together. Horses were in their blood, part of their everyday lives. The thought of anything happening to one of their animals cut deep. Would they find them?

After they passed through a cluster of trees, the packed clay ground was uneven, marked by jutting rocks and gnarled roots, the aroma of pine dominated the shaded trail. Unable to wait, Troy and Felicity began to jog, picking up their pace as they raced through the canopy of green toward the new sta-bles. A creek trailed along their path, the babble nearly inau-dible as fear and uncertainty rang in her mind, the pound of boots jarring her body.

Blue knew this land as well as Felicity, but the hotel sta-bles were new to her, having moved in only weeks ago. Sure-ly Blue wouldn't run off. She might wander, but she wouldn't go far.

Unless she had been frightened. But her mother didn't relay any such detail. Probably because Felicity hadn't given her the chance. The minute she heard Blue was missing, she ended the call, jumped in her car and peeled out of Casey and Troy's driveway in two seconds flat. She'd been visiting with them and the baby when her mother called. As manager of the stables, the horses were her mom's responsibility. It was a job she took to heart. Like Felicity, Delaney Wilkins Harris adored horses. She lived and breathed them. If anything happened to any one of the animals, her mother would be devastated. Felicity glanced to her side. As would Troy. He was a horseman through and through. He could work a horse quicker and better than anyone, retrain them for riders or break them in for the first time, his recent performance in the stables of Hotel Ladd proof positive. Hired by her mother, Troy had been in heaven. It was his second chance, his dream come true. Until her father stole it from him.

Her father, Jack Foster. An evil man, he had attacked her mother one night and Troy jumped in to defend her. The two fought, a gun was fired, then afterward her father lied like the devil to have Troy wrongly charged with assault. Assault with a deadly weapon. Troy had pointed a gun at her father—her mother's gun to be precise—using it as a way to protect the two of *them* from the real criminal. Her father. Could he be responsible for setting the horses loose?

"Are you okay?" Troy asked.

Felicity was falling behind. Now they were out in the open air, the August sun was taking its toll, as was the incline. The trail was graded but steep. Lengths of white four-board fencing lined their path up to the stables. At the top of the hill the distant tin roof reflected silvery white.

Urgency clawed at her. "Fine," she muttered, her chest heaving under labored breath. Troy slowed and she cried, "But we have to get there!"

"You sure you don't need to slow down?" he asked.

Perspiration gathered at her neck and beneath her blouse, a sure sign her fair skin would be flushed red. "Yes," she replied and pushed at him to continue forward. Blue needed her.

Her mother needed her.

Within minutes they reached the level ground surrounding the stables and paddocks. Her mother emerged from an open doorway of the stables, her bearing rigid, tense. Long white blonde hair was pulled back into a ponytail; her low-waisted jeans hung snug on her slender frame, her body fit from a life outdoors. She wore a navy tank top, her bare arms buff. But that was her mom. Delaney Wilkins Harris would rather be out hiking, throwing sweet feed or sitting on the back of her horse, Sadie, than primping with fuss and makeup.

As she approached her mother, the chip of fear in her brown eyes stopped Felicity cold. Was her mom's Palomino gone, too? "Is Sadie okay?"

"Fine. But the others are still missing. I've got several of the hands out looking, but you two are the ones I need." Delaney glanced between Felicity and Troy. "The horses will respond to the sound of your voices."

"What happened?" Felicity asked.

Delaney slid a hand over her shiny head of hair, then dropped it to her waistband. "Someone came in this morning and unlatched the gates. Several of the horses stayed around but most of them left."

Because they were new to Ladd Stables. Because the animals came from other ranches and weren't fully acclimated to their new home yet. As though reading her thoughts, her mom said, "Blue is probably down by the old stables. But Spirit..." She turned to Troy and his expression went slack. "Spirit is a different story."

"He's not ready for release."

Delaney returned a minor shake of her head. Spirit wasn't ready for riders, let alone free range.

"He could be anywhere," Troy mumbled.

"You're the one he'll respond to, Troy," Delaney said. "If anyone can find him and bring him back home, it's you."

Felicity looked to Troy. He'd been working with the horse since the animal's arrival. He'd come to Ladd Stables from a rancher friend in Georgia with a warning. He wasn't suitable for accommodating guest trails rides. But her mom took the animal anyway. Said she fell in love with the mahogany Quarter Horse the minute she laid eyes on him, and she was taking him. It was an emotion Felicity understood. And her assessment appeared to be right on, once Troy got his hands on the horse. He'd made huge progress but it was a process, one he hadn't quite finished.

Because he lost his job. Because of her father. Felicity closed her eyes. *Please don't let him lose the horse, too.*

"Who would have done such a thing?" Felicity demanded in a surge of anger.

"I have my suspicions, but right now we need to find those animals."

Something moved behind her mother's gaze. Did she know?

Troy responded immediately. Looking to Felicity, he asked, "You goin' down to the old stables?" She nodded. "Okay. I'll take the north side. Call me if you see anything, you hear?"

"Will do," she replied.

"Felicity!"

At the sound of her name, she turned. Travis Parker jogged up to them, his gaze darting between her and her mother. "I came as fast as I could. What's going on?"

Felicity circled her palm around his bicep, drawing him close. The smooth round of his muscle was reassuring in its strength, his calm level-headed presence comforting to her nerves. Travis was an identical twin to Troy, the brothers sharing the same build, sporting the same dark eyes and over-grown layers of brunette hair complete with a strong jaw line and determined gaze. Unlike Troy who never left home without his cowboy hat, Travis saved his for rides and hikes.

Yet both shared her love of horses.

Travis honed in on her mom. "Do we know who did this?"

"I think Jeremiah Ladd had something to do with it. Someone paid his debt to the casino, making him a free man." Delaney glanced briefly to Troy. "He's out and he's back in town."

Travis raked a hand through his hair, a fiery gaze landing on his brother. "You'd better watch your back."

"Oh my gosh—" Felicity's pulse tripped. Frightened for Troy's safety, she darted a glance between the two of them. "You don't think he would come back to cause trouble, do you?"

Travis glared at his brother. "Troy didn't exactly befriend the man while he was in town."

"Back off, brother."

"Well, it's true," Travis shot back. "What did you think would happen when you tried to sleep with his girlfriend?"

Troy angled toward Travis. "I did no such thing."

"I caught you in the act!"

Delaney stepped between the boys. "Stop it you two. Infighting will get us nowhere."

Felicity thought Travis had some nerve bringing up the past at a time like this. Jeremiah Ladd was not a man to take lightly. Sure, Troy might have gotten mixed up with the man's girlfriend, but it didn't give Jeremiah the right to hurt him. Didn't Travis care that Troy could be in serious danger? Didn't he remember what happened the last time Jeremiah was in town? Not only had he tried to take Ladd Springs from Felicity and her mother, but he threatened Uncle Ernie's life! Thank goodness her uncle was a tough old goat and didn't take grief from anyone, including his own son. He'd signed the property to her and that was the end of that. Uncle Ernie didn't care what Jeremiah wanted or why he wanted it.

Memory cut loose a flurry of angst. According to her mom, Uncle Ernie had even gone so far as to have Jeremiah beaten and left for dead in the street to stop him from interfering. Felicity centered on Troy. Would he now receive the brunt of Jeremiah's revenge?

"He's back," Delaney intervened, "and I don't think this it's any coincidence, but it has nothing to do with Troy." She paused, settling a heavy gaze on Felicity. "It has everything to do with us."

Chapter Two

Travis stepped back, tugged at his plaid shirt and doused his anger. Felicity needed him. She needed to find her horse, and that's why he was here. He'd deal with Troy another time. "C'mon," Travis said, taking his girlfriend by the arm. "Let's go after Blue."

Felicity didn't resist, though he could see the hesitation in her soft green eyes. As usual, her strawberry blonde hair was pulled back into a French braid, a frame of fine strands curling around her face. In the afternoon heat, her fair skin was flushed pink, brightening the spray of freckles across her cheeks. Felicity had always been sensitive at heart, but being hung up on Troy's well-being, currently jeopardized because of his own stupid actions, was plain wrong. If Troy hadn't tried to make it with Jeremiah Ladd's trashy girlfriend, he'd have nothing to worry about. He wouldn't be wearing a bullseye on his back. But that was Troy. Act first, think second. Travis deemed it would ultimately be his undoing.

"Go on," Troy told Felicity. "I've gotta go after Spirit."

"But what if Jeremiah finds you?"

"We don't know it's Jeremiah," Travis interjected. Sending a dodgy gaze toward Felicity's mom. Running off half-cocked was Troy's specialty, not his. Miss Delaney should know better. Unfortunately, she shared Troy's hair-trigger impulse control.

"Travis is right," Delaney said. "We don't know for sure who did this. The more important matter is finding those horses."

Relieved by her retreat, Travis asked, "How many others have gone missing?"

"Other than Blue and Spirit, we've got five unaccounted for. One of the guys called and said he located two of the animals grazing in a field on the other side of the river. The other three might be of a similar mind. I've asked the men to check all the clearings."

"Spirit won't be in the open," Troy said. "He's too skittish."

Delaney looked to Troy, and Travis felt an admiration string between them. "I'm going to let you decide on where to look for Spirit."

"Yes, ma'am."

Delaney Wilkins Harris was like a mother to them. Hanging out with Felicity since they were kids, Travis and Troy spent nearly every day at her house or on horseback along the river. They'd been a team, an inseparable trio. The first cracks in their bond didn't show up until high school when it became clear as a mountain stream both brothers harbored feelings for Felicity, feelings that went beyond friendship. In the beginning he and Troy joked about it, but one afternoon it came to fists. Travis insisted Felicity wasn't Troy's type. She was more like him. Studious, more sophisticated. Troy flew out of control and the two hit the ground, rolling and punching. It had been ugly, both walking away with bruises. In the end, Felicity chose him. Travis had won and Troy couldn't get past it. He'd stewed over the loss for weeks. Until he decided to hook up with Casey—right after he was messing with her father's girlfriend. Disgust roiled in Travis' gut. Sometimes he wondered how they could be brothers.

"Be careful, Troy," Her gaze held immense affection as Felicity said, "I don't want anything to happen to you."

Travis' stiffened as Felicity's words lit into him. *Maybe I chose the wrong brother. Maybe Casey's the smart one and I'm the loser.* The remarks from months ago still cut raw. Felicity seemed more concerned with Troy than him. And Casey and her brand new baby, too. She brought clothes for the kid, played the flute for her. She went to their cabin practically every day. Staring at his girlfriend, Travis felt the pinch. Since when did they rank higher than him?

"I'll be fine," Troy replied. "You go on with Travis."

Travis agreed. "C'mon," he said quickly and led Felicity away.

She followed his lead, cruising down the trail, keeping pace with him. The sun was scorching today, not a cloud in the sky, and Travis was hot. Mostly from his run up the hill, but the temperature had to be pushing a hundred. Swiping a hand through the hair on his forehead, he slid it back. Grass was dry, more brown than green. There hadn't been much rain lately, and the fields were beginning to wear. Casting a sideways glance, he could see Felicity was hot too. Not only was her skin flushed from exertion, but her neck was slick beneath her braid, her green shirt spotted with perspiration. The crux of her concern could be found in her face. While orange-blonde strands of hair caught and reflected the sunlight, reminding him of many a day spent outdoors in the sunshine, her emerald green eyes were knotted with worry.

Travis hated that she was upset, but at least she called him to come over and help her look for Blue. Ever since Felicity had overheard the Foster wives gossiping about how her father hit her mother and that's why she dumped him, she seemed changed, as if what happened between her parents ten years ago had bearing on her life today.

It didn't. He'd heard the rumors. People talked. They whispered. Didn't change anything about who Felicity was today. He was only surprised she hadn't heard the talk before. But she'd heard the women that night and totally went off on her mother, reaming her a new one after he'd dropped Felicity off at the cabin. Travis heard them arguing before he made it down the porch steps and felt bad. It wasn't Miss Delaney's fault that her husband was a jerk, but Felicity didn't see it that way. She was mad because her mother never told her, that she had to find it out from strangers.

Strangers that were family. Travis could understand why Miss Delaney didn't say anything. How do you tell a kid her daddy's a monster? Then, as if his past transgressions weren't bad enough, the guy attacked her mom in the stables one night, and that's when Felicity woke up. She turned on *him*, forgiving her mother completely. Only Jack Foster decided to pin the crime of assault on his brother, because Troy happened to be in the stables and jumped and saved Miss Delaney.

"Travis, if we don't find Blue I don't know what I'll do."

He placed an arm around her narrow shoulders and pulled her close. "Don't worry. We'll find her."

"Do you think Jeremiah did this?"

"Don't know. But what I do know is that if it was him, we'll figure it out."

"How?"

The way he did everything. Clues. Research. Fit the pieces of the puzzle together. "We'll gather evidence. Whoever did it had to leave fingerprints behind. A hair sample, something."

Bodies bumping as they walked in close contact, Felicity glanced up at him. "I don't think my mom will call the police."

"Why not?"

"If she didn't call it after being attacked, I doubt she'll call them now. Especially after the way they treated her."

Travis nodded. Felicity might have a point there. Apparently Officer Gavin Shore didn't give Felicity's mom a warm welcome when she went down to the police station to give her statement. Of course, her ex-husband had already been there and filled the man's head with lies but still, that was his job. Gavin Shore was officer of the law, sworn to uphold The Constitution. Whether he believed her or not, whether he liked her or not, Officer Shore should have treated her with respect and dutifully taken her statement. The fact that he didn't could work against him in a court of law, a fact Travis had tried to explain to Felicity at the time.

But she didn't understand things like he did. She was an artist, a flutist. She dealt in feelings and rhythm. Not Travis. He dealt in facts and logic. He was going to be a lawyer. He was going to be the man who defended the wrongly accused. Even if it included the likes of his brother, who in this case happened to be innocent. While he didn't approve of Troy's choice not to attend college, or his actions that knocked up his girlfriend, the two having a baby out of wedlock, Travis didn't want to see Troy convicted of a crime he didn't commit.

Entering a wooded section of the property, Travis and Felicity headed off the main trail. He welcomed the shade, brushing the moisture from his upper lip. This was a shortcut through the original Ladd homestead, leading to the old stables Felicity and her mom used before Nick Harris built the new ones. Mr. Harris was the man who owned and built the hotel, transforming the natural beauty of Ladd Springs into a luxury retreat for wealthy guests from around the world. Specializing in "green" development, he made a business of carving properties into the land, incorporating his hotels into the landscape so guests could feel at one with the nature of their surroundings. While Mr. Harris didn't actually own Ladd Springs, leasing the right to use the land for his hotel from Felicity, he married Delaney's mom, which made him family. Felicity had received title to the property after her Uncle Ernie signed it over prior to his passing.

But she didn't own all of it. Her mom had her sign over half the property to Troy's wife, Casey. Apparently Casey was Jeremiah's daughter from a relationship he had in high school. Her mother had finally been able to prove the point when they hauled Jeremiah off to jail, making it real convenient to court-order a DNA sample. And when the results came back positive, the matter was settled. Casey deserved half because she was kin. Family.

Travis didn't care for Casey or her mother. He thought it greedy of them to fight for the land in the first place, but Miss Delaney saw it differently, and hers was the opinion that counted with Felicity. Not like anyone would argue with her. Miss Delaney was a kind woman, but she was a tough one.

"Blue!" Felicity called out randomly. Moving a branch from her path, she yelled again, "Blue!"

Travis followed close behind, trampling over underbrush as he scanned the sea of leaves and tree trunks. Blue wouldn't be in this area. The foliage was too dense.

Felicity cupped hands to her mouth and called out for the horse again.

"She's probably hanging by the stables," Travis said, "eating old feed from the ground."

"Blue wouldn't eat stale food," Felicity huffed.

"Animals don't care if it's stale. If they can smell it, they're gonna eat it."

Felicity stomped on a dead branch on the ground. The loud crack seemed to underscore her displeasure with him. Travis raised his brow. Was there anything he could do right these days?

Ahead, Travis detected the first sign of the old stables, the outline of black-brown decayed wood and sagging tin roof just beyond a group of tightly packed trees. He could almost smell the rotting structure from here. Felicity walked faster as they neared the stables, heedless to the boulders in her way. "Blue?" she hollered, leaping over the side of a huge rock, its gray surface covered with patches of white fungus. "Blue? Are you here?"

Scrambling over a fallen tree, Felicity hurried to the structure. A rusted-out wheel barrow was parked to one side, a busted fence post stood feet from the entrance. The place reeked of wet mold and mildew, mixed with the dank scent of rotting leaves.

Felicity dashed into the stable, then darted out just as quick. "She's not here."

Her crestfallen expression tore at Travis. "Maybe she's farther up, toward the cabin."

Felicity turned, took a few steps in that direction and murmured, "I don't see her."

"She's probably behind a tree," he suggested.

Trailing Felicity's steps, Travis tracked her all the way to the trail opening, the one that led to Ernie's old cabin and a small clearing that marked the trail up to her mother's place. No Blue. "Where else could she be?"

Travis came to a stop by Felicity's side, hating the heartbreak in her eyes. "A hundred places," he replied. "Maybe she's down by the river. If I were her, that's where I'd go on a hot day like this."

Where Travis intended the comment to lighten the mood, his remark resulted in the opposite. "Not by herself. She's never ventured that far without me."

Part of him agreed. Before the hotel stables were built, Felicity and her mom would let the horses loose, allowing them free grazing in the open pastures. Most of the time, that's where he and Felicity would find them when they went looking to ride. Occasionally the animals would hang out in the woods, preferring shade to the heat of the sun. Never once did they find them by the river. Placing hands to her shoulders, Travis looked her in the eye, willing her to believe him. "Blue is okay. We'll find her."

"How many horses have you recovered?" Nick Harris asked as he strode into the stable office. An air of quiet confidence flowed in around him, filling Delaney's working space with his masculine presence. Standing six-four in boots, his long legs rising into a tapered waist and broad shoulders, Delaney felt the weight of her concern lift. Where she once considered his black eyes swarthy and suspicious, she now found them attractive and soothing. When Nick walked into a room, it felt like he was lifting whatever ailed her at the moment. "Two. An Appaloosa and a Quarter Horse."

"The new one?"

She shook her head. "Troy's out looking for him now."

"Good," he said and circled her desk. Taking her hand, he pulled her from her chair enfolding her in a hug. Delaney melted into the hard lean line of his body, immersed herself in the woodsy spice of his cologne. She didn't consider herself a weak, needy woman, but next to Nick, she felt every ounce of her femininity.

Kissing the top of her head, he said, "I talked to Malcolm."

"And?" she asked, pulling away.

"He's going to call his pal in Vegas and find out who paid the marker for Jeremiah."

"Do you still think Jillian had something to do with it?"

"Damn straight I think she had something to do with it, and as soon as Malcolm calls his man, we'll know for sure."

Delaney hated to utter the woman's name, but it did seem she was the most likely culprit. A vixen of the highest degree, she'd already proven herself capable of such tactics. Nick's jilted ex-lover, hotel developer Jillian Devane, wanted nothing more than to see their lives filled with misery. It seemed like her life's calling had turned from building hotels to exacting revenge against Nick and Delaney. One phone call from Nick had iced her first attempt. Her last had been spoiled by none other than Annie Owens.

Jillian had tried to purchase Casey's half of Ladd Springs. Annie had tried to negotiate a sale so she and Casey could get their hands on the money, but reneged on the deal before closing. Seems Annie realized there was more to happiness than dollar signs, a lesson learned with the help of one Cal Foster. Jillian had been livid to hear she would not have the pleasure of ruining Harris Hotels from the comfort of the adjoining property and left town in a huff.

Unfortunately, it didn't stop the threats. And there was only one person who could pay fifty thousand dollars on Jeremiah's behalf—one person with a motive. Jillian Devane. Delaney swallowed back a rush of nerves. "What are you going to do if it was her?" she asked, battling a slew of mixed emotion.

Anger thrashed in the black of his gaze. The lines around his mouth hardened. "I'm going to make her wish she'd stayed in Brazil."

"You don't think she's coming here, do you?" Jillian was the last person Delaney wanted to see in Tennessee. Jillian Devane once held an attraction for her husband. Despite her tendency for revenge and cutthroat business dealings, Jillian had the looks and body that didn't quit. Delaney didn't consider herself an insecure woman, but putting Nick and Jillian in the same room might remind him of why they'd gotten together in the first place! After all, Jillian had tried to seduce Troy the last time she was in town. Why not take another swing at Nick?

Nick looked away, his gaze drifting through the pane-glass window and into the stables. "If she did have something to do with Jeremiah's release, she can't be far behind."

"But how could she know about Jeremiah? She never met him. Not that I don't trust you, but that part still doesn't make sense."

Nick turned back to her, his face devoid of pleasure. "Jillian has her ways. She's not a woman to be underestimated. And until she gets her revenge, she'll use whatever means necessary to do so."

Gets her revenge. On Nick. On them. Delaney glanced around the office, the stables beyond, her mind filled with horrific thoughts of flames and destruction. In the past, Jillian had chosen fire as the method to exact her revenge on a rival hotel. Delaney gulped. Would she do so again?

Chapter Three

Jack Foster pushed in through the front door of Whiskey Joe's bar in need of a drink. Twiddling his thumbs as he waited for his trial against Troy Parker was not his idea of fun, but his mother insisted he stay in town for trial prep. The attorney she hired out of Nashville had a busy schedule and Jack needed to be available. At the guy's whim, he mused sourly. The man might be decent when it came to a courtroom, but he was arrogant, refusing to give Jack more than an hour's notice when he or one of his people were in town to work on the case. Usually one of his peons. Too busy for menial evidence collection himself, the guy had only made two appearances, one in the beginning for a quick meet and greet and one a week ago, at his mother's behest. She wanted to firm things up, make sure there weren't any loose ends that needed tying—around Troy's throat.

During the meeting, the guy had the gall to try and convince Jack to drop the charges, on account of it was a "he said-she said" deal with two against one, compounded by the fact Delaney and Troy were longstanding members of the community. *And he wasn't?* Living in Nashville for the last ten years didn't negate the value of his family's reputation in town. Jack's daddy owned the biggest bank for a hundred miles and their ranch was the finest three counties wide. If that didn't equate to upstanding member of the community Jack didn't know what did. Especially against a kid with a troubled past.

Jack sized up the Whiskey Joe's lounge crowd. Unlike the bars in Nashville, this place was cramped in size, poorly lit and smelled like they hadn't cracked a window in years. Two couples were seated at high-tops located on the opposite side of a dance floor while a few guys sat hunkered over the bar. Pretty slim-pickings. What did he expect for a Wednesday night in a Podunk town?

As he cruised to an open center seat, a guy three stools over threw back a swallow of his drink. His profile caught Jack mid-stride and he practically stumbled. Medium build, sandy blond hair, bright royal blue button-down, but it was the guy's mannerisms that rang familiar.

Was that Ladd? Smacking a hand to the bar, Jack's focus zoomed in on the man. *Well, I'll be...*

It is! That's Jeremiah Ladd. Without hesitation, Jack walked over and asked, "Jeremiah?"

Maintaining a hand on his glass as it sat on the bar, the man looked up. Light brown eyes were framed by hard lines. It took a second, but the mistrustful gaze melted away. "Jack Foster?"

"One and the same," Jack replied happily.

Swiveling on his seat, Jeremiah opened into a smile. "Wow. How long has it been? Ten, twenty years?"

Jack leaned a hip against the bar and said, "Gotta be at least twenty. Last time I saw you, you were on your way out of town with the cops nipping at your tail."

Jeremiah chuckled, easing back in his seat. "Now you know I didn't have anything to do with robbing that gas station."

Jack smiled. He didn't care one way or another. "Did they ever catch up with you?"

"Nope. Never did."

Glancing to a bartender making his way over, Jack asked, "Mind if I join you?"

"Have a seat," Jeremiah offered and squared himself with the bar.

"What'll it be, sir?" the bartender asked. No more than twenty-one years of age, the kid looked barely legal to serve alcohol. For a moment, Jack felt old. A brief moment. Flicking a glance to Jeremiah's glass, the amber liquid glimmering in the dim light, Jack ordered, "Jack Daniels. Neat."

"Coming right up."

Jack half-watched the kid as he grabbed a black-labeled bottle, uncapped it and poured the whiskey into a glass. Jeremiah took another sip from his drink as the bartender delivered Jack's. "Start a tab?"

"Sure."

Without another word, the young man headed back down the bar to a cash register where he rang in the sale. Then he grabbed a paper ticket and jotted down a note. Jack pulled a deep swallow of whiskey, a whiff of alcohol flaring his nostrils as the liquid fired down his throat. *That was a long time coming.*

"So how the hell have you been, Jack? Last I heard, you were carousing the streets of Nashville."

"Was, until some sweetheart sicked her ill-tempered boyfriend on me." Jeremiah's laugh was quick and hearty. "Damn near busted my jaw and got me fired."

Raising his glass, Jeremiah smirked. "Broads."

Jack grunted. "Speaking of broads, I hear you and my ex had a bit of a run-in last time you were in town."

"Is that what she called it?"

Jack shrugged. "She wasn't doin' the telling, but I gathered you two went at it over the property."

"Ladd Springs belongs to me," Jeremiah said, a veil of anger dropping over his gaze. Thinly veiled, it was palpable. "She and her daughter swindled it from Ernie before he died, and I aim to remind them of the fact."

The venom spitting from Jeremiah's eyes gave Jack pause. Maybe the rumors were true. He'd heard Jeremiah had threatened to kill his old man. Looking at him, he believed every word of it. Jeremiah's hazel eyes were grayed. Flat. "Delaney and I had our own run-in a while back."

His interest caught. Jeremiah lifted his brow. "What kind of run-in?"

"She pulled a gun on me and had her little boyfriend jump me."

"Little?" Jeremiah sneered. "The guy's a monster."

Jack chuckled at the mistake. "Not her husband. Troy Parker. I think the two have something going on."

Jeremiah gaped at him. "The twin? The bullish one?"

"That's him," Jack said, sucking back another swig of whiskey, satisfied to see Jeremiah's wheels churn with malice as he connected the dots. Stoke the flame. Make waves. The more people sided against Delaney the better. "He's a punk and I'm taking him to court."

A grin swept the disbelief from Jeremiah's expression. "I wouldn't mind a crack at that kid myself. He was taking a hit at my woman when she was in town, and I'd like to see him pay. What's the charge?"

"Criminal assault with a deadly weapon should do the trick."

Jeremiah's pleasure deepened. "That's a felony."

"Should put him away for a while, give him something to think about."

With a shake of his head, Jeremiah chortled, then tossed back another swallow. "Nice to know I'm not the only one who isn't a fan when it comes to Delaney Wilkins." Nailing him with a fleeting glance, Jeremiah added, "I mean, I know she's your ex and all, but that woman needs to be taught a lesson."

"Agreed. I take it kinda personal when a woman points a gun at my head."

Jeremiah nodded. "And you say Troy helped her?"

"Backed her up and made it two against one."

"Damn."

"You know he knocked your kid up, right?" Jeremiah's expression closed, as though he didn't have a kid. "Annie's daughter, Casey? He got her pregnant then left town. Ditched her but he's back."

Jeremiah's gaze soured. "So I heard..."

"Did you also hear that Annie married my brother?" Jack rubbed his fingers together. "She hit the jackpot. Cal has money. Big money."

"Really?" Jeremiah drew the word out as he visibly appraised the situation. "Well, that sounds interesting."

"Yeah. He's managing the new hotel and thinks he's Mr. Big in town." Bitterness curdled on Jack's tongue. "Well I'm gonna take care of him, too."

"How so?"

"The good old-fashioned way. I'm gonna cause him grief right where it hurts. Delaney, too. I've had it up to here with her," he said, taking a swipe at his throat.

Jeremiah rolled his lips and finished the last of his whiskey. Plunking it down, he summoned the bartender. Jack finished the last of his and ordered another round with Jeremiah.

Talk of Delaney and Cal sharpened an edge in him. It grated on him that Cal had been given the position as General Manager. What experience did he have? Momma said he managed a retirement community in Arizona, a far cry from running an international hotel. Delaney was head manager of the stables, as if she knew anything about being a boss. She knew horses, he'd give her. But people?

Delaney's people skills left a lot to be desired. Felicity was the rising star. She was young and beautiful and talented... Jack had been looking forward to reestablishing a relationship with her and then rubbing Delaney's nose in it. He wanted to prove that his daughter took after his side of the family, with a future beyond the four corners of this stale town. Who was Delaney to stand between a man and his daughter, preventing them from forgiving the past and moving forward?

But she did. Delaney stepped in it thick, filling Felicity's head with lies so she turned against him, too. Grabbing the fresh glass of whiskey, Jack drank deeply. The alcohol cut across his tongue, raced down his limbs and pummeled the tension from his muscles. Delaney would be sorry. They all would.

"Well," Jeremiah offered, "maybe I can help you out with your Delaney problem."

"Help me out?"

"Seems to me we have a common goal—payback against Delaney."

"You have something in mind?"

Jeremiah's grin turned wicked. "Oh, I have something in mind all right, and the gears have started to shift."

Enclosing his palm around the low-ball, Jack cocked a brow. "You have my attention."

"Jack Foster." The familiar purr of familiarity yanked his cord, spinning him around in his seat. Jillian Devane smiled, a naughty gleam entering her tiger-eyed gaze as she said, "I didn't expect to see you here."

His pulse skipped. "Jillian. I didn't know you were in town." Dressed in skintight jeans and strappy gold heels, her fitted satin tank shimmered creamy gold in the subtle lighting.

Flashing cat eyes toward Jeremiah, she replied, "I only just returned."

Standing abruptly, Jack reached out for her. "What brings you back?"

"Business, darling. Urgent business that could not wait." She drew a finger along Jack's collar and up his neck, igniting his libido. Deepening her smile, she said, "It's nice to know you've missed me, *cariño*."

"Who wouldn't miss a beautiful woman like you?" Jeremiah asked.

Jillian turned her attention to Jeremiah. "Sweet talk will get you most everywhere," she said, her accent husky.

Jeremiah smiled, more comfortable than Jack would have liked him. Reaching for Jillian's hand, Jeremiah lifted it to his lips and kissed the satiny brown skin. Locking his gaze to hers, he replied, "It only gets sweeter from here."

Jack felt an instant resentment over Jeremiah's intrusion. This was Jack's score, not his. "Have a seat," he said, indicating the stool next to *him*. "I'll buy you a drink. Care for the usual?" he asked, making sure Jeremiah heard him loud and clear. The usual, as in *I know this woman, I know what she likes*.

Jillian smiled between the two. "Yes. That would be fine."

As she slipped onto the barstool, Jack took her in more thoroughly, surprised by her appearance in town. He imagined her previous hasty departure had something to do with Nick and Delaney, but he couldn't be sure. He'd heard talk of threats and past quarrels but nothing concrete. One thing he was sure of—he was glad to see her. "So how long are you in town?"

She smiled sweetly, then pursed her glossy lips. "Depends."

"Depends on what?"

"On how successful I find my time in your small town."

Upon the addition to their party, the bartender appeared. "What can I get for you?"

"The lady will have a Cosmo," Jack ordered.

The kid tipped his head and went to work, drawing a martini glass from an overhead shelf slide, then reaching for a bottle of vodka, a container of cranberry juice and some ice. "So," Jack began, savoring her presence, the spicy perfume emanating from her body. Her cleavage was prominently displayed for his enjoyment, impeded only by strips of her shiny black hair. "What's on the agenda? Another land purchase? Resuming your hotel plans?" Before she could answer, he waggled his brow. "I sure would enjoy seeing Harris Hotels struggle against some competition."

"They will get what's coming to them," she said, her thick Spanish accent catching on the "them."

"Sounds more ominous than business," Jack observed. Sounded to him more like a vendetta. Was Jillian jealous? Was that why she was here? During their time together last fall, Jillian had mentioned she and Nick used to be partners. Bringing his glass to his lips, Jack wondered if it included the bedroom. Knowing what little he knew of the woman, it wasn't a stretch to assume that partnership included a romantic interest.

Jeremiah sat idle, though clearly dialed into their conversation.

Jillian simply smiled, refusing to elaborate.

The ring of a cell phone rose from Jeremiah's waistband. Unclipping the phone, he answered, "Hello?"

Jack watched Jillian who was watching Jeremiah. A placid smile sat on her mouth, but Jack detected a keen interest in the depths of her dark gaze. Did she find Jeremiah attractive?

"See you in a few," Jeremiah said, then ended the call. Downing the last of his drink, he slapped a twenty dollar bill on the bar as the bartender arrived with Jillian's chilled red drink. "Been expecting that call and gotta go." Sliding off the rear of his stool, he stood and withdrew a business card from his wallet. "Good to see you again, Jack." Handing the card over to him, he said, "Give me a call. We'll talk."

Jack took the card and slipped it into his back pocket. "Will do. And good to see you, too. Glad to know we're of like mind."

Jeremiah tapped Jillian with a gaze and grinned. "You bet we are."

Jillian pulled the angular glass closer to her. "A friend of yours?"

"An old friend."

She sat expectantly, waiting for him to elaborate. Jack wasn't going to go into detail but figured a little couldn't hurt. She didn't know the man. "That's Jeremiah Ladd. Delaney's cousin."

"Ah..." she responded. Raising her glass ever so slowly, Jillian brought it to her lips and took the smallest sip, hardly leaving a lipstick mark. Setting it down, she looked to Jack. "You knew him growing up?"

"Sure did. We hung out—when he wasn't hanging around Delaney, that is."

"Kissing cousins?" she asked, a hint of mockery in her bronze gaze.

"No, nothing like that. Delaney was a Tomboy and Jeremiah close in age. They lived on the same property, so it made sense they'd spend a lot of time together. We all hung out together in high school."

"I see."

Jack wasn't convinced that she did, but at the moment he didn't care. He only had one thing on his mind when it came to Jillian Devane. "So where are you staying?"

Jillian pursed her glossy tawny lips, the move causing a tingle in his loins. "Is that an invitation?"

"You know you have a standing invitation, doll."

She smiled. "I thought I'd check in to the new hotel."

"Pretty brazen move, don't you think?"

Jillian raised her glass to him and replied, "Do you not think I will be welcome?"

"I do not, but I doubt that will stop you."

She winked, and sipped. "It won't."

Chapter Four

Delaney closed the door to her office. Walking back to her desk, phone at her ear, she said, "There's still no sign of the horses, Cal. I'm afraid they might have been picked up."

"Let's hope not, but I hear what you're saying."

"I was hoping you could give Beau a call. Put the word out in case any of them show up." Delaney didn't want to think the worst but facts were facts. Blue had not surfaced and she of all horses knew her way around this land. If she was gone, it might be due to foul play. Beau Foster was Cal's brother and head man over at Misty Mountain Ranch. Cal's family bred horses and knew the players in the industry. If someone picked up the horses and tried to sell them, Beau could find out.

Unless of course the person responsible kept the animals for themselves.

"No problem," Cal replied. "As soon as we hang up, I'll give him a ring. Besides Blue, how many others are you missing?"

"At this point only Blue and Spirit." The two animals that meant the most to Felicity and Troy. "We found the others in the forest, on the back side of the stables."

"Okay, and Delaney—"

"Yes?"

"Don't give up. We'll find those horses."

She heaved a sigh and rolled her gaze through the plate-glass window, where a view of a stable full of horses served as constant reminder. The lengthy corridor cut between two dozen stalls housing quality horses. Most were new to Delaney but Cal understood the implications. Felicity's horse had been with her since grade school and Spirit...well, Spirit was fast-becoming Troy's professional salvation. Delaney didn't want to lose either animal, but the loss would hit her kids hardest. Her kids. Troy was like one of her own. A kid who'd had a rough go of it lately, the only bright spot being the birth of his daughter, Cassidy Jo Grace. "Thanks, Cal."

Ending the call, memories of the emergency delivery in the barn pulled warm feelings of pride. Casey had gone into labor two months premature and Troy had saved the day, single-handedly delivering his child amongst the hay and dust. Fortunately Cassidy was healthy and happy, coming home from the hospital after only a few weeks. Delaney shook her head. Troy was amazing. There was no other word to describe him. But his hardships weren't over. Jack continued to press forward with his phony charges of assault, jeopardizing Troy's freedom. If she couldn't convince a judge and jury that Troy had only attacked Jack in the act of defending her, he would go to jail.

For a very long time.

A tremor raced through her, but Delaney shook it off. Wasn't gonna happen. Jack was a liar and he would not prevail. Gavin Shore might not have given her an open-minded reception when she tried to give her statement about Jack's attack, but a jury would. They'd hear every word she had to say, provided Jack didn't drop this stunt of his beforehand. Delaney scooped the day's schedule from her desk and perused it. A good chunk of her believed dropping the case was his plan, going to trial a ruse. He had no intention of going through with it because he knew he would lose. Doubt fluttered in her belly. *He had to lose*. Too much was riding on it.

Checking the time, she plunked the schedule back to her desk and left the office. She only had an hour between now and the first ride, and she had yet to check in on Albert. Since Uncle Ernie died, Albert had no one to look after him. Not that he did a whole heck of a lot to "look after," but Delaney swore the man wouldn't eat if someone didn't set a plate of food in front of him. Blowing strands of hair from her face, she set out for the trail to his place. Nick had a small cabin built for Albert near the river restaurant, accessible by a small winding road and wooded trails for those who knew their way around the property. Albert spent most of his time sitting on a front porch rocker, watching the water as it rushed over and around the boulders. When he wasn't outside, he was indoors watching the cable television Nick had installed. It was a lonely existence but one Albert insisted he enjoyed. Mentally preparing herself for the endless conversation about squirrels and trees, she entered the forest and headed downhill for her "visit."

Cal dialed the number for his family's ranch, calculating the odds of someone running off with Blue and Spirit. He doubted either happened. Spirit was too cagey to allow anyone near him—anyone but Troy—and Blue was as loyal to Felicity as the stripes on a flag. No one had ridden the horse but Felicity, and Cal would bet no one would ride her now. Like Delaney said, Blue knew this land. She could escape a horse thief without effort.

"Misty Mountain Ranch."

"Beau, it's Cal."

"Hey, Cal. What's up?"

"Nothing good at the moment."

"Come again?"

"We've had a problem here at the hotel. Someone unlocked our horse stalls setting loose the animals."

"*What*? You're kidding?"

"Wish I was. We've found most of them but two are still on the run and I need your help."

"Name it."

"I want you to be on the lookout for two Quarter Horses, a dark brown stallion about eighteen hands and a black mare approximately sixteen-five."

"Will do."

"Delaney seems to think someone might try to sell them."

"But you're not so sure."

"I'm not sure they're gone. One of them belongs to Felicity and knows the land. The other hasn't been mounted in two years and I doubt that will change with a stranger."

"Gotcha. Either way, I'll keep my eyes open, make a few phone calls."

"Thanks." Cal paused. Beau was a good man. Faithful, smart, a horseman to the bone. He ran the ranch for Daddy and did a damn fine job. Cal's other brother, Clint, worked at the bank alongside their father. Daddy was grooming him to take over in a few years, maybe sooner. The way Jack and Momma were causing friction, Gerald Foster might up and retire tomorrow to escape the town scrutiny. Daddy was a fine man, a decent man. But he wasn't above falling victim to his past, a past his wife seemed determined to unearth and throw in his face. "How's Daddy?" Cal asked.

"Hanging in there, but with the trial barely two weeks away, Momma is packing heat like a wildcat, lickin' her chops for the kill."

"What's Daddy say?"

"Nothing much. He's been pretty quiet, pensive. I'm afraid this might be the end of their marriage, if she keeps pushing."

Cal agreed. Victoria Foster was a proud woman, a society woman, but she was acting anything *but* these days. Cal chalked it up to Jack's seedy influence. He was her youngest, her baby, and she was using his problems with Delaney to dig up problems of her own, rehashing a past affair that had no bearing on her present-day life and family—other than what she was creating out of thin air. Susannah Ladd and Gerald Foster had been an item in high school. High School. Over forty years ago they shared feelings for one another and for some reason, Cal's mother was letting those old feelings tear her family apart.

But the more serious concern remained Troy. If Jack was successful at trial, Troy's life would end. A new baby, a new wife, a promising career at Hotel Ladd would all be sucked away.

It was criminal what Jack was doing. Raping and plundering all over again. Cal had been there the night of the assault. He'd seen Delaney, witnessed the fear and shock in her eyes. Troy had jumped in and saved her from a horrible fate. Two, in fact. Attempted rape and her near killing of the man. Cal clenched his jaw as anger knotted in his gut. Would have served Jack right, treating a woman like that.

"Let's hope Jack comes to his senses before it's too late," Cal said. When Beau didn't respond, he added, "Yeah, I know. Wishful thinking."

"Whatever, I'm here for you brother."

"Thanks. We'll talk soon?"

"You got it," Beau replied.

As Cal ended the call, he glanced around the hotel manager's office. Small, private, located off the front desk in the hotel lobby, this space had become his lifeline, his salvation. Leaving Arizona one year ago with nothing to his name but a bank account, Cal had returned to Tennessee to start over. He'd come home to prove himself worthy of his daughter's love. Newspaper headlines lit up in his mind's eye, dragging him back to those dark days of the accident, the lives he changed, irrevocably marring them forever. Cal had crashed his truck into another man's car because his reflexes were slowed. It had been raining, but not hard enough he couldn't see. He'd missed seeing the other car because he'd been drinking.

A man had lost the use of his legs because of Cal. His family had faced near financial ruin because of Cal. Didn't matter that Cal tried to help out by offering money. They didn't want his help. They wanted nothing to do with him. Same as Cal's daughter and wife. Despite the fact he gave up the bottle, his family had cut him from their lives.

But that had all changed when Malcolm Ward offered him the position as General Manager of the new Hotel Ladd. More than redemption and the chance to prove himself to his ex-wife Caroline, his daughter Emily, this job gave him purpose. Then he married Annie and his world grew more complete. They built a home together, forged by a bond strong enough to heal the past. Emily was on the road to forgiveness. With his ex-wife's help, Cal was going to see his daughter this afternoon for the first time in almost two years. Ribbons of nervous anticipation threaded through his belly. She was coming to visit him and Annie in their new home. If things went well, she'd be able to spend summers with him in the future.

Cal couldn't give voice to the gratitude he felt. Without a sense of purpose, the love of family, a man could be reduced to self-destruction. Troy faced the same battle. Drinking had cost him more than one job and nearly cost him his life with Casey. But like Cal, he'd given up the whiskey and focused on family. With the threat of criminal conviction hanging over his head, the missing horse that he'd worked so hard to retrain, Cal feared Troy might fall hopeless and give up. Cal had been there himself. Soon after the accident, he'd been tempted to hit the bottle. He'd been tempted to give up. Only thoughts of Emily kept him sober. With a looming trial and without a job with the horses he loved, Troy had no purpose to his days. Sure, he had a wife and daughter to care for, but a man needed more. He needed to provide for his family. He needed to be strong, reliable.

He needed to be needed.

Chapter Five

Travis took the lead for the morning search, intent on finding the animals before Felicity became totally unstitched. All evening she'd been consumed with the loss of her mare, a loss they didn't even know for sure was the case. She hardly touched her food during dinner, barely said a word afterword. Even when he left her house, the peck to his cheek felt like a bullet to his skin. Probably didn't sleep a wink by the looks of the bluish-black marks beneath her eyes, made worse by the navy blue of her shirt. It was unusual to see her look anything but fresh and bright, yet today she looked tired and worn.

But Travis understood. Felicity was a woman, and women tended toward the emotional. They worried and fretted and worked themselves up over stuff that hadn't even happened yet. Not him. He dealt in facts. "Okay, we've covered the river banks by the swimming hole, made the hike around the hotel, the old stables, the original homestead. The staff covered the back side of the stables and reported no sighting. What's left?"

"We haven't gone to the gold site," Felicity offered.

"Way over there?" Troy asked. "Don't you think that's a bit far?"

"Not at all." She looked between the two brothers, gaining momentum as she said, "Blue knows the way. We've walked through there a hundred times. Why wouldn't she go that way?"

"I guess Spirit could have ended up over there, too," Troy said, gloom coating his tone.

"It's a possibility," Travis agreed. At this point, he'd take any suggestions. The second day of searching needed to be successful. Leading the trio out of the stables and into open morning air, he cut around toward the back end. "We need to split up. Felicity and I will search the opposite side of the bridge, the forest along the lower river banks while you take the trail up to Zack's Falls," he told Troy. "Check the woods in and around the excavating sight."

He nodded. "I'll go all the way to the property line and into the USFS if I have to."

Travis hoped he didn't have to go that far. The USFS was public land. If one of the horses ventured into that area, they could have run into hikers, squatters... There were people who hid and lived in the forest and would like nothing better than to stumble across a horse and for any number of reasons. Several had been stolen of late; a fact that didn't bode well, under the circumstances. "Okay, it's settled then. We'll meet somewhere in the middle. You have your cell?"

Troy tapped his front pocket. "Got it."

"Okay. If you see anything before then, give us call. You might need help."

"Spirit ain't comin' to no one but me," Troy said, irritating Travis with his cockiness. Whatever. Troy wanted to run solo, let him. "C'mon, Felicity. Let's go." Setting off on their separate ways, Travis took two steps and stopped, his attention snagged by a shiny flash on the ground.

"What's the matter?" Felicity asked. Troy hung back, waiting for a response.

Travis walked over to the spot and bent over. Scrutinizing the grassy ground, clumps of hay here and there, he picked up the object. It was a lighter. Flipping it backward and forward in his hand, he turned to the others. "Someone lost a lighter." The slim silver body was rimmed in gold where the top part opened. "An expensive lighter."

Felicity zeroed in on it and burst, "That's my father's lighter!" She yanked it from Travis' grasp and scrutinized it more closely. "It is, I'm sure of it." Her eyes rounded. "What would it be doing here?"

Troy was by their side in an instant. "Maybe Jeremiah wasn't the one who let the horses free. Maybe it was Jack."

"Don't you think it's more feasible that he lost it that night?" Travis posed, then directed to Felicity, "He hasn't been around here lately, has he?"

"No. He wouldn't dare come around here."

"Unless he was tryin' to cause trouble," Troy interjected.

Felicity looked to Troy and her gaze sharpened, as though she were connecting the dots. "It is *our* horses that are missing. Do you think he did it? To get back at you and me?"

"How would he know anything about Troy's training Spirit?" Travis asked.

Felicity became defensive. "I don't know what he knows, but it's possible. Who else?"

"Jeremiah?" Travis proposed. "That's who your momma thinks is responsible."

"Why would Jeremiah care anything about my horse?" She slanted a glance to Troy and said, "Troy's maybe, but not mine."

Travis took the lighter from Felicity and shoved it in his front pocket. "Jeremiah has a motive for revenge against you, your momma, the hotel..."

"So does her father," Troy snapped.

Travis didn't like the way Troy was taking Felicity's side when it made no sense. He was only doing so to cause trouble between Travis and her. "Yes," Travis said pointedly, "but he's already pursuing his revenge. You have a court date in less than two weeks, remember?" Glancing between the two, avoiding the obvious displeasure radiating from Felicity, he continued, "Jeremiah is the more reasonable assumption."

"Don't give me that 'reasonable assumption' business," Troy shot back. "Jack Foster is here and has plenty of motive. When I find those horses, I'm gonna show him exactly what he can do with that motive, too."

Travis stared at his brother. The bulge of his neck vein was a sure sign Troy was going down his usual path. If he wasn't careful, the hothead was going to land himself in even more trouble.

"Really?" Travis mocked. "Your answer is to add to his list of charges? Why don't you learn to use the proper channels and bring the perpetrator to justice instead of settling everything with your fists? You might not be in the predicament you're in if you'd learned your lesson the first time."

"I didn't have a choice but how would you know? You weren't there. As usual, I was solving problems in the real world instead of throwin' fancy words around like I was already some kind of lawyer man—which you aren't. You're just a—"

"Guys, stop it!" Felicity exclaimed. "This isn't a competition!"

Travis and Troy retreated to their respective imaginary corners. Troy's nostrils were flaring and Travis knew he wanted nothing more than to punch him in the face. Well, go ahead. *Bring it on, brother. I'm in the mood to belt you one back and good.*

"It could be Jack or Jeremiah," Felicity insisted, her aggravation thinly veiled. "Both have reason and both could have done this. But at the moment it's irrelevant. We need to find those horses."

Travis clenched his jaw. "Agreed."

Troy gritted his teeth and put as much space as possible between himself and Travis, storming down the mountain to the trailhead that led into the forest and up to Zack's Falls. Located across a grassy meadow, it was a good forty-five minute hike from here to the rock, a time he would cut in half, his pace fueled by anger. Travis was a jerk. Everything had to be his way, like he knew best. He always had to be in charge, always had to be right. Well, he *wasn't*. Troy knew a thing or two when it came to people, and Jack Foster could easily have been responsible for letting the horses free. He was the one with motive to hurt Felicity, hurt him. Those horses that were missing were theirs, weren't they? They were, which should be proof enough.

Stomping over a field littered with purple and yellow blossoms, Troy needed to forget Travis and focus on Spirit. The animal would respond to him and him alone. Not Travis, not Felicity—not even Miss Delaney. Spirit would come to him because he was the one who'd invested the time and energy, the only one qualified to do so. Travis might know how to ride but he didn't know nothin' about working a horse. He was too busy sticking his nose in books.

Entering the shaded trail, Troy scanned the forest around him. Roughly a car width wide, the clay-packed terrain was burnt orange in color with grooves carved out in various sections by fast-flowing water racing down from the mountaintop. The ground was layered with rocks and roots, fallen twigs and decomposing leaves, the air laced with musky earth. If Spirit was around here, he'd have to be on the trail. There wasn't enough room for him otherwise.

Up ahead was a different story. In about hundred feet the trail would narrow, opening into a valley to his right. If Spirit had wandered off the trail and hung by a tree, he'd be hard to spot. Dark brown, the horse would blend in with black trunks, the mass of branches and the occasional boulder. Troy cupped his hands to his mouth and called, "Spirit! Spirit, you here?" Watching for signs of movement—response—Troy sharpened his gaze and slowed his step. If he wasn't careful, he might miss the animal. "Spirit!"

Troy continued the process for the next fifteen minutes, passing a flat wall of rock, a sure sign that he was nearing the excavation site. Nick and Delaney had authorized an outfit out of Johnson City to come in and cut the gold from the rock, mine as much as they possibly could so they could have gold pendants made. Wishing wells. They'd hired the local jeweler to make them and sold them in the hotel gift shop as souvenirs. Felicity said they were supposed to represent eternal hope and spiritual fulfillment. Crazy, if you asked him. Wishing wells were supposed to represent wishes for dreams to come true. Where did they get spiritual fulfillment out of that?

Troy froze. Glimpsing movement up ahead, he stopped, but rather than call out, he simply searched for the source. No sense in spooking Spirit into bolting. He was already out of sorts in unfamiliar territory. Troy needed the animal to remain calm if he was going to be successful in retrieving him. At the moment, he saw no sign of him.

Inching closer to the trail's edge, Troy narrowed in on the landscape, specifically the midway point on the forest floor. Setting a hand to a nearby stone, the surface cold and grainy beneath his skin, Troy slowed his breathing.

"Those greedy bastards took it all!"

"What?"

"That ain't no horse," Troy muttered to himself. *That's a man*!

Troy crouched behind the boulder, noting there were three men, not one. Two black-haired men with beards dressed in jeans and T-shirts next to a lighter brown-haired guy dressed in a red button-down.

"But you said there was enough gold here to pay us for the rest of our lives!" one of them scowled. "We was relyin' on you."

The second dark-haired man spoke up, "We took a big risk for you cuz you promised!"

"Shut your pie hole. I need time to think."

"Think? Think about what—it's gone!"

Instinct scissored through Troy's lungs as the third man came into full view. It was Jeremiah Ladd.

"You better think," said one of the strangers. "And you better figure a way to pay us back."

"I'll get you your money," Jeremiah growled.

Surprise, surprise, Troy mused. The man was back and seemingly up to his old tricks. He was here to steal the gold, only there was one problem. Nick and Delaney had already removed most of it. Troy suppressed the urge to reveal himself and rub it in the man's face. *That's right, Jerry. The rightful owners actually secured their fortune before you could come and steal it.*

The taller stranger straightened and poked a finger in Jeremiah's chest, surprising Troy with his authority over Jeremiah. "You'd better find a way. This here gold belonged to us and it's gone. Stolen right out from under us."

Mighty presumptive, Troy thought, savoring the defeat in their voices. Just because a man owes you a "gold mine" doesn't mean it was his to give. Troy chuckled. Maybe Jeremiah would get another beating. Seemed tall man had no fear of Mr. Ladd. Delight streamed in like sunshine on a cloudy day. Oh, wouldn't Troy enjoy watching a good payback beating.

"Don't worry. I will," Jeremiah declared, then stalked off through the brush in the opposite direction. Troy looked beyond the men, through a mass of tree trunks and leaves. The other side of this area was the Ladd property line with the USFS. The men were leaving via public land, most likely the same way they'd arrived. Depositing his gaze on the exiting trio, Troy decided a call to Cal was warranted. He'd know exactly what to do with the news of Jeremiah's appearance on Ladd land. Felicity's land.

A low whinny erupted behind him. Troy whipped his head around, his heart slamming against his ribcage. Spirit! Pleasure swamped him. Tossing a final glance toward the departing men, Troy focused his energy on the horse several yards away. "How'd you find me, Spirit?"

The horse raised its head and shook its mane, dark eyes honed in on Troy. Course, just because he'd found him didn't mean he would leave these woods willingly. Troy grinned. Spirit was a determined one. But then again, Troy could be pretty determined, too. Turning a shoulder to the horse, Troy took a slow step backward onto the trail. Spirit watched, wary, but didn't move. "How've you been, boy?" Troy asked pleasantly, casually, adopting a submissive stance to the animal. Troy stood at a slight angle, not facing the horse head on or turning away in passivity. He already had a relationship with the horse as a leader, a comfortable figure for the animal, but after being on the run, Spirit might need reminding.

This was Troy's invitation to come check him out.

As if on cue, Spirit dipped his head, then raised it, giving another shake. He didn't make a move toward Troy. Seemed he wasn't ready. "No problem, buddy. I got all the time in the world," he said, remaining in place. Patience was his ticket to success. "You and me can hang out here for as long as you'd like."

Spirit's ears pricked forward and back. He was thinking. Deciding. Troy understood. It was rooted in the predator-prey instinct. The animal wanted to follow a leader but was fearful, uncertain. His "flight" capacitors remained charged. Troy couldn't blame him. The ordeal of running loose in strange territory had to be unsettling for Spirit.

A branch cracked loudly in the distance and Troy cursed under his breath. Spirit's ears stiffened, twitched as he backed away. *Dad gummit.* Troy wasn't about to turn and see if the sound had come from returning men. He was relyin' on Spirit and his response to the situation for his answer.

Spirit looked around, settled on nothing in particular, then returned his attention to Troy. "Nothin' to see over there," Troy said softly. "Just Mother Nature cleanin' house. You and me...we're just a couple of friends gettin' back together."

Troy dropped a shoulder and turned away from the horse, simultaneously taking a step. Spirit reacted, taking a step, too. "That's it, boy. You remember me." Troy halted, reversed direction, then took a few more steps away. Again, Spirit did likewise. Troy stopped, turned, and faced the animal directly. Keeping his voice gentle and soothing, he encouraged Spirit to abandon his natural fear response and let down his defenses. "I'm not here to hurt you. I'm here to take you home."

When the horse hesitated, glancing away, Troy took it as a sign Spirit still wasn't ready. Angling his body away from the horse again, Troy worked to reassure the horse he wasn't a threat, communicating the message with body language. Spirit needed to understand that he was safe with Troy, that no harm would come to him. For several moments, man and horse stood motionless but fully engaged in one another. Troy rotated back toward the animal in a slow and methodical fashion. He didn't stop for a head-on posture but rather continued his body's rotation for a three hundred sixty degree turn until he was facing in the opposite direction in an effort to get Spirit reacquainted with his presence. Comfortable. "That's it," Troy cooed. "All is good here."

Feeling the moment was right, Troy maintained his angle-away stance and took half a dozen steps from Spirit. The animal immediately pursued, emerging from the woods and onto the trail. Troy smiled. The horse wanted to reunite. It was his job to instill in the animal an emotional security that would take him all the way to the stables. Circling his body in place again, Troy liked that Spirit was watching his every move. Ears pricked forward, the animal was fully intent upon what Troy was doing. They were close enough that Troy could smell the animal, the scent mixing with the earthy scent of clay and pine. When he took a step, Spirit took a step. When Troy stopped, Spirit stopped. Troy walked several paces down the trail and the animal trailed him, closing the space between them to mere feet.

Troy stopped and Spirit stopped. Turning, Troy took a step toward the animal and slowly extended a hand to touch Spirit's snout. The horse didn't draw back but allowed him the contact. Troy purposefully kept it brief, turned and took a few more steps away. Spirit followed. Like a horse on a lead line, the animal was in sync with Troy's every move. Troy could walk out of this forest right now and Spirit would probably track him every step of the way, but Troy didn't want to push it. He worked too hard to build a relationship of trust with the animal and he wasn't going to blow it now. Instead, he returned to face the horse, establishing contact again, ruffling the black mane between Spirit's eyes. "You're a good boy," Troy praised, his voice light and easy as if he were talking to a child. "You're a very good boy."

Spirit blinked. Unalarmed, standing still, the animal was demonstrating his acceptance.

Troy quickly walked down trail and then stopped. Spirit stopped. Troy chuckled. "I think we're officially back together, Spirit." Turning, Troy smiled and patted the animal once again. "What do you say? You up for a hike home?"

Spirit rewarded him with a low rumbling nicker. Troy laughed. "I knew you missed me." Stroking his neck, the round length of his sweaty muscle, Troy added, "Now let's say you and me get back to the stables. Miss Delaney is gonna want to see you."

Mindful of the forest around him, the possible intrusions and potential surprises, Troy headed down the trail the way he came in, Spirit on his heel. Miss Delaney wasn't gonna like what he had to tell her about Jeremiah Ladd being here, but she was gonna love seein' Spirit.

Chapter Six

"Blue!" Felicity's boots crunched over the gravelly riverbank as she jogged toward the water. "I can't believe you," she cried out breathlessly. There in the middle of the river stood her horse, the animal's body half submerged in the slow-moving depths of the river. Blue whinnied, then shook her mane like a nuisance fly had buzzed her.

"Told you it was a possibility she'd be here," Travis said.

"But she's never come this far on her own." Felicity clicked a call from her mouth and her mare responded, plodding carefully over the rocky river bottom, her slick black coat shiny in the bright sunlight. Felicity went quickly to her, boots splashing in the shallows of the river's edge as her horse walked out. Felicity grabbed hold of Blue's neck and hugged her, the round muscular body comforting to the touch. "Oh, Blue, I'm so glad we found you." Felicity buried her face in the coarse hair of Blue's mane. The horse was stinky with sweat and Felicity's blouse was soaked through, her jean shorts, but she didn't care. Heartbeats kicked in her chest. *Blue was safe*.

Her baby was okay.

"Probably came here to cool off," Travis remarked.

Pulling away, Felicity slid a hand up and down Blue's neck, rubbed the curve of her jaw, the pillow of her snout. The mare groaned and Felicity giggled, relief spurting through her limbs. "Oh, girl, you had me scared." Blue nudged Felicity who cupped a hand to her velvety muzzle. "And you're so spoiled," she said. "Look at you. Here you've been gone for two days and all you want is a good scratch."

"She's probably hungry," Travis noted.

"I'll bet she is," Felicity said, instantly concerned over Blue's well-being. Had she been hurt? Had she been scared? Was she starving?

"Why don't you call your mom and tell her you found Blue."

Felicity nodded, instantly wondering how Troy had fared. Had he found Spirit? Taking a few steps from the river with Blue loyally following, she said, "You call Troy. I'll call my mom."

Travis plucked the cell phone from his waistband while she pulled hers from her back pocket. Her mom would be so relieved to know Blue was safe and Felicity could only hope the same held true for Troy.

As Felicity and Travis entered the stables, an elated Delaney immediately filled a bucket with water. Striding over, she deposited the bucket on the ground, slid a hand down the stretch of Blue's back and examined the horse from head to toe. "She looks okay. Doesn't appear to be dehydrated."

"We found her in the river."

Delaney smiled. "Figures." With a pat to Blue's hind quarter, she said, "Decided to go for a swim, did you?"

The animal jerked up its head and shook its mane.

"I was surprised," Felicity said. "It's not like her to go that far."

"Probably wanted to steer clear of the stables, seeing as how they've been a source of instability of late."

Felicity knew her mom was referring to the incident with her father. When he attacked her and the gun had discharged, the horses had been spooked. Add a stranger entering their midst and shooing them from their stalls and her mom was right. Anxiety pushed in Felicity's stomach. Blue wouldn't want to be anywhere near here. "Have you heard from Troy? We called but he didn't answer." It could have been due to bad cell reception. Service was spotty in the mountains. Nerves flitted through Felicity's breast. It might be that he'd found Spirit and was on his way back right this minute. At least she hoped so.

"Haven't heard a word," her mom replied.

"Listen," Travis said, placing a hand to Felicity's shoulder. "Now that we know Blue is okay, I'm going to run down to Mr. Dakota's office and see if I can't do a little digging."

"Digging into what?" Felicity asked.

Shooting a brief glance to Delaney, he said, "I want to find out who did this, who might have helped pay Jeremiah's debt."

"How are you going to do that?"

"There are ways to find the information, and Mr. Dakota's computer has access I can't get anywhere else."

Not fully understanding but relieved to know Travis was intent on doing something, Felicity nodded. "Okay. I'm going to hang out here a while with Blue."

Lightly kissing her cheek, he said, "I'll call you."

As he walked away, Felicity called after him, "I'll let you know if Troy calls with news about Spirit."

Travis waved a hand but didn't look back, bothering Felicity with his apparent disinterest in all things Troy. What was going on with him? Why was he being so detached?

"Troy will find him," Delaney said.

"I hope so."

Between them, Blue slurped from her bucket, then snorted. Drops of water sprayed onto Felicity's jeans. Placing a hand to her horse, she looked at her mom, emotions pulling and tugging in her heart. Felicity didn't want to think about the consequences of not finding Spirit.

"What's the matter? You sure look unhappy for a girl just reunited with her missing horse."

Felicity shrugged, glanced in the direction of the open doorway. "It's Travis. I don't know what's gotten into him lately."

"Why? What's going on?"

"It's like he doesn't care about his brother at all."

"Oh, I don't know about that. They're just different people," her mom defended. "Troy's situation is not easy. It's putting stress on the family and Travis is reacting. It'll pass."

"It's more than being different. It's like he disapproves of Troy's choices and has cut him off from his affection."

"Travis is headstrong. He believes what he's doing is right." Her mom frowned. "And to be honest, Troy has made some mistakes."

"*Mistakes*," Felicity emphasized. "It's not like he has to be tied to them for the rest of his life. What ever happened to forgiveness?"

The corner of her mom's mouth tipped into a smile. "You have a bigger heart than most, Felicity. Travis will come around. Give him time."

Grunting, she returned focus to her horse and ran a hand along the animal's neck. Not all things healed with time. Some people didn't want to mend fences. Travis sure didn't seem like he was interested in pounding any nails back toward his brother.

"Now that Blue's back, I have a favor to ask."

Felicity looked to her mom. "What favor?"

"Will you run down to Fran's and pick up a lunch order? One of the guy's is celebrating his birthday, and I offered to buy lunch for the crew."

"What about the hotel kitchen? Don't they serve food up here?"

Delaney shook her head. "This man wants fried steak and cornbread, and he only wants them from Fran's."

"Oh..." Felicity checked her attire. A bit smudged, her shirt had dried, though if anyone came too close, they'd surely smell her horse on her. "I guess I can go."

"Thanks." Picking up on Felicity's concern, she said, "Maybe you can run up to the cabin and change first?"

"Do I smell that bad?"

"Not to me. I love stinky horse smell but Fran..." Delaney shook her head. "She might mind."

Felicity sighed. With nothing keeping her here other than a hungry horse, she replied, "Okay. Maybe I'll pick up some carrots for Blue on my way."

Her mom grinned. "Good idea."

After changing into a fresh T-shirt and jeans, Felicity drove to the diner, engrossed by thoughts of Blue and whoever could have been responsible for her release. It had to be someone that knew Felicity. It couldn't be a coincidence that her horse had been one of the ones targeted. Troy, too. Sure, a few other horses had been set free but maybe that was for distraction purposes. Maybe the perpetrator was trying to cover his real intent.

The perpetrator.

Slowing for a red light, Felicity still believed it was her father. He was the only one with ties to both Troy and Felicity. Why he didn't release Sadie was a question left unanswered, but maybe he ran out of time. Maybe someone walked in on him, and he had to get out quick before he was discovered.

A kid on bicycle sped across her path. Barefoot and shirtless, the kid couldn't be more than ten. Peering at the boy, she glanced around for a nearby adult. Spotting no one who appeared to be with him, Felicity wondered about his safety. Were kids allowed to bike through the center of town on their own at that age?

Her mom would have had a fit. Even Travis' parents wouldn't have allowed such a thing. With no parent in sight, Felicity watched as the boy jumped the curb and turned down a side street, pedaling as fast as his legs would take him. Trailing his figure, Felicity caught sight of a familiar face. She stilled. *Two* familiar faces. Up above, the light turned green but Felicity remained fixed in place.

Was that her father?

And Jillian Devane?

Her pulse skipped as she zeroed in on the couple. Lingering outside a two-story building, Jack and Jillian stood idle by his truck. Felicity recognized and assumed the silver sedan next to it belonged to Jillian Devane.

Jillian Devane. Her mind still couldn't absorb the fact. What was she doing here? Running a hand up Jack Foster's chest, the woman leaned into him and kissed his cheek. *Oh my gosh*--Felicity's gaze darted upward to the hotel sign. Had they spent the night together?

At the honk from behind, she jammed her foot to the accelerator. She had to call her mother. As soon as she arrived at Fran's, she had to let her mom know what was happening. Jillian and her father, *together*. Revulsion shimmied through Felicity's midsection. Could the news get any worse?

Jeremiah Ladd dropped his cohorts at a waffle joint then drove back to the motel to clear his head. He needed time to think, to plan, and he needed it without the annoying presence of those two idiots. The gold was gone, the land raped by Delaney and her arrogant husband. As if they weren't making enough money with the hotel they built on the property, they had to dig out every last flake and sell it. He'd needed that money. After getting his marker paid, the debt he'd racked up against the casino, he needed money for payback and to start over. Money that belonged to him. Ladd Springs was his family's land, not Delaney's. She was a Wilkins. She didn't deserve Ladd Springs.

Anger and resentment coiled through his chest as he drove familiar streets on autopilot. If Delaney and her daughter hadn't conned his old man out of the land, Jeremiah would have inherited it upon his death. A death that couldn't have happened early enough. Thinking back to his last encounter with his father, Jeremiah recalled the hatred in the old man's eyes, the rage.

Too bad they didn't finish the job.

In the space of one sentence, Jeremiah had suspected his father was responsible for the anonymous beating he received, left for the dead on the streets of the worst section in town. Bile rose at the memory. Ernie Ladd had thrust his gun into the screen door, threatening to pull the trigger of the shotgun he held. Heart thumping, Jeremiah was disturbed the thoughts still drew a reaction from him. Growing up with Ernie Ladd for a father had been a rotten existence. It would have been the icing on the cake to cause his death, but he never had the chance. The old man died while Jeremiah was sitting in a jail—sitting in a jail because Delaney's rat of a husband called the authorities in Vegas, alerting them to his whereabouts, leading them by the nose to his hometown where that weak-kneed Gavin Shore arrested him for the money he owed a casino. Anger surged.

Well, guess what? Time to pay up, boys. Plan B was about to go into action. Yanking his cell phone from the center console, Jeremiah dialed the number and waited through the rings.

"Hello?"

"Time to ramp it up," Jeremiah said, staring ahead through his windshield, the roofline of his motel coming into sight.

"Talk to me."

"Can you meet later this afternoon?"

"Shouldn't be a problem."

"Good."

"What's your plan?"

"I'll call you back," Jeremiah clipped, then ended the call. He didn't know exactly how he was going to make Delaney and the rest of them pay, but pay they would. Jeremiah would hit them where it hurt. He'd do whatever it took. Passing a seed and feed store, he honed in on a horse trailer parked out front. A slow smile crept onto Jeremiah's lips as an idea began to form in his mind.

Jack Foster and his mother Victoria sat in the waiting room of Hank Dakota's law firm. His mother paid to have Hank on retainer, even though he wasn't representing them. His office would serve as a meeting place for their attorneys out of Nashville who were representing them in the case against Troy and Delaney.

"I'll talk to you then," Jack said into this cell phone then slid it back into his pocket.

"Who was that?" Victoria asked.

"An old friend."

"What kind of old friend?"

Jack smirked.

Victoria glowered at his evasive response but Jack couldn't care less. He wasn't about to reveal the identity of his "old friend" because it could muddy the waters of her support—support he needed. The trial was set to begin in two weeks and the firm his mother hired was finalizing their attack plan, meeting today to go over strategy. Jack glanced at his gold watch. Eleven fifty-nine. They were late. Fifteen minutes late.

"Don't get into any kind of trouble before the trial," Victoria warned.

"What's the matter, Momma? Don't you trust that I know how to stay clean?"

She flashed an angry gaze that said she did not. Jack chuckled. Patting her arm on the armrest between them, he said, "There's nothing going on that will jeopardize our case. On the contrary, I've got allies that can only work to help our cause."

"What allies?"

"Secret weapon allies," he said, glancing up as a flood of sunlight spilled in through the opened front door. The Nashville team had arrived. Jack rose to his feet, assisting his mother to do likewise.

Three men dressed in full suits, all dark, all pin-striped, filled the modest lobby of the Dakota Law Firm. Two wing chairs, a potted plant and a cheesy landscape picture hung on the wall lined with wainscoting, the office appeared beneath them. The tallest man in the middle took charge, his gray hair implying a senior status. "Good afternoon, Mrs. Foster. Mr. Foster."

"Good afternoon," his mother replied politely, though Jack knew she wasn't happy to be kept waiting.

Dispensing with all pretense, the man asked, "You two ready to get started?"

"I was ready fifteen minutes ago," Jack replied, ignoring the displeasure curling his mother's gaze. *Manners should always be maintained, despite one's personal feelings.* He'd heard the mantra day in and day out growing up with her. He didn't need the reminder.

Unaffected, the man glanced toward the conference room just as Hank Dakota emerged from his office.

"Good to see you, Samuel," Hank greeted warmly, his navy blue and green plaid button-down a stark contrast to the professionally dressed men. He looked more like a farmhand than an experienced attorney.

"Sorry we're running late," the man replied. "Traffic accident on I-24."

"No problem," Hank replied. "Shall we get started?" Hank flicked the light on as he entered the conference room, the gentlemen filing in behind him.

Jack grumbled to his mother about the likelihood of the man's excuse, but followed them in without further protest.

In the back office, Travis sat hunched over the computer, legal pad and pen to the right of the keyboard. As expected, Hank Dakota offered no protest to his request for computer access. Over Christmas break he'd offered his computer, saying Travis had an open-door invitation to do research. Mr. Dakota said he was glad to see another sharp mind entering the field of law and was counting on Travis working summers for him, a deal to which Travis readily agreed. Interning for an attorney would be an invaluable asset on his application to law school, not to mention the experience he'd gain. While Mr. Dakota had indicated he was meeting with clients this morning and couldn't be of help to him directly, he didn't mention who they were. But as he excused himself, voices carried, easily identifying those in attendance as Jack and Victoria Foster.

Clenching his jaw, Travis clicked through screens on the monitor before him. The Fosters were here to meet with counsel regarding the impending trial against Troy and Felicity's mom. According to Felicity, Mrs. Foster had hired a firm out of Nashville to argue their case, most likely in response to Mr. Harris' decision to hire a group out of Chattanooga for Troy's defense—a blockbuster group with a reputation for winning even the toughest cases.

Travis hoped they raked the Fosters over the coals, leaving lasting marks. It was disgraceful what they were doing to Troy, Mrs. Foster in particular. Felicity's father was saving his own skin. Criminals like Jack Foster always lied to save their butt from jail, but his mother's involvement is what enabled the travesty. Without her money and connections to Gavin Shore and other members of the police department, Jack Foster would have gotten nowhere fast. Travis might have his differences with his brother, but he would not stand by and allow people to make a mockery of the justice system or a fool of his family.

Shaking off the frustration, Travis worked to clear his mind, concentrating on the information displayed on the screen. Someone paid Jeremiah's marker to the casino and that payment could be traced. He'd called the casino and learned the bank used for such purposes. Now he had to get the routing number. Every bank had one, kind of like a person had a social security number. It was specific to them. Clicking through screens on the Federal Reserve's website, Travis searched for the bank in question. He knew the amount of money in question. Knew Jeremiah's name, his driver's license number, his last known address in Atlanta, though he wasn't sure the latter was necessary. The man had been in jail in Nevada. That was an easier find.

Once he pinpointed the bank, he could work backwards and find the debit bank. A phone call with the beneficiary bank information and recipient's information should get him one step closer to discovering who originated the transaction. Then he'd be one step closer to tying a direct line between Jeremiah Ladd and his accomplice. Next, Travis would work to establish motive. Despite Felicity's assertion that her father was responsible for setting the horses free, Travis believed her mom was on a better track. Jeremiah was the one who promised revenge. He was the one who hated the hotel and everyone connected to it. It was likely him behind the horse fiasco.

But who paid the money to get him out of jail? Travis clicked his mouse as he scrolled through screen after screen, speed-reading the names and lists. It would take a bit of time, some well-placed phone calls, but Travis was confident he could get to the bottom of it. Then he'd share the information with the authorities, and Felicity and her mom would know who was responsible and take the appropriate actions.

Chapter Seven

Troy walked clear of the trail and into the meadow, Spirit plodding methodically behind him. In the distance, the hotel was barely visible. Hidden away in the mountain, its walls were partially obscured by trees and underbrush, windows allowing guests to see out better than passersby could see in. It had been an amazing transformation. He hadn't been here for the entire process, but he knew this property like his own. He loved it like his own. The fact that someone was trying to destroy it rubbed him raw. Whoever tried to harm the horses was going to hear from him. First stop needed to be the stables. He needed to deliver Spirit safe and sound to Miss Delaney, but he also needed to consult with someone regarding the appearance of Jeremiah Ladd in the forest. He could tell Miss Delaney, but Troy felt her attention would be better fixed on her horses. Hopefully Travis and Felicity found Blue, and her hands would be full caring for the animals. Troy pulled the cell phone from his pocket and called Felicity.

"Hello?"

"Did you find Blue?" Troy asked.

"Yes. She was down by the river. How about you?"

"Spirit's with me now. I'm walkin' him back to the stables."

"Oh, good!"

"Where are you?" he asked, flattening flowers and grass as he and Spirit plodded along the tree line.

"At Fran's. My mom sent me here to pick up lunch for one of the guys at the stables."

Troy nodded, his stomach growling at the mention of food. "I could use a little lunch myself," he said, noting a shiny silver car turning into the hotel's parking lot.

"Want me to pick something up for you?"

"Nah. I'll go home for lunch, but thanks."

"Okay and Troy..."

"Yeah?"

"I saw my father this morning..."

When she didn't elaborate, Troy asked, "What was he doin?"

"He was with Jillian Devane."

"Jillian Devane? What the heck is she doin' here?" he asked, memories of the cat woman gurgling to the surface. The last time he saw her she was tryin' to wrap her arms around him like a noose. He'd been waiting for Casey at Whiskey Joe's and the woman latched onto him like white on rice. Casey had walked in on him and nearly dumped him over the incident. Which burned his hide. That vixen wasn't even worth the headache.

"That's what I was wondering, but it's worse."

"Worse? What could be worse than the she-devil being in town?"

"I think she spent the night with my father."

Troy groaned. Felicity was right. That couldn't be good.

"Gotta go," she said. "I'm pulling into the lot for Fran's."

"Okay. Thanks."

Troy picked up his pace, more determined than ever not to share what he saw in the woods with Miss Delaney. If she knew Jillian Devane was in town, she would not be happy. She already suspected Jeremiah was up to trouble. What would it do to her to know she was up against a double-whammy?

Crossing the bridge, Troy took the turn for the trail leading up to the stables, stopped sudden by the call of his name.

"Troy, hold up!"

Cal Foster descended the front steps of the lobby and jogged over to him, wearing a light green button-down and khaki pants, his standard manager wear. Combined with his fair skin and light brown hair, the colors made him look soft, but Troy knew the man to be anything but. Pausing, Troy glanced back to Spirit, who tugged at the lead. "Whoa, boy."

The horse stopped, shook its mane and swatted a fly from his rear.

"You're okay. We're only here for a second," Troy said.

Mr. Foster grinned as he reached them. "I see you found Spirit. Good job!"

"Yes, sir. He was wandering in the forest."

"Delaney will be thrilled by the news."

"Headed up her way now."

"Let me take a look at him." Troy stepped aside as Cal assessed the animal behind him. Walking the around the back of him, he inspected Spirit's body and legs, ran a hand the length of his mid-section. "He looks good. Did you have any trouble rounding him up?"

"No, sir." Troy paused. Spirit's ears twitched forward and back, he kicked a hoof restlessly at the ground as he kept an eye on Mr. Foster. "But there is something I have to tell you."

Mr. Foster's expression stilled, his hazel gaze clouding with concern. "What?"

"I saw Jeremiah Ladd in the forest, out near the gold site."

"What?"

Troy nodded. "He was with two men."

Cal raked a hand through his hair. "Do I need to ask what they were doing?"

"I don't know for sure, but they weren't real happy to find the gold had been mined."

"I'll bet they weren't! Do you know who the men were?"

"No, sir. But I think Mr. Ladd must have promised them some of the gold."

"They probably paid his marker."

Troy glimpsed a black head of hair and his heart stopped, then punched into motion. "There's something else you need to know," Troy told him, his gaze catching on a sight over Cal's shoulder. His heart began to pound. "We got company."

"What's that?" he asked, turning to see what Troy was looking at. Cal's demeanor coarsened. "What the hell is she doing here?"

"That's what I wanted to tell you."

Both men watched as Jillian Devane picked her way through the natural terrain, carefully walking over the dirt and gravel trail in her heels. Her very high heels and skintight pants. She wore a short jacket made of some kind of animal print, the sleeves stopping just past her elbow. She glanced over at them, gave a short wave and served up a fat smile.

Witch. "Felicity called me and told me she saw her outside a hotel downtown with Mr. Foster."

"Jack?"

"Yes, sir. Seems the two have hooked up."

"Great." Cal's displeasure was visceral. "As if we didn't have enough trouble already. Talk about dastardly duo."

"Can't be good," Troy agreed. Beside him, Spirit whinnied, prodding him to resume his trek to the stables.

Cal looked at the horse and said, "Appreciate you telling me. How about you go ahead and take Spirit back to the stables while I take care of Jillian Devane." Glancing over his shoulder, his tone dropped. "See if I can't shorten her visit."

"There's one more thing, sir."

Lines formed across Cal's forehead. "More bad news?"

"We found a lighter outside the stables."

"A lighter?"

"Yes, sir. When Felicity, Travis and I set out on our search this morning, we spotted it on the ground outside the side entrance." Cal stared at him expectantly and Troy swallowed. "Felicity said it belonged to her daddy."

Cal's gaze cooled several degrees. Mr. Foster was thinking what he was thinking. Lighter. Fire. Jillian Devane.

Revenge.

"I need to call Nick right away."

Troy figured he might. Snapping a glance up the hill, Troy asked, "Should I say anything to Miss Delaney?"

"I'd prefer you not. Let Mr. Harris do the honors."

Relief swept through him. "Yes, sir."

Without another word, Troy started for the trail up to the stables. Mr. Foster would handle things from here. He was General Manager of the hotel. He was in charge. He knew what needed to be done. Avoiding eye contact with Jillian Devane as he passed, Troy could feel her hot gaze beating down his back. She wanted nothing more than to taunt him, to tease him. To cause him trouble.

It was a pleasure he would deny her. Pulling his hat forward, Troy said, "C'mon, boy. We're goin' home."

Cal Foster walked over to Jillian, curious as to her presence. Was this a pleasure visit to see his brother? Cal doubted it. While Ms. Devane might indeed be playing around with Jack, Cal didn't think it stopped there. No. Ms. Devane was a woman of means, a woman nursing a vengeful heart. She was here for one reason and one reason only.

Ruin Hotel Ladd.

Jillian Devane stood out of direct sunlight, waiting for Cal beneath the shade of towering oaks, a cluster of dogwoods mixed in. Azaleas dotted the landscape along with clumps of hydrangea, their leaves a deep, healthy green. Against the backdrop of Tennessee country, Jillian looked out of place, adorned in gold jewelry, her sunglasses oversized and very black, a near match to her shiny hair falling in sheets past her shoulders. A stick figure, her long legs were clad in form-fitting jeans, her shirt a combination of gold mesh and creamy silk beneath a leopard-print cropped jacket.

"Good afternoon, Mr. Foster," Jillian said, addressing him formally.

"Afternoon." Cal stopped feet from her. Masking his emotions with a detached professionalism, he asked, "What brings you out our way?"

Jillian smiled. "Why, I'm here to check-in."

"Check in?"

Her eyes held a deliberate goad. "Of course. Why else would I be here?"

Cal could name a thousand reasons, none of them good, but refused to give her an ounce of satisfaction. "Of course. A woman of your intelligence knows there's only one place worth staying in this part of the country. A Harris Hotel."

Jillian's smile hardened but remained intact. "Yes. You would say so, wouldn't you?"

Genuine pleasure coursed through him. Seems he'd struck a chord. "Facts are facts," he said, adding without pausing, "and we've got the booked schedule to prove it. Do you have a reservation? If so, I'd be happy to assist you with your check-in."

"I do."

Too bad. Cal extended a hand toward the hotel "Shall we?"

Cal followed Jillian as she walked to the lobby, employing a full hip swagger, most likely for his benefit, though he wasn't interested. She could shake and shimmy all she wanted, Cal preferred his woman down-to-earth and real. Neither of which applied to Jillian Devane.

While he didn't find her presence threatening, there was no mistaking the look in Troy's eyes when he spotted her. He was not happy. Knowing Jillian, Troy had a right to be upset. With a new wife and baby on his hands, the last thing he needed was Jillian working to upset the mix—a real possibility, especially if she was working in cahoots with Jack. Wasn't it enough Jack was taking Troy to trial? Did his brother need to provoke tension between Troy and Casey by re-injecting Jillian onto the scene?

Troy was under a lot of pressure these days. Trial was scheduled for week after next and without a job, the boy had nothing to do but think. Think about everything he stood to lose should he receive a guilty verdict. Think about his wife and new baby going it alone without him. Think about his horses. Cal was glad he hadn't lost Spirit. Granted, it wasn't technically his horse, but Troy connected with the animals, treating each and every animal he worked like it was his own. Troy built layers of trust, bonding with the horses in a way most people never experience. He'd given up drinking, but Cal knew how hard a battle it could be. It was a job you attended every day of the week, every week of the month, every month of the year. Sober himself now for nineteen months, Cal understood the challenge. Desperation pushed a man to his limits. It made him shift priorities. If Troy broke under the pressure, he could easily seek relief from a bottle.

Troy wasn't the only one caught in a vise-like grip at the moment. Cal's daughter Emily was arriving in Chattanooga this evening. His ex-wife had agreed to allow the visit, a week-long stay that could turn into two, provided Emily was in agreement. Cal was excited. Nervous, excited, he was set to drive to the airport in a few hours and meet Emily at the gate. Annie wouldn't be joining him. She decided it was best if he and his daughter took the initial reunion solo. There'd be plenty enough time for visits with her new family during her stay.

A visit complicated by the likes of Jeremiah and Jillian. Jeremiah had made a point of threatening Annie during his last trip to town. If he had thoughts of repeating the gesture, Cal was going to make him wish he'd done otherwise. Her too, Cal mused, following Jillian as she ascended the front steps to the lobby. It wasn't a coincidence Jillian was in town. Or that Jack's lighter was found outside the stables. The two had been seen together. Lighter. Fire. A shudder passed through him. Jillian set fires. Jack was facing jail time. Sure, it was possible he'd dropped the lighter back when he attacked Delaney, but if it was in good condition and relatively unscathed, it could be the clue that put Jack in the guilty seat more recently.

Someone deliberately set those horses free. Someone who knew the animals, someone with a motive.

Opening the door for Jillian, more out of habit than courtesy, Cal decided that someone could be his brother, Jack.

She, his willing accomplice. Cal didn't want to even think about what the lighter represented. Not with Jillian on premises. She had a reputation for arson and a heart black with envy and malice.

Chapter Eight

Nick Harris spied the narrow backside of Jillian Devane's figure as she stood in front of the bar at Whiskey Joe's. Not his preferred meeting place. Unfortunately he wasn't in a position to quibble. She'd insisted on the bar and lounge and he accepted. Actually, venue mattered little. This wouldn't take long, he mused, raking his gaze over the length of her body, her tapered legs draped in denim, her four inch heels par for the course. Nick could envision her face. Cat eyes would turn up at the ends when she smiled, spit daggers when she was angry, accompanied by a flash of temper. Full lips would pout or part, depending on her mood. She'd held an intrigue for him once, an adventure onto dangerous terrain, but when her heart turned spiteful and she turned the sharp end of her blade toward him, the thrill had ceased. She was threatening his family now, and Nick had zero tolerance for her games.

"Jillian," he murmured, keeping his voice purposefully low as he drew up beside her.

Sliding a hand down the counter, she turned, peering up into his face with a practiced calm. "*Amorzhino.*" She smiled, her eyes slanting in pleasure. "I was so glad to get your phone call. I knew you'd come to your senses eventually. Your country wife must be leaving you alone much too much," she purred, tiptoeing her fingers up his chest.

Removing her slender hand from his body, he pressed it back against her chest. Planting his hands to his waistband, he said, "This isn't a friendly visit. I want to know why you're here and how you're mixed up with Jeremiah Ladd."

"Are you jealous?"

"Couldn't care less," he retorted.

Jillian slid her arms around his torso and pushed into him. "You have nothing to worry about. I've never heard of the man."

Roughly pulling her arms from him, Nick brought them together, securing them in a single-fisted grip. "I'm not playing games with you, Jillian. Jeremiah was bailed out, with *cash*. Where did he get it?"

Anger lit up the gold in her eyes, emotion thrashing openly before she snuffed the flames and smirked. "Perhaps he went to a bank?"

"I think it was you." Nick leaned down, whispering harshly, "I think you contacted the casino in Vegas and paid his marker for him."

Jillian didn't shrink from him. He knew she wouldn't give him the pleasure and certainly not for public consumption. Instead, she held her ground and softened her tone. "Why would I pay money on behalf of someone I don't know?"

"Because you and Jeremiah share a common goal."

Hypnotic eyes turned up at the ends as she ushered forth a pout. "Does he want you like I want you?"

A bartender walked up behind Jillian, depositing a martini glass filled with aquamarine liquid. The young man cast a hesitant eye toward Nick's hold on Jillian's arms. "Can I get you something to drink, sir?"

Nick shook his head. "No, thanks. I won't be staying."

The kid moved down the bar, attending to other patrons.

"You should stay," Jillian hummed against her burgundy-glossed lips. "I will make it worth your while."

He wasn't interested in her tease. Only her end game. "I will figure it out. I will put you two together."

"Don't waste your time. The only 'two' you should be putting together is you and me." She winked. "Like the old days."

Nick released her in a sudden thrust and stepped away from her. He was getting nowhere. While he thought he could detect the lie in her eyes, Jillian's practiced deception was a mask he couldn't penetrate. No problem. There were other ways to get at the truth besides attempting to extract it from her up close and personal. "Oh, and by the way, how did you get here so soon? I only called your father forty-eight hours ago."

"I am a woman of means." Reaching for her drink, she explained, "You know how I feel about you. When I heard you were looking for me, I rushed here as fast as I could."

Nick believed her slippery leer suggested differently. "Hope it was worth the expense."

She brought the Cosmopolitan to her lips, tiger eyes becoming slits as she replied, "Every *centavo*."

Jeremiah Ladd sat in his parked car. Tucked away in the heavily wooded section of the property, Cal Foster's log home was big. Rambling almost. And expensive. Jeremiah didn't know much about building materials, but he didn't have to. Two stories in height, the house was lined with porches and connected to smaller structures by breezeways. Late afternoon, the trees around him were drenched in gold, shadows growing across the yard as night came to call. Huge plate-glass windows lined the front and sides, allowing for an unobstructed view of the forest around them. Lights illuminated the walkways, casting glowing beams up trees from their placement along the ground. Bushes and trees around the home had to be newly planted, but appeared as if they'd been there for years. It took money to accomplish that—and lots of it. Jack had been right. His brother was loaded.

But Cal had no right to build his home here. This land rightfully belonged to him. It was his family's land, not Cal's. Not Annie's. Not even her bastard child's. Old resentment percolated in Jeremiah's gut. This was his land, yet *they* were the ones living on it. They were the ones who looted his gold, leaving barely a flake behind for him to salvage. Jeremiah tightened his fist around the steering wheel of his truck. Well, those day s were over. Their high-living at his expense was about to come to an end. He would make them sorry they ever pushed him out of his rightful inheritance.

Startling him from his reverie, Jeremiah's cell phone rang. He yanked it from the center console. "Talk to me."

"He's gone."

"Gone where?"

"I followed him to the highway."

Jeremiah smiled. "Keep following him."

"*What*? For how long?"

"Until I tell you." Jeremiah pressed the End button.

Until I finish my business here, that's how long. A little probing of Jack Foster told Jeremiah everything he needed to know. Cal and Annie lived here. Her daughter and punk husband lived in a cabin located farther back. Jeremiah couldn't see it from here, but he didn't care. He was here for one reason and one reason only.

Sliding free of his truck, he rallied his anger and walked up to the Foster home. Hustling up the steps, he peered in through the front window and smiled. Annie was home. She was standing in the living room by a desk of sorts, a narrow table pushed up against a wall near what looked to be the entrance to a kitchen. Dressed in a hot pink blouse and white cotton skirt and flats, she looked young and fresh. Pretty. Grinning, he rapped on the door. This should be fun.

Several seconds passed and the door opened. Annie gasped, flinging a hand over her mouth.

Staring into widened blue eyes, Jeremiah chuckled. "Hello, Annie."

She tried to ram the door closed, but Jeremiah shoved a boot inside, blocking her efforts. He needed some time with her and he was going to enjoy it. "What? Not happy to see me?"

"What are you doing here?" she demanded.

"I'm here to rekindle an old flame."

Alarm surged in her gaze. "Get out of here, Jeremiah. You're not welcome here."

"Awe, Annie. We're family, you and me. We have a daughter together. Can't a guy come and pay his respects to the grandmother of his grandchild?"

Her black brow furrowed in suspicion. "Casey told me you showed up at the hospital."

"I did. Too bad her baby looks like a raisin. Must take after your side of the family."

Regaining some of her old spite, Annie pushed back, "You get out of here, Jeremiah, before I call the police."

He laughed, intentionally sharp and derisive. "Oh, you floor me Annie, you really do. Call the police? Doesn't your family have enough to worry about with the police these days?" Realization instantly cooled her indignation, and he took full advantage. "That's right. I know about your son-in-law's legal troubles and I know the law isn't on your side." He meant Gavin Shore. Jack boasted about his mother's connections to the police department and how they did everything but turn Delaney away and kicked her to the curb. *Go home, Delaney, and suck it up.* He savored a private smile. Jeremiah only wished he could have been there to witness the exchange. Not to worry. He'd be witnessing some of his own glory and soon.

Pushing his way inside her home, Jeremiah looked around and let out a low whistle. "Looks like someone married up in the world."

Annie marched over to a phone by a plush leather sofa. Supple smooth and littered with pillows, it looked comfortable. Taking stock of the interior, Jeremiah noted the fancy lighting, the rich wood furniture, oversized paintings and cowboy bronze statues and thought this guy had money to burn. Annie set her hand to the phone receiver and glared at him. "If you don't leave right now, I'm calling the police."

Jeremiah sauntered in farther, tempted to drop to a seat and make himself at home. "Why don't you call your hubby?" He snickered. "Oh, wait. He's on a highway on his way out of town."

The comment served its purpose. The color drained from Annie's cheeks, her skin ice-cold against the bright flush of her blouse. "What do you want?" she asked.

"Like I said, I wanted to stop by for a visit, rekindle old times."

"No one here is interested in visiting with you."

"Tsk, tsk. So different than the girl I used to know in high school. That girl would have kissed my boot if I asked her."

Annie returned a hooded gaze. "Like you said, so different than today."

"Too bad. We're kin, now," he said, walking toward her, dragging his fingertips along the top of the sofa as he approached her. Keeping a wary eye out for unexpected intruders, he noted the leather was as soft as it looked.

"Funny how we're all of a sudden kin," she said, "when for the last twenty years I've tried to prove exactly that and you shut me down. Where was your desire to be 'kin' then?"

"Oh, Annie. You're too hard on a man. I only dodged you because you were trying to extort money from me."

"Extort money from you? How about do what's right and pay for your child?"

Jeremiah laughed softly. "I never said I wanted a baby with you." Nearing her, he could feel a palpable fury radiating from her body. Every cell seemed to be vibrating hot and wild. Recalling their days together, it occurred to him she had a passionate side, a very willing passionate side. She certainly knew how to please a fellow when she wanted to. "You and I should've spent more time together."

"Should've thought about that before you ran off with my sister, Lacy."

Jeremiah laughed. Thoroughly enjoying himself, he almost hated to leave. But leave he must. He had bigger fish on his pole than Annie. Though looking into her eyes triggered an old arousal. She had been one of the prettier ones, one of the pure ones in his past. "Didn't she tell you?" He leaned forward and whispered, "Lacy and I were never more than friends."

Knowing he had sufficiently incensed Annie, Jeremiah turned on his heel and walked back to the front door. Pausing, he turned and winked. "Don't worry. We'll see each other again before I leave town." Closing the door on his way out, Jeremiah took pleasure in the sound of her angry shriek. *Miss you too, Annie.*

Chapter Nine

"May I help you please?"

Staring down at the young woman behind the counter, more girl than woman, he smiled. "Are these real gold?"

"Oh, yes," she replied. "Fourteen carat."

Gazing at the gold pendant pulled from the display case, he fondled it between his fingers. It was small, no larger than his thumbnail, but felt solid. "And you said this here was made from the gold they found on this land?"

"Yes, sir. Mr. Harris had it mined for the sole purpose of selling here in the hotel. A souvenir from the very earth you visited."

She smiled, and he smiled back. Replacing the pendant on the small velvet tray, he scanned the case below where rows of similarly formed pendants were displayed. They varied in size, but all were formed in the shape of a wishing well. He stroked the thin tips of his beard and pondered how he was going to pull off his heist. Jeremiah said to steal as many as he could. Take them by the box full if he could swing it. Peering into the big round eyes of the innocent country girl, he dubbed it would be child's play. But first he had to get rid of her.

"Would you like to purchase the pendant?"

"Uh... I need to think about it for a minute."

"Okay," she chirped, happy as a bird flittering through treetops on a spring morning. "Let me know if there's anything I can help you with."

"I will," he replied, realizing he knew exactly how he was gonna do it. Snagging a peek toward the front desk, he counted two clerks. Add this one and there were three girls on shift tonight. Three. Dropping a possessive hand over the pendant, caressing the gold chain attached to it, he knew the store was supposed to be closing soon. Sign said five-thirty.

It was about that time, now.

As though giving him time to think over his purchase, the girl moseyed down to the opposite end of the counter, pretending to organize some postcards along the wall. When she turned her back, he bumped his Styrofoam cup. Coke spilled in a rapid slide across the glass counter and onto the floor. "Dag nabbit!" he exclaimed.

She whirled and cried out, "Oh!" Rushing over, she grabbed the oversized cup he bought from a gas station and began wiping ice into the palm of her hand. "Don't worry about it—it's okay!"

"I'm so *sorry*," he said in the most sincere voice he could muster. Rounding the counter, he crouched down and began making a mess of trying to clean up the dark brown cola currently spreading like a sheet of molasses over the beige stone tile.

"It's okay. I can grab some towels from the spa." Bounding up, she ran out of the gift shop and down a hall—in the opposite direction of the front desk.

Chuckling to himself, he remained on his haunches so as not to call attention to himself from the girls at the front desk. Quicker than lightning, he swiped a hand through the case grabbing hand fulls of pendants and chains and anything else that stuck to his fingers. There were three levels of 'em and he stuffed every single one into his pockets—front, back, wherever they would fit—until the case had been wiped clean. When he yanked open a drawer beneath the shelves, his eyes lit up at the sight of large boxes. He knew from previous experience there would be extra jewelry stored below, and sure enough, here it was. Why she hadn't locked it was a surprise to him. Maybe the one key that opened the case unlatched the lower drawer at the same time. He'd seen it work that way in a store in Georgia.

But this wasn't gonna fit in his pockets. Hauling a box free, he looked around for a bag. Bingo. A stack of them were housed neatly in a cubby beneath the register. In two minutes flat he had cleaned out the case and the drawer. Oh, wouldn't Jeremiah be pleased!

Slowly he rose from his position on the lookout for witnesses. Neither front desk girl was looking his way. Breathing a sigh of relief, he stood fully. Straightening his coat, he sidled out from behind the counter. Exiting the store with gift shop bag in hand, he controlled his pace, careful not to draw attention to himself. Despite the hammer of pulse, he knew no one would give him a second glance if he strolled out of here at a leisurely pace. No direct eye contact, he kept watch from the corner of his eye. The helpful cashier girl would be back any second. His job was to be gone.

"We've been robbed!"

Malcolm Ward bolted from his seat in the manager's office. While hidden from public view, it didn't prevent him from hearing what went on at the front desk. Rounding the corner, he demanded, "What's going on?"

The gift shop attendant stood shaking, her doe eyes pricked by fear. "All the jewelry is gone."

"Gone?" Malcolm hated to press the girl when she was obviously distraught, but he needed answers. "What do you mean, gone?"

"Gone," she replied. Her lower lip began to quiver. Tears swam into her lower lids. "It's been stolen."

Anger split Malcolm straight down his middle, but he held his temper. The front desk clerks stood like statues by his side, neither daring to say a word. "Stolen?"

She nodded.

"Do you know who did this?"

"I think so." Glancing sideways, she said, "There was a man in the shop. He was looking at a pendant. He spilled his drink and I ran to the spa to get towel and when I came back—"

"The pendants were gone," Malcolm finished for her.

She bit down on her lip and nodded.

"How many did he get?"

"All of them."

Damn it! Malcolm muttered under his breath, striding to the gift shop to look for himself. Sure enough, the case was clean, a few empty blue velvet boxes scattered about the floor, soaking up a mess of spilled soda. The open drawers tangled insult and injury in his gut. The girl couldn't have been gone that long. Whoever did this knew what they were doing. They understood they had to get in and get out and knew how to do so without igniting suspicion.

Walking back to the front desk, Malcolm asked, "Did the guy give you a name?" The girl shook her head. "Could you identify him if you saw him again?"

"I think so," she murmured. Tears were streaming down her face, streaking her cheeks with runny lines of black mascara.

Turning to the young women behind the front desk, he asked, "Did either of you see anything?"

The older blonde replied, "I saw a dark-haired man walk out. He seemed normal enough..."

The second clerk chimed in, "I saw him, too. He was carrying a gift shop bag," she added, visibly fearful the words were a condemnation of her friend. "He had a beard."

"Am I fired?" the girl asked.

"No, "Malcolm said automatically, upset with himself for losing his cool. When the boss lost it, the staff quickly followed. "You did nothing wrong. But I will need you to make a statement to the police." The police. The minute he uttered the word he regretted the need to call them. After what that officer put Delaney through, Malcolm had little expectation for better treatment though he damn well was going to push for it. Hotel Ladd had been robbed. It was a crime that would not go unpunished.

Cal did his best to keep focus on the road. The drive home was only an hour, but he couldn't keep his eyes off her. Emily was beautiful. The changes over the past year and a half were incredible. No longer a young girl, she had the look a teenager. Her blonde hair had lost its curl, straightened with the telltale precision of flat irons Annie used so frequently these days in her salon. Emily didn't wear makeup, save a small gloss on her lips, yet the pink shade made her mouth pop against her fair skin. The sight tugged at his heart every time she smiled. No longer sullen and angry, Emily seemed to skipping on clouds. She was bright and eager and talkative, wielding an impressive vocabulary for a twelve-year-old.

Twelve. Emily had turned twelve last month, and while he wished he could have been there to celebrate with her, he had the next best thing. It was a gift for her. Cal had one of the wishing well pendants from the hotel store engraved with her name and adorned with tiny diamonds. He wanted it to sparkle and dazzle. He wanted his daughter to love it. It being the first piece of jewelry she received from her father. Her daddy. That's what she had called him when she walked off the plane. *Hello, Daddy.*

"How much farther?" she asked.

"We're almost there," he told her, excited for Emily to meet Annie. He'd texted her when they left the airport so she'd know when to expect them. Cal had wanted Casey and Troy and the baby to be there when they arrived home, but Annie declined. *Slow and easy wins the race, Cal.*

Cal smiled to himself. His wife was so much like him.

Emily turned in her seat. "Do you think we can go horse-back riding, sometime?"

"We can go every day, if you'd like."

"Really?" Her brown eyes rounded. "I'd *love* to go every day!"

He laughed. "My Daddy is gonna love you!"

"Does he like horses, too?"

"Sure does. Owns a ranch full of them!"

Funny how Cal hadn't talked much about his family while living in Arizona. Looking back, it seemed like he'd been living in a cocoon. He had Caroline and Emily, a job that he enjoyed. There had been no reason to talk about Tennessee other than in terms of "one day." One day we'll spend a summer there. One day we'll visit the family. But that "one day" never materialized. Other than a brief visit when Emily was a year old, Cal and Caroline had been content to spend their time in Arizona. They took long weekends in the mountains, picnics along the rivers. Her parents lived nearby. It seemed enough at the time.

"It's so beautiful around here," Emily said with a sigh, gazing at the landscape like she was star-struck. "There are so many trees."

Glancing at Emily, he soaked in her enthusiasm. He loved that she loved the landscape, but it wasn't enough anymore. Cal wanted Emily to *know* Tennessee. His home. Her family. This was the land of her ancestors, these were her roots. Pulling into the driveway for his and Annie's home, he thought, his family tree might have its share of gnarled roots but they were his—hers. They were family. "Wait until you see the house," he said. "It's smack dab in the middle of forest!"

Winding through the woods, the drive opened and Emily blew out her breath and pointed. "Oh my gosh! Is that where you live?" He nodded. "It looks like a picture from a magazine."

Cal considered the observation, relived the months of construction, the miscellany of decision after decision. Annie had always wanted cathedral ceilings, the higher the better, as she claimed living in her apartment had felt like living in a box. It was a feature he was willing to oblige, allowing him to incorporate the walls of windows to open their home to nature. He had insisted on the stone façade out front because he felt it gave the house a feel of strength, impregnable, like a man's castle should be. Azalea bushes lined the front porch, a wide covered patio wrapped around the entire house. In the spring, when all the blooms were blazing, that was the place they wanted to sit, looking forward to watching Cassidy laugh and play. But it wasn't only Cassidy they were looking forward to watch grow up. They hoped Emily would share her life with them, too. "We had it built special for us, including a room especially for you."

"There is?" she asked, her mouth agape.

Pleasure coursed through him. "Sure is. Annie had it decorated with all your favorite things." Gently tapping the brake, he said, "And there she is."

Annie walked out of the house and stood waiting on the front porch. But rather than tossing out the welcome mat with a warm and friendly smile, she look pained, rigid. Rounding the circular drive, Cal detected angst in her smile. Was something wrong?

"Is that her?" Emily asked, her voice soft but eager. "Is that your new wife?"

"Yes," he murmured in reply, fighting the ramp of nerves in his gut. "That's Annie."

"She's so pretty."

"Thanks," he replied absently. Throwing the gear into park, Cal pushed out his door and rounded the hood. "Everything all right?" he asked Annie. She nodded, her gaze tightly encircling his daughter, Emily.

Cal opened the passenger door and helped Emily hop down from her seat. She straightened her cropped jean jacket over her emerald green T-shirt, ran a hand down her matching floral-patterned skirt, then swept the straight blonde hair over her shoulders where it fell midway down her back. Annie walked down the steps and straight to Emily. Thankfully, whatever had been eating her seemed to be forgotten as she reached out a hand. A smile formed on her lips. "Emily, so nice to finally meet you."

"Hi."

Cupping both hands around Emily's one, Annie drew her near. "I love your outfit," she said, flashing a glance to Cal.

"Thanks." Emily accepted the compliment easily.

"How was your first drive through Tennessee?"

"Great. It's really pretty here."

"It sure is," Cal agreed, and grabbed his daughter's suitcase from the backseat. Heading inside, Annie and Emily followed. "And you're going to see a lot more of it," Cal said over Emily's head, searching for signs from Annie as to her earlier discomfort.

Responding with a brief, *we need to talk* look, Annie asked Emily, "Do you like horses?"

"I love them! My dad says we can go riding. Can we?" she asked Annie, as if accustomed to checking with the female head of household before all was said and done.

"We sure can. Do you ride back home?"

Cal opened the door and set Emily's luggage by the staircase as she and Annie continued talking horses. Reflexively, he glanced around the living room. Everything seemed to be in order. He would have preferred conducting a full search, on account of Jeremiah being in town, but that would be overkill. No sense in worrying Annie about the possibility of trouble. Best to wait until there was something to worry about.

"Are you thirsty? Would you care for something to drink?" Annie asked Emily.

"No, thanks. I'm fine. I ate dinner on the flight over."

Annie sat, offering Emily a place beside her on the sofa cushion. Cal thought she appeared okay, but he could tell there was something working behind those blue eyes of hers. Something she wanted to share but clearly could not. He wanted to take her for a detour in the kitchen, probe Annie about what was going on, but this was Emily's first visit. A visit he wanted to go well, smooth as a hay field swaying in a summer breeze. So Cal took a seat on an adjacent sofa and stuffed his concern in a back compartment, concentrating on his girls. There'd be time enough later for a private interrogation.

"Have you thought about other things you'd like to do or see while you're here?" Annie asked.

"Well, I've heard about panning for gold," she said, her eyes glittering with curiosity. "Is there really such a thing?"

Annie laughed. Rich, genuine, the sound eased Cal's mind. "We do. We have gold and rubies, too."

"Rubies?"

Annie nodded. "You can find them in the rivers, or we can visit one of the nearby mines."

"Is that like Ruby Falls?" Emily glanced between them. "I saw signs for it on our drive here."

"No, sweetheart," Cal answered. "Ruby Falls was actually named after the wife of the man who discovered it. His name was Leo Lambert and he was a local cave enthusiast in the area who discovered the falls while he was drilling a hole for an elevator." Relaxed by talk of history, the common thread to people and events today, Cal went on. "The falls are one of the top tourist destinations in Tennessee. Located deep in Lookout Mountain, you have to walk for an hour through underground caves to see them but once you get there, you'll never forget them."

"Wow..."

"Did you tell her about the bonfire?" Annie prompted.

"Sure did." Leaning forward, he set elbows to knees and explained, "Every Sunday the hotel hosts a bonfire for guests. We play music, tell stories..."

"Kinda like a campfire?" Emily asked.

"Pretty much. But we gave it a fancy name and call it Serenity Scape."

"Sounds awesome! Can we go this weekend?"

"You bet," he replied, warmed by her interest. The three settled in for a discussion of things to do and see while Emily was in Tennessee.

"It's getting late," Cal announced an hour later. "I bet you're tired after your long flight."

"Not really. It's only seven o'clock my time."

Cal grinned. Kids would be kids. No matter the hour, it was never too late in their mind.

"Why don't you take a shower and get ready for bed?" he suggested. "You don't have to go to sleep."

Annie rose from the sofa. "I'll show you where your room will be."

"Okay."

Annie took Emily upstairs and returned a few minutes later.

Sweeping around the base of the banister, she sighed in a heavy stream. "She's precious, Cal."

"She's a sweet one," he agreed. Taking Annie in his arms, he wanted to hear about her at the moment. "What's up, Annie? You seemed a little off when we arrived. Is everything okay? You don't mind having Emily here, do you?"

"Oh, Cal, of course not. I'm thrilled she's staying with us, and I hope we can keep her the entire two weeks before she has to go back to school."

Relieved, the knot in his chest loosened. He wanted Annie to like Emily. He wanted Emily to like Annie. It would mean more time together with his daughter, and next to the woman he held in his arms, there was nothing he wanted more. "Then what is it? Something was eating at you when I drove up." Annie pressed her lips into a line and the tension returned to her gaze. "What?" Cal pressed. "What's got you so worked up?"

"Jeremiah."

"*Jeremiah*?"

"He was here," she said.

The revelation ricocheted in his skull. Images of him ripped through his mind's eye. Bits and pieces of Annie's story about Jeremiah escorting her and Lacy from the forest at gunpoint exploded in his heart. If Jeremiah Ladd had the nerve to think he could force two women against their will in a sick attempt at revenge and then come here and invade his home and family's privacy, he had another thought coming. Cal ground his emotion into a ball of fury, and cinched it tight. Jeremiah would not set foot in his home again. If he did, he'd be stepping over Cal's dead body.

Chapter Ten

Cal strode down the hall from the spa on his way to the hotel lobby, the scent of eucalyptus persisting in his senses as he savored the vision of his daughter eagerly hopping up into a big leather chair for her pedicure. After her tour through the salon, she'd declared her favorite part were the spring-fed, open-air showers, particularly the disappearing ceiling. Cal chuckled, warmed by her thrill. Malcolm's creative genius strikes again! Cal would have loved to have shown her more of the property like the strange labyrinth formations in the forest, the swimming hole just past the riverside café, but there would be time enough for that later.

Right now he had to man the front desk until Malcolm's noon return. He and Nick had a meeting with Troy's legal team this morning which could not be rescheduled. Thankful for their support of his son-in-law, Cal agreed to handle administrative duties for the morning, the most important of which was signing payroll checks. It wasn't a huge inconvenience, not with Annie and Emily tucked away in the spa next door. Cal was only glad he didn't have to leave the two at home alone. Jeremiah's surprise visit yesterday was a bad sign. It meant the man had no fear. When Annie had threatened to call the police, he laughed. The arrogance grated on Cal. Somehow Jeremiah had known Cal was on his way out of town. *Knew it.*

Well, if the man thought he had free roam in this town and could taunt whomever he wanted, he was wrong. The visit with Annie yesterday would be Jeremiah's one and only. Cal was going to make sure of it. At the moment he had business to attend. Closing his mind to thoughts of Jeremiah, Cal shifted into manager mode. Walking behind the front desk, he slowed, surveying the hotel lobby in a swift evaluation. The fountain was gurgling softly in the early morning calm, wood floors were satisfactorily polished to a subtle shine, the windows were clear and clean, appearing almost non-existent as he took in the lush green mountainside.

"Good morning, Mr. Foster."

Smiling at the front desk clerk, he replied, "Good morning, Patti." Eight-thirty in the morning, there was only one clerk on duty. The second wouldn't arrive until ten. Slowing, he asked, "How does the schedule look for the day?"

"Six check-ins and one departure."

Cal nodded. Fairly normal for a forty-room hotel. Fridays were a popular day for arrivals, though Saturday was their heaviest. Headed to his office, he considered occupancy rates for the month, scheduled activities, generating a quick mental profit and loss statement... They were completely booked through Christmas, and Cal couldn't be more pleased. Business was good.

"Mr. Foster?"

Cal paused and turned. "Yes?"

Patti approached hesitantly. Glancing around the vacant lobby, she asked, "Did Mr. Ward tell you about the gift shop?"

"The gift shop?" She nodded but didn't elaborate. "No, he didn't. Is there a problem?"

"It was robbed last night."

"Robbed?"

"Yes, sir. A man came in and stole all the gold pendants."

Disbelief swirled through him as questions rose fast and furious. "What man? When?"

"We don't know who he was," she replied. "It happened around five-thirty, just before closing time."

Cal cursed inwardly. "Did Malcolm report the crime to the police?"

"Yes, sir. They're scheduled to come by this morning and get a statement. I wanted to be sure you knew."

"What time?"

"Nine."

Cal checked his watch and mentally cleared his agenda. "Okay. Thanks, Patti. Let me know when they get here. Until then, let's stay on high alert."

"Yes, sir."

Jeremiah Ladd strolled into the dumpster of a house, the interior saturated with the scent of old cigarette smoke. The boys were laid out across the couch, the typical bored expressions pasted on their faces. Well maybe this would spark their mood. "My pal says those pendants you snagged are worth a good twenty grand or more. Not bad for a ten-minute heist."

Seated on opposite ends of a soiled couch, his two cohorts exchanged a look of satisfaction. "So where's my money?" Rob asked.

Of course that would be his first question, missing sight of the big picture, Jeremiah thought, pausing in mid-room. But then again, the brothers weren't the sharpest tools in the shed. Never had been. They were thieves, not rocket scientists. Jeremiah was the brains of this trio, which meant he had to do everything, including the thinking. "You'll get your money and then some. Twenty grand is squat when you look at the hole they carved out of the ground." According to his friend at the pawn shop, the gold Delaney scored from the site had to be five times that much, a hundred times. "The rest has to be in a safe somewhere and it's our job to find it."

The men looked at him expectantly. "I didn't see no office when I was there." The younger brother scratched his head, his dark brown hair a greasy mess of nasty strands. Even his beard looked knotted and nappy. The two would not have been Jeremiah's first choice for partners in crime, but after two dozen phone calls, these boys had been his only hope. Clem Sweeney had been useful the first time around, cluing Jeremiah into the gold's existence. But he'd caught on quick and was of no use to him anymore, not once he realized Jeremiah wasn't interested in sharing the loot. The guys he used to run with during high school were of no use. They couldn't break into a piggy bank, let alone a real one. That's where these two fit in. It took some effort, but he'd managed to locate them south of Bryson City, living in a trailer with two biker babes. The duo had been more than willing to help. All it took was a few words. *Gold. On Ladd Springs.*

Grabbing a cold beer from the refrigerator, Jeremiah returned to the living area and popped it open. "The office is behind the front desk. And I'll guarantee you there's a safe inside."

"How we gonna get in there without anyone seeing us? They'll know we ain't guests if they see us behind the counter."

Jeremiah stared at him, his palm iced by the cold beer can. Moron. The man was a complete and utter moron. "Diversion," Jeremiah said bluntly. "Diversion 101."

"Diversion?" the younger asked with a blank stare.

Glancing sideways, his brother tossed him a look of disgust. "Distract them so you can get in while they're busy doing something else."

"Oh... But how we gonna do that?"

Both men looked to Jeremiah. Pleasure unwound his mouth into a grin. "I know how to get everyone's attention."

Travis sat in his parked truck, his lungs pressed tighter than the pages in a legal journal. After discovering Jeremiah Ladd's marker had been paid from a bank in Tennessee—a local bank—Travis decided to follow the man and find out who his source might be. It had to be someone from Jeremiahs' old crowd. If the money came from here, it had to be someone he knew from the old days. Couldn't have been Clem Sweeney. Despite the two hooking up during Jeremiah's last visit to town, Clem was still in jail and broke as a bone-dry whiskey barrel. Clem might have been the one responsible for leading Jeremiah to the gold on Ladd Springs, but he couldn't help him steal the precious metal. Couldn't help him pay his debt either. No, it had to be someone else.

Glancing around the desolate streets, the run-down hous-ing and litter-ridden streets, Travis wondered who around here could have helped Jeremiah pay his way free. This area was poorer than poor, but this is where Jeremiah had come. Travis had followed him from a local motel near Fran's Din-er. He had no problem learning where Jeremiah was staying. A few blind calls inquiring to speak with Mr. Ladd turned up the right motel when the clerk offered to connect him with his room. Focusing on the lean-to of a house, Travis wondered who might be inside with Jeremiah. As he sat, the humidity built within the confines of his truck cab. Not a cloud in the sky, it was sunny and warm. Swiping the back of his hand against his forehead, he hoped Jeremiah wouldn't stay inside all day.

The front door of the place swung open and Travis in-stinctively ducked, his heart shooting beats into his ribs. Jer-emiah knew what he looked like, and Travis couldn't risk being seen while he was spying on the guy. There was no doubt in his mind that Jeremiah would not take it well. Over the rim of his dashboard, he chanced a peek. Two men walked out behind Jeremiah. Two dark-haired men with faci-al hair, medium build. By the looks of them they were defi-nitely locals. One hung at the top of the steps while the other trailed Jeremiah to his truck. The two had words before Jere-miah climbed in and drove off. As Travis watched, something struck him as oddly familiar. Were they workers in town? Had they helped with the construction of the hotel?

Heart pounding hard within his chest, Travis snapped a few quick shots of the men with his cell phone. Maybe some-one else would recognize them. Debating whether or not to follow Jeremiah, Travis hesitated. The one man remained outside. If Travis drove by him now, he might call attention to himself and arouse suspicion. But with Jeremiah putting distance between them, Travis might lose his primary target. Pressure compounded as he silently counted the seconds. Jer-emiah's taillights illuminated, then disappeared as he turned a corner. Unfortunately the stranger remained in place. No longer looking around as though distracted, he seemed to notice Travis' truck. Probably not used to seeing a vehicle in decent condition around these parts.

But when the man's expression changed, Travis took that as his cue to depart. *Get out of Dodge before the man was able to place a face with the truck.* Throwing the gear into reverse, Travis made a three-point circle in the middle of the street and took off in the opposite direction. No sense giving the guy any more detailed description than necessary. Too bad it came at the price of losing Jeremiah. Glancing in his rearview mirror, Travis was torn. Bothered. The man continued to stare after him. Not good. If the guy told Jeremiah a black truck had been parked on their street, a man inside watching them, it would be all Jeremiah would need to come looking for him. Young brunette guy in a black truck could lead him straight to Travis.

Or Troy. They shared looks and they shared vehicle description. Slamming a palm to the steering wheel, Travis cursed his mistake. *How could he have been so stupid?*

Chapter Eleven

Injecting as much enthusiasm into his voice as possible, Cal asked, "How was the spa treatment, girls?" He wanted nothing more than to focus on his wife and daughter and their pleasure, but thoughts of Jeremiah and the robbery gnawed at him. Cal knew they were connected. Sure as he was breathing, he knew the two were not a coincidence.

"Great!" Emily squealed, waving fluttering fingertips for his perusal. "I got a facial, and my nails done in sparkles."

Sure enough, Cal mused, her nails glittered pearlescent cream in the overhead lighting. "Those are mighty pretty."

Annie smiled. "Emily insisted her toes match, so be careful if you think you're losing your mind later at home when you catch glimpse of a disco ball bouncing from her feet." She laughed, adding, "She had every toe done in a different shade!"

"Wonderful. It will remind me of my old dancing days."

"Really?" Emily asked. "You know how to dance? Can you teach me?"

Placing an arm around her shoulders, Cal led Emily from the spa and winked. "I don't think my moves would be very popular with the 'in' crowd today. You might want to watch some of those online videos instead." Glancing at Annie over Emily's head, he remarked, "Or maybe we could find a dance class around here?"

She nodded. "I'll ask Candi. She's full of good ideas when it comes to what's in."

"Sounds like a plan," Cal replied. Candi was Annie's best friend and very hip. If anyone knew it would be her. Now that she worked in the salon with Annie, she'd be easy to consult with on the matter. "Are you gals hungry?"

"I am," Emily answered unequivocally.

Annie nodded. "I could use a bite to eat."

"I've got a little more work to do around here," Cal lied, "but how about you two head on over to Fran's and I'll catch up with you?"

Annie looked to Emily. "Best cheeseburgers in town."

Emily grinned. "Works for me."

Cal escorted Annie and Emily to the truck and sent them on their way. Returning to the lobby, he picked up a set of keys for one of the hotel vehicles and made his departure. It was sort of a complimentary rental car program the hotel offered for guests interested in taking a spontaneous trip to town yet had no car of their own. While most folks didn't need it, they all appreciated the gesture. Now that Malcolm was back, he could head out. "I'll have the car back this afternoon," Cal said.

Malcolm Ward waved him off, his light blue eyes warming within the tanned brown of his skin despite the pressure Cal knew him to be under. "Take all the time you need," he replied. "You know we have two more for the taking."

Cal nodded thanks, cupping his hand closed over the keys. But that was Malcolm. Not only calm under pressure, the man was personal, genuine. Similar to the gel that kept his shock of white hair smoothed back in place for his southern California hairstyle, Malcolm was the invisible glue that held the business together. He was subtle yet effective. You couldn't miss Nick Harris coming from a mile away but not Malcolm. He beat a softer path.

"Let me know if you hear anything from the police regarding the break-in."

"Will do," Malcolm replied.

Cal had his suspicions about who was involved, despite Jeremiah's alibi. The intent of his little impromptu visit with Annie suddenly became clear, and one way or another, Cal was going to prove Jeremiah's involvement with the robbery. Until then, he was employing a backup plan. If Jeremiah had any more thoughts of confronting Annie, him—or God help him, Emily—Cal was going to greet him with barrel of a gun.

Not a man of violence, Cal understood some men only understood the threat of physical harm. They pushed the boundaries until someone stopped them cold. Dead cold. Hardening himself to the possibility, Cal knew he would shoot Jeremiah if the situation warranted. If there was no other way to get the point across to back off and leave his family alone, Cal would shoot.

First on the agenda, collect his guns from his parent's home. Boxed up before he'd moved to Arizona, he had yet to move the guns from the attic. His and Annie's new home had only recently been completed, and the guns had been not a high priority when it came to moving in. Cal planned to transfer them when he got around to it.

That day would be today.

Driving the half hour to Misty Mountain Ranch, the Foster family estate, Cal contemplated a confrontation with his mother. He hadn't called to warn them of his arrival. There was no need. He had a key. He'd let himself in. Still, the thought of seeing his mother so close to the impending trial chafed him. The insanity of her support for Jack made no sense. Bringing Troy to trial, airing Jack's dirty laundry would do more harm to her reputation than good. Contrary to her continued assertion that she and Jack were in the right, the Fosters had a reputation to uphold, a community profile to manage, and this trial would do nothing but soil it. Everything she claimed to defend would be ruined.

It was lunacy. Sheer lunacy.

But that was his family. Everyone had their "crazy" in the gene pool, and apparently his mother was revealing theirs. Years of impeccable dignity and aplomb would be ripped and churned by the gossip mill, plastered all over the papers. Victoria Foster would be mocked. She'd become the face of pity. Families would shun her once they learned about Jack's real actions. The secrets from years of whispers would become shouts in the streets. People had speculated about Jack's and

Delaney's divorce. Many had the details right. Jack Foster was an abuser. An abusive alcoholic and he was the reason Delaney baled on their marriage. Afterward people had flocked to Delaney and Felicity like they were warm pie blowing through an open window. Women offered to take Felicity while Delaney was busy working. Men and women alike had made a point to give Delaney a start with her new accounting business, his brothers leading the way, their wives included, and word was spread.

As Cal turned onto the drive to his childhood home and took in the acreage, he was flooded by bittersweet memories. Wide open spaces called to the horseman in him, the mountains in the distance beckoned his outdoorsman side. Not only beautiful with its rolling hills of green, Misty Mountain Ranch was known for quality horses sold by rock-solid members of the local community. The Fosters were part of the town's fabric. They lived and breathed the country and people around them. From the densely-packed earth beneath him to the starry skies that blanketed his nights, Cal loved this land. He loved the ranch and everything it stood for.

But once the facts about Jack's attack on Delaney spread, it would taint the entire Foster family. Because his mother had chosen to involve herself. Because she had chosen to take up for Jack, the business of Misty Mountain Ranch would suffer. His brothers and their families would feel the repercussions. Shoot, *he'd* feel it too. Cal didn't kid himself. He was knee-deep in the center of this mess and he and Annie would not escape the talk.

Only Cal didn't care. He would stand up to the lot of them and face them with a clean conscience and a pure heart. Troy had done nothing wrong. Delaney had done nothing wrong. Together, they would stand strong against this assault of lies.

Roaming the confines of the toasty attic, the air suffused with heat and dank, Cal counted his blessings. He'd avoided

contact with his mother on the way in. She was here but in
her bedroom. Retired for a cat nap, Thelma had told him.

Before lunchtime? Cal could only hope it was simply a
lack of sleep and not a prescription-induced slumber. His
mother had been known to partake in the past. She might do
so again considering the stress she was under. Pausing in the
center of the plywood-lined space, Cal searched for sight of
his boxes. He was certain he'd left them in the corner, but
now, they weren't there. Glancing around, he examined boxes
according to size. His guns were packed in a pretty big box.
The myriad stacked around him could not belong to him.
Taking a few steps, he ducked his head for a timber frame
and continued his search. There were pieces of furniture arranged neatly in a line, accompanied by empty frames and a
miscellany of household items. A lot of this stuff should
probably see the inside of a thrift store, he mused, but it
wasn't his place to toss out junk. Cal's job was to find his
belongings and move them to his new home.

In the back, behind an old hutch, Cal spotted his box. At
least he thought so. Walking over, he squatted behind the
wooden crate and, sure enough, believed the box was his.
There were several lightweight boxes piled on top of it which
he carefully moved aside. As he brushed the dust from his
box, featherweight fumes of dirt particles billowed into his
face and he coughed. Reading the label, this was definitely
his box. His gun collection. Satisfaction unfurled, mixing
with a swarm of anticipation. Inside he would find not only
an   assortment   of   shotguns,   but   pistols,   ammunition...everything he needed to protect his family from the
likes of Jeremiah Ladd.

When he slid the box free from its position, the bottom
stuck, immovable as if it had been glued in place. Too long in
dormancy, he thought, giving the box a good shove. Breaking
free, the corner hit Cal's knee. "Ouch!" Dropping back, his
hand landed on a slender wooden box.

It split open and the contents spewed free. Cal swore as
he stared at a bunch of letters strewn about the floor. Rubbing

the spot on his knee, he noticed they were addressed to his father in handwritten script. Gathering them, Cal re-organized the envelopes as he'd found them, the stiff paper flaps catching on one another. Taking greater care, he peered at the fronts, realizing they weren't all addressed to Daddy. Some were addressed to Susannah. Comprehension snapped his senses together. *Susannah Ladd?*

A flush of adrenaline inflamed his thoughts. His father had kept letters from his old flame? Cal hurried to put the letters back in place, but curiosity pulled at him to slow down. What did this mean? Why would Daddy keep these after all these years?

Pausing, drawn to the handwriting scrawled across the front, he realized there was no address. Only a name. Susannah. Guilt swept over him. Odd. He'd done nothing wrong, but the mere touch of the envelope filled him with guilt. Shame. Like he was looking at something he shouldn't. Unable to stop himself, Cal opened a loosened flap and tugged the letter free.

My Dearest Girl...

Cal held his breath as he read. *Last night meant more to me than anything in this world. Nothing can raise my spirits the way you do. You fill me with ecstasy. Joy. You make me feel like the world is my oyster, your heart is my soul. Dear Girl, do you know what you do to me when you say those things? They are indelible in my mind, seared in my heart like a hot iron brand to the hide. Your love completes me. I am nothing without you. I will never be anything without you. You are the light of Heaven, an angel of His. You are a gift, a holy blessed gift and I am yours. Faithfully and forever I pray you know I will always belong to you. Gerald.*

Cal's heart stopped beating—but, oh, how his father's must have beaten for Susannah! Holding the delicate page in hand, Cal couldn't breathe. The rumors were true. His father and Susannah. Cal reached for another letter. He couldn't stop. Even if he wanted, he couldn't stop from reading on.

Gerald, you floor me. You have no idea how you carry me with your wit and intelligence! Every day is more fun than before. How could a girl ever be so lucky as to share your heart? And your soul? My word, but I am blessed. Truly. How did I get so lucky as to win your affection? It doesn't seem real. It seems like a fantasy. My friends are filled with envy and I pray for them. They could only wish for a man like you to entertain and delight them. Looking forward to our picnic this weekend. Susannah

Sorting through a few more, Cal was mesmerized.

My Dearest Girl, your lips are a succulent aphrodisiac. Pardon my saying it but I can't help myself when I'm around you. Your green eyes ensnare me, your golden hair is like spun silk from the heavens. This afternoon by the falls was incredible. It will live inside me forever. You are my sustenance, the very beat of my heart, the breath of my lungs. I find I can only think of you...

Cal sifted through letter after letter from his father, transfixed by the words inscribed, words that tied a knot in his heart. *I want us to be together. I want our lives forever entwined. I understand it will be hard. I know your father is a difficult man, but I am fortified by your love. With you by my side, we can overcome any and all odds...*

Cal dropped letters in hand to his lap, his gaze glazing over as he stared into the blackness. Dark corners of the attic felt like an abyss of secrets, crevices where lies and love hid from sight. His father and Susannah. Had they been lovers? Did Delaney know the extent of their relationship?

Compelled to find the truth, Cal continued to read. He read until his heart began to break. *My Girl... You cannot let your brother stand in the way of true love. You cannot let his arrogance prevail. We are meant to be together. In time he will come to accept it. Yes, he is your blood, but I am your soul. We are destined to be together as one. Please do not dismay. We will work through this challenge and grow stronger for it. There is nothing we cannot overcome.*

My Dearest Gerald, I cannot go with you. I cannot ignore Ernie's wishes. You know where I would be without him. You know the pain he has suffered on my behalf. I cannot disappoint him. It would be disrespect of the mightiest regard. I worry for your safety. He has promised to kill you and I have no doubt that he means it. You know I care for you. Deeply. I love you, Gerald. You will always have a special place in my heart. But I cannot go against my brother's wishes. I will not. Nor can I ask you to stand in harm's way on my behalf. I pray for your understanding.

Susannah, You have ripped the heart from my body. I can only believe you are of weak mind at the moment to do such a thing and I pray you regain your strength. Every day I watch you, I pray for you. I want you to know that I am here for you. I will never forsake you. There has been and never will be another woman in this world for me. I will wait for you. I will be strong enough for the both of us and I will wait for you.

Gerald, You must let go. You deserve better than me. You were right. I am weak, unworthy. You deserve a woman who is strong enough to stand by your side through life's storms. It pains me to see you sullen and alone. I understand you are angry, yet you must find your love with another. I have.

According to the dates, it was the last letter from Susannah, the last private correspondence between them. Cal ached. For his father, for a young woman who felt afraid to step clear of her brother's protective shield, the heartbreak they both must have suffered...

Neatly folding the letter, Cal slid it back in place. A crushing sensation overcame him. Obviously he should conceal the letters once again. He should hide them from sight as they were hidden by his father. But something inside him resisted. His mother was renegotiating the past. She was waging old battles on new terrain because of what lay in the pages of these letters. Cal settled a weary gaze on the open box.

Should he broach the subject with his father? Should he implore him to work through these issues his mother?

Cal felt guilty for the mere knowledge, but clearly he had stumbled upon the lynchpin. These letters, this relationship, lay at the core of his mother's struggle. If his father would work through them with her, show his mother half the devotion he had to Susannah, perhaps she would reconsider her pursuit of false justice.

But as soon as Cal thought it, he realized there was no way to bridge this divide. If his mother had ever laid eyes on this correspondence, she would forever be doubtful.

Meticulously, Cal replaced the letters in the box as he had found them. Annie and Emily were waiting for him. Right now, he needed to find Beau and enlist his help to load the crate of guns into his truck. Collecting the shoe-box size container of letters, Cal rose. There would be time enough to decide later. A man could only put out so many fires at once.

Chapter Twelve

Three o'clock in the afternoon, Jeremiah sat at the bar
hunched over his third drink and contemplated his next step.
The boys were impatient, continuing to make noise about getting their money. He'd told them he had a plan, but the two
fools wouldn't listen. *Money. We want our money.* Money he
didn't have. Because Delaney had carved out the entire site of
gold and taken it for herself, making him look like a two-
timing liar for promising it to the guys in the first place. The
stolen pendants were chump-change in comparison.

The thought cut like rot-gut whiskey. She had no right to
take it all. Ladd Springs was *his* land, not hers. Throwing
back another swallow of alcohol, he clenched his jaw against
the strong fire of liquid as it snaked down his throat. More
than take his money, her theft had put him in a bad position
with his boys. If he didn't deliver the goods, no telling what
those guys would do. He couldn't trust them to wait. Hell, he
couldn't trust them period. Lifting his glass, he held it before
his lips and stared into the amber-brown liquid glowing
against the backdrop of light. It was time to get serious. Time
to up the ante.

Finishing his drink, Jeremiah tossed a fifty onto the bar,
grabbed his keys and walked out. Shouldn't be too hard to
cause the hotel a little grief. According to Billy, the robbery
had been easy. Almost *too* easy. As he walked out into the
bright sunshine, the overhead sun warmed his face, felt like
an iron to his hair. Hottest damn time of the day. Sliding on a
pair of sunglasses, Jeremiah adjusted his vision from the dark
interior of Billy's Bar as he took off for his truck.

The robbery had been simple because of a lack of experience and naiveté in the people involved. Delaney and her
rich husband had hired a bunch of hicks to work at the hotel,

and if the main lobby was staffed by neophytes, it made sense that the stables would be too. And the stables were where Delaney's heart dwelled. Jeremiah smiled to himself. Pressing the key fob, Jeremiah popped open his door lock. He'd known her a long time and if she had a weak spot that would be it. Her horses.

But first things first. He had to get back to his motel and shower. Lady Luck had delivered a sweet piece flesh in his lap and he was looking forward to learning the reason why. Not that he much cared much about why the lovely Ms. Devane had called, only that she had. Jack's "friend" was as hot as they came and if she wanted to hook up, Jeremiah wasn't about to say no. He'd never been with a South American before and couldn't wait to get his hands on her deeply browned skin, kiss those big luscious lips... Desire surged in his loins as salacious images peppered his mind. Oh *yes*, he was definitely looking forward to getting his hands on Jillian Devane and he wasn't about to be late. Whiskey Joe's, five o'clock *sharp*.

"Take the Appaloosa," Delaney told the stable hand. "The trail ride leaves in an hour and they're one short."

"Yes, ma'am," the young man said. Turning on his boot heel, he went to round up the horse.

Last minute sign-ups were nothing new for trail rides. The minute guests heard a ride was heading out, they wanted in. Delaney smiled as she headed back to her office. Just like she thought, her horses were turning out to be the star attraction for guests. Who wouldn't want to hang out with these gorgeous animals? She chuckled. Stinky, but gorgeous.

"Hello, Delaney."

Delaney stopped mid-stride, jerking her head toward the voice. *Jillian Devane*.

"So this is where you spend your time all day?"

"What are you doing here?" she demanded, glancing over Jillian's attire, thigh-high boots and leather miniskirt. She most assuredly wasn't dressed to ride.

"I came to look around."

Delaney smacked her hands to her hips and said flatly, "You're not welcome here."

Jillian smiled. "Are you this rude to all your guests?"

Struck by a drift of sweet feed from the buckets behind her, buckets that needed to be delivered to the barn, Delaney steeled her posture. "When they're here to cause trouble, I am."

With a roll of her eyes, Jillian said, "So paranoid. Do you see strangers outside your windows, too?"

"The question stands," Delaney replied, growing agitated by the woman's presumptive air. If Jillian thought she was going to waltz in here and cause Delaney and her staff grief, she was mistaken. They had work to do and this woman wasn't going to stand in their way.

"You are so *rough,"* Jillian returned haughtily. "Your clothes are torn, you don't bother to improve your looks with makeup or any effort to your hair... What does Nick see in you?"

"Apparently enough to put a ring on my finger—something he chose *not* to do with you."

Anger flashed in her eyes but Jillian remained calm. Drawing her expensive designer purse close, she snipped, "You think you've won, don't you? You think because he married you that I have become nothing to him." She smiled, loathing dripping from her gaze. "Well, you're wrong. Nick and I will be together again."

"In your dreams."

"Did you know he asked me out for drinks the other night?" Pausing only briefly, Jillian added, "Doesn't matter. Once you're out of the picture, we will find our way back to one another. It's only a matter of time," she said, glancing around the stables as though she were sizing them up.

Or casing the place.

Intuition curled up her spine. Slightly unnerved by the women's audacity, Delaney pitched back, "One problem. I'm *in* the picture. For good. Stuff that in your field of dreams. Now if you don't mind, I have work to do."

Jillian raked a hot glance over Delaney and sniped, "Temporary inconvenience. Nothing but a nuisance obstacle I can remove without effort."

Delaney was about to tell Jillian exactly what she thought when the woman's phone rang. She watched as Jillian withdrew it from her oversized bag, strolling off with a girlish wave of her fingers. But not before Delaney heard the word, *amorzhino*.

"Yes?"

"Jillian. It's Jack."

"Hello, *amorzhino*."

Now she was talking, he mused. Jack hadn't cared for the fact that when he showed up for their last rendezvous, Jillian had been working her second drink of the night, the first of which she drank alone or more likely, with someone. Could that someone have been Jeremiah?

Jeremiah was supposed to hook up with *him* tonight to go over their revenge plan against Delaney, but he'd backed out at the last minute. Said something unexpected came up. Jack didn't give a crap about his unexpected business unless it involved the man moving in on his woman. Jillian was his score and he didn't care to share. "Let's say I show you a good time in Chattanooga," Jack said with practiced ease. "You up for it?"

"Not tonight, darling. My schedule is booked."

Booked? What the hell could she be doing? It's not like she knew anyone in town, and those she did know had no interest in spending time with her. Which begged the question once again, why was she here?

Only it was a question Jack didn't care to ask. He wasn't concerned with the *why* as much as the *where* and the *when*. "No problem. Tomorrow works for me."

"I'm sorry," she replied throatily, "but this whole weekend is bad. Maybe next week?"

"Since when did a Sunday in this town become so exciting?" he asked.

Jillian laughed softly. "Next week. You will still be ready and willing, no?"

Jack didn't like to beg. Worse, he didn't like it when a woman made him feel like he was begging. Made him look desperate. But hell... After the other night who could blame him? "Fine. Sure. Monday?"

Jillian laughed again. "Maybe Monday."

As Jack hung up the phone, his gut tightened. Ladd better not be two-timing him. As he pulled Jeremiah's card from his wallet, it occurred to Jack that he should have taken the card Jeremiah gave Jillian when he had the chance. It would have ensured no contact between them.

Jack's instincts hummed. It was too coincidental that Jillian and Jeremiah both had plans tonight, plans that *didn't* include him. Envisioning the two of them cozied up over drinks settled it. Maybe catching them in the act would ice their libidos, huh? Maybe walking in on them would put them on notice that he was a man not to mess with. It wasn't like there were a ton of places they could go, leaving him a good chance at running into them. Shoving the card back into his wallet, he made the decision. He would pay a visit to some of the more popular establishments in town and see for himself. Something was luring Jillian away. Time to find out what that "something" could be.

Pulled up to the granite center island of their new kitchen, Nick Harris stretched out his legs. His lower back ached, his head hurt. He was angry over learning Jillian had tried to goad Delaney this afternoon. "I'm throwing her out."

"You can't," Delaney objected. Standing beneath the overhead recessed lighting, she wiped down a stainless steel pot and placed it alongside the cast iron pan she'd used to cook the cornbread. They'd designed the home together but this space was Delaney's favorite, claiming the kitchen was the gathering place, the heart of any home. It's why she insisted on the expansive island, the host of chairs lining it on three sides. "If you do, then she'll think she's won."

"She hasn't won anything, but I'll be damned if she scores any more points."

"It was no big deal. She's a vindictive woman who knows she's been beaten. I, for one, refuse to let her get to me."

Nick cocked a brow. "Not that I'm upset to hear the change of heart but why? I thought you didn't want Jillian anywhere near the hotel." Or him for that matter, but Nick wasn't about to salt that wound. Jillian was taunting Delaney and Nick didn't like it. Allowing it to continue was a show of weakness.

Setting her hands to the counter, Delaney dropped her weight into them with a heavy sigh. "Isn't there a saying, it's better to keep your friends close and your enemies closer?"

"Not in my book. Keep your friends close, your woman closer and put your enemies out of business."

"Jeremiah is the one I'm concerned about. Have you been able to put the two together with the money? Do we know if she paid his casino debt?"

Nick shook his head. Pushing off from the island, he stood. "We can't prove it was her. Malcolm looked into it and the money came from here."

"*Here*?" Delaney straightened. "Are you sure?"

He nodded. "Cash transaction. It doesn't rule Jillian out completely, but it does open the door to your ex."

Delaney gaped at him. "You think Jack had something to do with bringing Jeremiah onto the scene?"

"It's a possibility." Nick walked over to her and took her hand. Delaney allowed herself to be led to the sofa. Leather furniture was arranged beneath a massive overhead chandelier, exposed beams criss-crossed above, interior walls revealed genuine log construction, this was his favorite spot—other than their master suite. Heavy wood tables and shaggy floor carpets made the room feel solid, warm and comfortable. Easing down, Nick guided his wife onto his lap, wrap-

ping his arms around her narrow waist. Her cabbage and onions and cornbread might count as comfort food, but *this* was
his. The last thing he wanted to be discussing was their exes
but facts were facts—these warranting his urgent attention.
Squeezing her to him, Nick said, "Jack knows the players. He
would know the connection better than anyone. Someone
paid Jeremiah's marker, someone with a reason to see him set
loose. You have a better idea?"

Leaning into him, Delaney dropped her head onto his
shoulder. "I wish I did. The thought of Jack and Jeremiah
teaming up is almost worse than Jillian and Jeremiah."

"Triple J for triple jinx."

Chapter Thirteen

Consumed with thoughts of his father's letters, Jeremiah's unexpected visit and his daughter Emily, Cal Foster knew what he had to do. With his gun collection secured and stowed away in his new home, he had to prepare himself for what came next. If Jeremiah set foot on his property again, it would be his last visit. If he caused trouble anywhere else, Cal would see him put in jail. It was a man's job to defend his homestead, his family and it was a job he took to heart.

Heart. Cal's ached for his father. He hadn't seen him while at the house retrieving his gun collection. Thankfully, he hadn't seen his mother either. Cal wasn't sure he could look either of them in them eye without divulging that he knew. Susannah Ladd had been Gerald Foster's greatest love. She had been his first, his strongest, and from what the letters implied, his only true love. It broke Cal's heart to think his mother knew, to think she felt second-best all these years. But if she had ever laid eyes on those letters there would be no doubt in her mind.

There was no doubt in Cal's.

But Daddy couldn't be still pining after all these years. He had a family. Four sons and a wife who loved him. That meant something to him, didn't it? Reflecting on his childhood, Cal couldn't recall any discord between his parents. They didn't fight and argue, were always there for Cal and his brothers. Sure, first love burned hot in a man's heart, but eventually it turned to embers. A man moved on, found the woman of his adult dreams and built a life with her. Like Cal had done with Caroline.

And now Annie. You made a commitment to a woman and devoted yourself fully until life stepped in the way or until "death do us part." It was the way of families, bonds that tied the generations together. Cal couldn't imagine keeping any love letters for all these years. It was one thing to understand the rapture and power of first love, but to keep it alive and well and stored in the attic of the home you shared with your wife? Was Daddy insane?

Maybe he forgot them. Maybe Daddy had stowed them away when he was young and invincible and plain forgot about them over the years. The house had been in his family for generations before him. It was possible. Cal hoped that was the case. Either way, it was a topic he planned to discuss with him. Him *and* Delaney.

But it was a discussion that would have to wait for another day. Tonight was Serenity Scape and Emily was dying to go. The minute she'd heard there were going to be banjo players, she lost it. Banjos were something she'd only seen in the movies. To see them in real life would be *amazing*. Cal smiled. Well, they lived and breathed right here in Tennessee he'd told her, and she'd get to see them in the flesh.

Slowing for a red light, Cal's attention was drawn to a big red truck. Shiny, it looked brand new. *Don't see too many sweet rides like that one around these parts*. A man came out of the gas station's mini-mart, stuffing a wallet in his back pocket as he walked toward the truck. He was wearing a light purple shirt, his blond hair shining in the sunlight. Fair-skinned, medium build, he looked about forty. Cal honed in on the man. Something struck him as familiar. He watched as the guy plucked the gas pump from his vehicle and hooked it back in place.

Cal's insides hardened. That was Jeremiah Ladd. The light above turned green and Cal jammed his foot on the accelerator. Swerving from his turn lane, he barreled across the intersection and into the parking lot. As she slammed his brakes, his truck lurched with a squeal of tires. Cal leapt out and stormed over to Jeremiah.

Alarm seized Jeremiah's features as Cal approached.

"I want to have a word with you, Ladd."

Surprise cracked in Jeremiah's gaze. "Well, what do you know? Cal Foster!"

"This isn't a pleasure visit," he snapped, hit by a whiff of gasoline. "Annie told me about your visit to the house, and I'm here to warn you it was your last. Stay away from my family or you'll be dealing with me."

Jeremiah laughed. "Jack said you were playing big man these days."

"Jack?" Cal asked, taken aback the two had spoken. When had Jeremiah and Jack reconnected?

"He said your new job was going to your head, and I guess he was right."

"Forget about Jack," he thrust, getting in Jeremiah's face. "It's me you need to be concerned with—me and my family. I know what you were up to last time you came to town, and I'm here to tell you it won't fly. Not this time."

"Save your idle threats, Cal. You don't have it in you. Jack maybe, but not you." Jeremiah dropped a brief glance to Cal's chest. "Never did."

"Go ahead and test me," Cal grumbled, longing for Jeremiah to start something. Right here, right now, in broad daylight. "Go ahead and see exactly how much has changed."

"Don't tempt me," Jeremiah bit back. "But speaking of Jack, I ran into him at Whiskey Joe's the other night. Seems he and I are of like mind when it comes to Delaney and that Parker kid." Jeremiah chuckled, pausing before he opened his car door. "Guess it's true what they say, 'what goes around comes around.'"

"It is," Cal said evenly, watching Jeremiah slide into his truck. "Mark my word."

"Thanks for coming tonight," Felicity said, walking alongside Travis as they headed for the Serenity Scape bonfire. "No problem," he replied. "You know I think it's pretty cool what they do."

Held every Sunday night, the event was one of her favorites. Musicians assembled to play pieces ranging from simple and country to complex and sophisticated, using instruments common to the region. Malcolm Ward had invited Felicity to perform a flute solo one evening, and while she had been nervous at first, unaccustomed to performing in public, she'd lost herself in the composition, playing three encore pieces for a delighted group of guests. Travis had to hand it to Mr. Ward. He knew his venue. Even to Travis' untrained ear, music seemed to dance in the sky, float through the trees as it drifted upward into the starry night. And while Felicity thought the cooler evening temperature would adversely affect the sound and pitch of the instruments, it didn't. Not to any significant degree. Both agreed the music sounded great.

Though to be honest, Travis would rather be discussing his findings with Mr. Harris than hanging around listening to music. He had lost his tag on Jeremiah's whereabouts, but he knew he could pick up the tail any time he wanted. He knew where Jeremiah was staying. It would only be a matter of waiting for him to show before he could follow him again. But he couldn't talk to Mr. Harris because Felicity insisted Travis be a part of the festivities tonight. Cal Foster's daughter would be in tow and everyone should meet her. While Travis didn't particularly care about meeting some twelve-year-old girl, he knew Felicity did. More importantly, he knew Felicity felt he should *want* to meet the girl.

Because she was family. His family.

Sort of. Travis thought it a stretch to call his brother's wife's stepfather's kid a member of his family, but Felicity didn't. She stretched the ties and looped the knots, and so long as she didn't choke him with it, Travis didn't mind. Lately Felicity seemed hell bent on getting him and Troy to make amends, which made for tension. It wasn't like he hated his brother. He didn't. But he wasn't interested in closing the space between them either. Not yet. Not until Troy proved himself worthy. Stable.

In order to do that, Troy needed to secure his freedom. If Travis helped Troy beat the charges against him, maybe Felicity would see that he didn't hate his brother. Only his choices.

He held a branch from her path as they walked, the scent of pine served up by a misty breeze. It wasn't cold by any stretch of the word, but when the sun dipped below the horizon, so did the temperature, even this time of year. Soon he'd be headed back to Nashville for his second year at Vanderbilt, and the winter weather wouldn't be far behind.

"So did you ever find anything out about who paid Jeremiah's debt?" Felicity asked.

"Yes and no. It was someone around here, but I wasn't able to pinpoint it."

"Here?"

"The money was transferred from a local bank."

"But they didn't give you a name?"

"They don't give you names. The routing number indicated the wire transfer originated from here, but the sender's name was blocked."

"Blocked?"

"Yeah, like someone didn't want anyone to know they were sending the money."

"So it could have been anyone," she said, her eyes filling with disappointment.

"Anyone," he repeated, though he had a feeling Mr. Harris would be able to track the information further than he could. He and Mr. Ward seemed to have their ways. Hopefully, their methods were legal. In the past he'd believed them capable of crossing that line. Until Ernie Ladd confessed to hiring a couple of thugs to beat up his son and leave him for dead in the streets of town, rumor had it Mr. Harris and Mr. Ward were the responsible party. It'd been an easy rumor to digest.

"Do you think Mr. Foster can help?"

"Cal?"

Felicity nodded. "His daddy owns a bank in town. Maybe he could look into it for us."

"And break half a dozen privacy laws in the process? No thanks." Travis wanted the information but not at the expense of jail time. Kicking a stone from the trail, he picked up the scent of wood smoke. The green landscape was drenched in hazy shadows, the sky a heavy purple and gold. Nips of misty air signaled that festivities would begin soon. "I'm gonna talk to Mr. Harris about it later. Maybe one of his people can find out."

"Will he be at the bonfire?"

"Not sure. The girl at the front desk didn't seem to know where he was."

Rounding a bend in the trail, the clearing for the bonfire was visible about twenty yards in the distance. A few hotel guests were mingling near the fire pit, the glow of flame lighting up their figures. A niggle of impatience pulled at him. Sitting around for the next two hours listening to nightscapes was going to be a challenge. Maybe Mr. Harris and Miss Delaney would be here. It would at least give the evening some purpose.

But as Felicity and Travis emerged from the trail, his spirits sank. There was no sign of them. Travis searched faces of the people gathered around a considerable fire in full flame. Those in attendance were comprised mostly of guests. Makeshift log benches were assembled around fire. Casey and Troy had taken up residence while Cal Foster and his wife Annie stood nearby with a young girl, presumably his daughter. Circling the perimeter, Travis spotted Casey's Aunt Lacy. She married Mr. Ward last summer and now the two had a baby. On the opposite side of the fire, she was carrying her baby and pointing at flames, her face aglow as she spoke near the child's ear. Lingering on her, Travis always thought it weird how much she looked like Casey's mom without being a twin. Both women had the exact same blue eyes and white skin. Both had the exact same black hair, kinda like Casey, but Miss Lacy was always dressed pretty fancy, even though tonight she wore a short skirt and boots. He guessed the women were attractive enough, except he preferred blondes.

"There she is," Felicity said excitedly, tugging Travis to look as she pointed. "C'mon, let's go say hi."

Groaning inwardly, Travis obliged. Where was Mr. Ward? Travis doubted Mr. Foster would be working the event, not with his daughter in town. Who was officially in charge?

"Hi, Felicity!" Casey waved with one hand, the other cradling her sleeping infant, the baby wrapped in a light-weight flannel blanket. A plaid mix of blues and reds, the material blended in with Casey's jeans and denim button-down as she held the baby close to her breast, the ends of her dark hair brushing over the kid's body. Sporting his usual T-shirt and jeans, Troy flanked her side. From beneath his black hat, Troy's eyes made a bead on him and Felicity.

Walking over, Felicity greeted them happily. "Hi, Casey. Hi, Troy."

"Hey, Felicity," Troy replied, more nod of his head. There was no similar greeting extended to his brother.

Whatever. Travis could care less. He was only here be-cause he had to be.

Bending at the waist, Felicity touched the bundled baby in Casey's arms. "How's Cassidy Jo?"

"She's good. I was hoping she'd be awake to hear the music."

Felicity laughed. "Oh, there's time. When the fiddle player starts playing, I doubt she'll be able to sleep through it!"

Casey smiled. "You're probably right."

"Where's Mr. Ward?" Travis asked. "Isn't he supposed to be here?"

"He's coming," Casey replied, absently tucking the cor-ner of her daughter's blanket beneath a fold. "Aunt Lacy said he was held up at the hotel but he's on his way."

Good. Travis would get his opportunity after all. While it wasn't Mr. Harris, Mr. Ward would surely do.

"So when do we get to meet your new sister?" Felicity asked, stealing a glance toward the trio standing several yards away. Mr. Foster was casual tonight in jeans and boots, while Casey's mom wore a bright blue dress with frilly layers of material hanging down the front. Beside them the girl was sporting a brand new pair of cowboy boots and skinny jeans, a summer plaid shirt with the sleeves rolled up her forearms. Of average height for her age with stick-straight hair, she looked the same as most girls her age. Travis assumed she bought the outfit specifically for tonight since he doubted they wore plaid and boots in the city.

Casey rose from the bench, Troy mirroring her movements with a hand to assist his wife. "How about right now? I'll introduce you."

Following Casey over, Travis noted the girl perk up as the four of them approached. He was struck by an intelligence dancing within her brown eyes. It was a maturity that seemed beyond her years.

"Emily, I want you to meet my cousin, Felicity."

The girl was quick with a smile as she reached out a hand. "Hi."

"Hi," Felicity replied. "It's nice to meet you."

"Nice to meet you, too," she said, a curious eye darted his way.

"This is my boyfriend, Travis. He's Troy's brother—if you couldn't already guess," Felicity teased.

"Wow... You look exactly like him."

Not exactly. Anyone who knew them could easily tell them apart, but Travis merely replied, "Nice to meet you."

Emily giggled, erasing any maturity her gaze might have bestowed.

"Glad you could come out for the event," Cal said to the two of them. "It should be a lively evening. I've heard these fellas play before, and they really know their instruments."

From her studies, Felicity had learned that although the fiddle had been around the mountains for centuries, it had its roots in Scotland, Ireland, even France. And Mr. Foster was right—when the fiddles broke in, the fun broke out. Actually a violin, the difference came in how you played the instrument. Folks in the country played the violin with high-energy, and lots of movement. Symphony players worked the strings more methodically, resulting in sweeping notes that lingered and carried. Felicity figured that's where the name originated. Someone "fiddling around" with a violin gave birth to a brand new genre of play. Certainly a great first concert for a girl of Emily's age.

"So," Felicity began, interested in getting to know more about Casey's new kid sister, "what have you been doing since you've been in town? Have you had a chance to ride horses?"

"We're going tomorrow," she said. "My dad and Annie are taking me for a trail ride."

Felicity looked to Cal and asked, "Do you mind if I join you?"

"Not at all. We'd love it." He turned to Emily and said, "Felicity is an excellent rider. Been riding since she was a little girl."

"You weren't afraid to get on a horse?" Emily asked.

Felicity laughed. "Not a bit! When you grow up around horses, they're no scarier than a puppy dog."

Catching sight of Mr. Ward, Cal excused himself. "I need to speak with Malcolm. Ya'll get seated and I'll join you in a minute." Annie and Emily took their seats, Casey and Troy beside them. Felicity lowered into place, tugging Travis to do likewise. "Aren't you sitting?"

Staring after Mr. Foster and Mr. Ward, he replied, "Yeah. But first, I want to grab a word with Mr. Ward."

"What for?" Felicity asked. "The show is about to begin."

The two musicians were placing a pair of stools beyond the circle of logs, an open area designated for performers. Another fellow had joined the two fiddlers, a surfboard-shaped piece of wood in his hand along with what looked like a drumstick. "It won't take long," Travis said and headed for the men before Felicity could stop him.

"Travis!" she called after him.

Ignoring her, he exited the seating area and slowed to a stop near the men.

Casey leaned close. "Is everything okay?"

"No," Felicity snapped, staring at the backside of her boyfriend. "Actually, it's not."

"What's up?"

Watching Travis as he stood idle near Mr. Foster and Mr. Ward, one of the musicians joined them. What did Travis have to do with them? He didn't work at the hotel. He was over there, because he didn't want to be here, with her, with Casey and the Fosters. With Troy. "I don't get him. It's like he's so detached these days, like he doesn't care about the stuff I care about."

"What do you mean?"

"I *mean*, coming here...hanging out with family." Felicity slapped her palms to her jean-clad knees. "He acts like it's a chore, like I'm forcing him to come." And she didn't appreciate it. If he had better things to do, then say so.

"Are you?"

Felicity drew back. "No, I'm not *forcing* him. I *invited* him to take part." Glancing back to Travis, his body rigid in the dark of night, reflected shades of golden light swaying over the black of his shirt, she added, "He can do whatever he wants, for all I care. Including stay home."

"That doesn't sound good."

"Because it isn't." A cold certainty of decision tunneled into Felicity's heart. It had been something she'd been considering of late, ever since Troy spent the night in jail. Travis had approved his parents' decision. He knew his brother was innocent of the charges, yet he agreed they should let him sit in jail to teach him a lesson. The way Felicity saw it, Troy wasn't the one in need of a lesson. Travis was. He was so arrogant these days, as though he knew better than anyone what was right, what was wrong. Felicity was sick of it. It was fine to be rational and logical but quite another to be rude and judgmental. "I think I'm going to ask him for a break when we go back to school."

"You are?" Casey asked, her tone of disbelief echoing in her gaze.

"I think it's for the better. If Travis can't share in the things I think are important, what's the point?"

Casey followed Felicity's gaze to Travis and the other men. The musician was excusing himself, but Travis remained. With them, Felicity mused, not her. Summer break flashed in her mind's eye as she drifted in thought. She'd been so happy to see him at Ashley's Memorial Day party, their ride the next day...the private time they spent hanging at Zack's Falls. It had been wonderful, amazing. They'd caught up on school, planned the entire summer together, talked about their upcoming sophomore year... But now?

Felicity's heart pitched, then burst as a loud boom thundered across the quiet of night. The calm had evaporated. Shock seized hold as they stared at one another in question. *What just happened*?

Chapter Fourteen

Travis whirled at the noise. For a second he thought he'd imagined the sound. But every expression around him registered the hit. In the distant sky, a golden red glowed above the tree line. *Oh no...*

It was the direction of the stables. Travis took off running.

"Travis!"

Someone yelled his name, but he didn't stop. He had to get to the source of the glow. *Fire!* There was no longer a question in his mind as to what had happened. That sound had been an explosion. Images of a lighter flashed in his mind. Lost horses. Paid markers.

A meeting in the slum of town.

"That's coming from the stables!" Troy shouted, running to catch up with him.

Jeremiah Ladd. Jack Foster. Felicity. Her mother—

Pumping his arms and legs, Travis pushed himself through the darkened trail. Shadows swallowed the woods, can lights the only illumination on their path. The stables were on the other side of the forest. This trail would take them there. Both knew the way by heart. Both knew what was at stake. Travis' heart beat wildly as he powered over the gravelly trail. He could hear his brother's breathing, could feel the pound of their boots as they raced toward the stables.

Let it not be the stables. Let it not be the horses or Miss Delaney.

The exertion tightened his lungs. Adrenaline fired his limbs. He couldn't stop. They couldn't stop. Troy passed Travis as the trail opened up. Across the clearing, the impact of what happened punched him in the chest. Flames licked high into the night sky. The stables were on fire. Struggling to keep up with Troy, Travis understood his brother's drive. Hay, wood, locked stalls—there wouldn't be time for the animals to get out.

Shutting the thoughts from his mind, Travis hammered forward. He could only hope the damage could be contained.

Troy made it to the stables first. Through the main opening, flames could be seen spilling from Delaney's office. Smoke rose from the scene, a chalky orange billowing up into the black of night. A sickening mix of shrieks and whinnies pierced the quiet. Troy's dark figure hesitated for an instant as he changed direction, entering from the side. He was headed for the stalls.

Travis barreled straight in. Lights were on. People were here. If Delaney was here, it's likely she would've been in her office. "Delaney!" he shouted as he ran. Shooting a glance down the corridor, he felt relief to see the fire was confined to this section. But ripping across the ceiling, it was quickly making its way toward the stalls.

He neared the stable office, where the doorway was engulfed. Unable to gain access, Travis prayed she wasn't inside. Catching sight of movement, he turned and saw her running from stall to stall, unhooking gates. An Appaloosa reared as Delaney charged in, shooing the horse clear.

"Delaney!" he yelled. That's when he noticed the flames climbing the back of the building. The fire had spread farther than he thought. Or had it started in multiple points?

Travis had no idea. None of it mattered. He had to get her out of here.

Beyond her, horses cried out in fear. Travis could hear Troy's shouts as he forced the animals, one by one, from their stalls. Running toward Delaney, Travis noted several remained locked in place. One was a black horse. Travis froze. Licks of flames jumped in the reflection of the animal's wild eyes. *It was Blue*.

Rushing for Felicity's horse, Travis heard Delaney cry out. He turned in time to see a frightened horse storm from its stall, knocking Delaney to the ground.

Delaney.

"Travis!"

He whirled, coughing against a thickening smoke. Felicity ran toward him. "You have to save Blue!"

Blue. Yes, the horse was still locked in its stall—but Delaney could be hurt. Travis' heart caught. His gaze shot to the ceiling. A rafter was pulling away, flames coiling along its timber. Delaney lay directly in its path. Felicity, following his gaze, shrieked, "Mom!"

Delaney looked up. Felicity rushed toward her.

Wood cracked and Travis sprang forward. Ramming a shoulder into Felicity, he shoved her out of the way in a dive toward Delaney. He tackled her in a roll as the beam swung down, sinking its fiery mass into the stall. Flames crawled up wooden siding, raced over and around everything in their path as Travis remained huddled over Delaney's body. Heat blazed hot against the bare skin of his arms, the shirt on his back. The fire was devouring the stall beside him. He had to get Delaney away but where was Felicity? Was she okay?

"Felicity!" he cried out.

She didn't respond.

Fear pummeled him. Was she okay? Travis choked in a chest full of smoke, the acrid smell burning his throat. He buried his face into Delaney's body, noting with alarm that she wasn't moving. He had to get her out of here. But where was Felicity?

Felicity's shrill voice called out to him, "Travis!"

Thank God she was okay.

"Where are you?"

Warning bells sounded in his skull as her voice neared. She couldn't come over here. She had to stop. It was too dangerous. "Go away!" he commanded. "Stop—go back!"

"Travis! Mom!"

Men were shouting. Commands punctured the chaos, Troy's voice distinct among them. Horses whinnied and ran. They had to get out of here before they were trampled. Or burned. The fire was growing. Spreading. In a split decision, he scooped up Delaney's petite figure and yelled, "Troy, get Blue!"

"Travis?"

Felicity's voice snapped him to a halt. "Felicity."

As they locked gazes through the smoke-filled air, time stood still. He peered into her face. The chaos around them dissolved. Her horse was in danger. Felicity needed him. Delaney lay unconscious in his arms. Instinct warred with need. Felicity's mom could be seriously injured. He had no way of knowing the extent of her condition without thoroughly evaluating her. He had to get her out of here but he couldn't leave Felicity. Sirens echoed in the distance. "You've got to get out," Travis urged her.

"My mom—is she okay?"

"I don't know. I've got to get her out of here. You, too. We've got to go."

"But what about Blue?" her voice quaked.

"Troy will get Blue." Suddenly sucked in by the sight of her mother's lifeless body, Felicity hesitated. "Felicity, go. Run!" When she didn't respond, Travis yelled at her, "Move, Felicity! Get out. *Now!*"

"I can't leave Blue here!"

Travis couldn't grab her but they had to get out. "C'mon. Let's go!" he ordered, running determinedly from the stables. He had no other choice. Delaney was hurt. Unconscious. He had to get her to safety. Felicity would follow. *She had to.*

Carrying Delaney clear of the building, Travis looked back, disturbed Felicity had not followed him. Where was she?

As soon as he thought it, the answer occurred. She's saving Blue. At risk to her life, she was staying behind to get her horse. Dammit!

Troy would get Felicity. One of the men. Someone!

But he couldn't think about Felicity. Delaney wasn't moving. Closing his mind to everything but her, he set her gingerly on the ground, scanning her body for signs of injury. Was anything broken? Was she breathing?

Despite the backdrop of frantic shouts and whinnies, the jeopardy of his girlfriend and her horse, Travis forced himself to remain calm. *Think*. Check her vitals. Placing an ear to her mouth, he searched Delaney's chest for signs of movement. For a moment he thought he detected a faint breath, a slow rise and fall of inhalation. Could she be moved? He didn't recall the horse kicking her head. But the fact she lay unconscious said otherwise.

"Travis!" Malcolm's solid voice cut through as he rushed over. Dropping to a knee, he skimmed over Delaney's body. "Is she all right?"

"I don't know," Travis replied. "She was unlocking the gates when one of the horses ran out, knocking her to the ground. A rafter above was on fire and about to fall. I pushed her out of the way. She's breathing." It was the quickest summation he could manage.

Malcolm nodded, the growing fire casting his tanned face in golden tones. "Ambulance is on its way. Let's not move her."

Travis rose to his feet. "Are the horses out?"

"I think so. Troy and a few of the stable staff were in there getting the last of them."

"I've got to go find Felicity." Delaney would be okay now that Malcolm was here and he had to go after Felicity.

"Go." Malcolm set a hand to Delaney's lifeless body. "I'll stay with Delaney."

Guilt and duty washed through Travis. Delaney wasn't out of danger but she was in good hands. Unlike Felicity. Travis had to get to her. "Thanks," Travis said, then bolted off to find his girlfriend.

Making it to the front of the stables, a squawk of siren blasted from the valley below. Flashing red lights flared against a wall of dark forest. The fire department was here. Searching the faces of those leading horses from the stables, he saw no sign of Felicity. Travis' heart sank. Half the building was consumed by flame. *Felicity*. Running to the edge of the building, there were no more shouts, only sheets of smoke billowing free. He panned over the growing crowd of faces, dread lodging in his throat.

Felicity was not among them.

As firefighters decked out in full gear leapt from the fire engine, Travis ran to the opposite side of the building, inundated by "what ifs." What if one of the rafters had fallen on Felicity? What if he'd managed to save her mother at expense of her life? Travis wouldn't be able live with himself. If Felicity suffered because of his actions he didn't know what he would do. Fighting a rising tide of panic, he looked inside the stables. The flames had yet to reach the back end. "Felicity!" he called out, his heart pounding anew with panic. "Felicity!"

Behind him staff members were corralling horses, leading them to the paddocks, a few being taken to the barn. Backing away from the stables, Nick Harris raced up from the trail. Travis knew he'd be looking for Delaney and waved him over. "Mr. Harris! Mr. Harris—she's over there!" Travis shouted, pointing in the direction of Delaney and Malcolm.

His sharp eyes drilled into Travis as he demanded, "Where?"

"Over there. Near the fence."

At sight of Delaney's body lying on the ground, alarm swamped Nick's gaze. "Is she okay?"

"I think so," Travis replied. But Mr. Harris didn't hear him, already en route for his wife.

Travis' heart skipped a beat as he glimpsed Troy's black hat. Sprinting toward his brother, he wondered, had he gotten Blue? Did he have Felicity? Dodging firefighters lugging hoses, Travis made a beeline for Troy. Cutting around them and a collection of curious guests, he called out, "Troy!" Frozen expressions didn't so much as register his passing, transfixed as they were to the inferno before them. "Troy!"

His brother was leading a horse in circles as Travis ran to him. "Troy!" Recognition sharpened in Troy's gaze as Travis neared. "Where's Felicity?"

"Headed for the barn," Troy replied, his voice taut and controlled.

"Did you see her?"

The horse yanked its head against Troy's tight grasp on a lead rope fastened around its head. "Yes." His attention was clearly aimed on his animal, not Travis or Felicity.

But the animals needed Troy right now. Spooked by the fire, they were understandably jittery. But Felicity needed *him*. As he glanced in the direction of the barn, the knots in his chest loosened. If Troy said she was by the barn that meant she was safe.

Jogging past a few loose horses, Travis shifted his focus between the fire and Felicity. He hadn't asked Troy about Blue. Had she made it out? Would he find Felicity in tears?

Pulling up to the barn, he scanned the exterior. No sign of her. Striding inside, he saw a couple of horses with one of the older staff members, but no Felicity. Hurrying over, he asked, "Have you seen Felicity?"

The man looked to him briefly, the horse he held bridling between skittish and calm, and shook his head.

No? Travis whipped his head around. But Troy said she was here. If not here, where?

Travis turned on his heel, his frustration over Troy's misdirection welling hot and fast in his chest. Hustling outside, he paused at the sight of burning stables, the sky above them glowing orange-gold, spits of charred wood floating into the black. Where had Felicity gone? Where was Blue? Without wasting another second, Travis ran back toward the stables. Troy had seen her, which meant she was okay, but Travis couldn't relax until he laid eyes on her himself.

Around the edge of the building, Travis caught sight of medics wheeling a gurney toward the ambulance. Nick's imposing figure trailed behind, partially obscured by the emergency personnel. They were transporting Delaney. At the pace they were rolling her, Travis thought it must be critical. His heart pinched. *Please let her be okay.* That's when he saw Felicity. Lagging behind the cluster of medics, her face appeared blank. In shock. But relief flooded him. She was safe. Travis rushed over to her. "Felicity!"

She glanced up at him. Her mouth was set in a firm line, her usually soft gaze hard and impenetrable. Unable to read her expression, his pulse jumped. *Was she upset with him? Was Blue okay?*

When she didn't stop or call out to him, he yelled, "Felicity!" As if the sheer force of his voice would stop her in her tracks. It didn't. The group continued its course, leaving Travis no option but to follow.

Catching up with them as they arrived at the ambulance, Travis hovered by Felicity's side, watching in silence as three men hoisted the bed up and slid it into the rear of the vehicle.

"I'm going with her," Nick declared to the lead medic. Meeting no protest, he climbed into the back of the ambulance and they closed the doors.

Felicity raced forward. "I'm her daughter—I want to go, too!"

Securing the door shut, one of the medics replied, "I'm sorry. There's not enough room."

Travis grasped her arm. "I'll drive you, Felicity. I'll take you to the hospital."

Trembling, Felicity stared at the rear of the ambulance. It was as though he hadn't spoken, like she took in the closed doors with a chilling finality. Felicity cried out beneath her breath, "I have to go. I have to be with her!"

Travis firmed his hold of her. "I'll take you. She'll be okay."

Felicity looked up at him, a vein of anger pulsating to life in the soft heather of her eyes. "She's not okay, Travis. She's not okay!"

Chapter Fifteen

Felicity wanted to scream, she wanted to shout, yet she could hardly move. Her mother was unconscious! She had not responded to the paramedics. Nick was the calmest man Felicity had ever met. Nothing ruffled him. Yet he was ruffled now, she mused, staring in despair after the departing ambulance.

"C'mon, Felicity." Travis tugged her arm. "Let's go. We'll get to the hospital right behind them."

The hospital. Felicity's breathing grew shallow. Her mother was on her way to the hospital, yet none of it felt real. Red lights flashed through the night sky. Firefighters aimed arcs of water over the building, heavy streams that doused leaping flames. Guests gathered around them, gawking as the stables succumbed to fire.

"She's not okay."

"She will be."

"They said she's unconscious. She might be in a coma." Felicity felt gutted by the words. Her mother looked dead. She didn't move. She didn't respond. Not to the medics, not to Nick.

"They'll take care of her at the hospital."

"She shouldn't even be at the hospital!" Felicity exclaimed. "This should never have happened!"

Her mom would not let the animals burn to death. They were her life. Her world. Felicity shuddered. A horse had been burned. She'd seen it trotting out with several others. At least Blue had escaped harm. When Travis left the stables, Troy had grabbed her, shouted that he had Blue. Resentment twisted Felicity's heart. Travis had not come back for her. She was grateful to him for saving her mother but after he rushed outside with her mother he never came back. It was Troy who had come to her rescue, not Travis.

Her heart split. Troy had saved her when Travis had not.

"We need to go," Travis pressed.

The desperation in his voice pulled at her. Thoughts of her mom lying on that gurney, being whisked away by strangers began to unravel her. Latching onto sight of Troy, her heart started to pound. He was walking two horses around the inside perimeter of one of the pens, calming them, reassuring them everything was okay. The horses had been hurt. Her mom had been hurt.

Behind them, Malcolm approached. He was usually so easygoing and relaxed, but at the moment his eyes were scored by concern, the blue paled to a flat gray. His expression was hard, his posture tense. Was it a wonder? His hotel stables were going up in flames. "Aren't you going to the hospital with your mom?" he asked.

"Yes. Yes, as soon as I make sure that Blue is okay, I'm driving over."

"She's fine. Troy has her and several others over at the paddocks."

Felicity felt light-headed. Dizzy, relieved, her head felt like it was spinning.

Glancing between her and Travis, Malcolm asked, "Is there anything you need?"

"Where's Casey?" Felicity asked abruptly, struck by the thought she hadn't seen the others since she abandoned them at the bonfire. "Are she and Cassidy okay?"

"They're fine. Cal sent them home with Annie. He's down at the hotel now, fielding questions and directing response teams."

Felicity imagined the confusion guests must be experiencing. A fire of this magnitude would certainly undermine the "serenity" of their stay. It was unsettling, frightening. People would want to know what was going on, if there was any danger to them.

"The police are on their way now to investigate," Malcolm said.

The fire started with an explosion. Felicity's chest suddenly hollowed. *Her father*.

"I need to go," she said, then turned and ran.

"Felicity!"

Travis followed Felicity as she walked from the ER to a waiting room upstairs. It was for patients having an MRI. He understood it was a piece of equipment doctors used to detect brain injury. Delaney was unconscious. There was no way to know what happened without some sort of internal scan. When he called ahead, they said Felicity's mom was having one, but he couldn't get any other information. He wasn't family. He was a friend, but even that was beginning to feel uncertain based on Felicity's attitude. It was like she didn't want him around her, didn't want him accompanying her to the hospital. Which was crazy. He'd saved her mother's life! She should be grateful to him but instead she was shunning him. She ran to her car and when he caught up with her, she threw his arm from her shoulder, refused his offer to drive. The whole scene had been insane. From the explosion and burning stables to the crazy actions of his girlfriend, Travis' entire world felt flipped upside down.

As they exited the elevator, they saw Mr. Harris conferring with a middle-aged doctor wearing khaki pants beneath his white coat, his hair graying at the temples. Mr. Harris looked ten years older, his expression long and drawn, his black eyes deadweight in his face.

Felicity hurried toward the men. "Is my mom okay?"

Turning, emotion churned the depths of Mr. Harris' gaze. "She's in a coma."

"A coma?"

"Yes," he replied dully. "It's due to the trauma done to her head."

Standing idle, Travis wondered what could have caused her head injury. The beam hadn't hit them. Had she hit her head against the stall? Had it happened when he tackled her to the ground? He moved his gaze to the open doorway, his thoughts going to Felicity and Mr. Harris. The two people closest to Miss Delaney were hurting. Had this been his fault?

"She's critical," the doctor added. "We're keeping her overnight."

Felicity fell back a step. "Overnight?"

Exchanging a glance with Mr. Harris, the doctor seemed hesitant, but Mr. Harris nodded. "Your mother has some swelling in the brain. We need to watch her for a few days before deciding what to do."

Felicity gaped. "A few days?"

"It might resolve itself sooner," the doctor replied quietly, "but it's a wait-and-see proposition. We're doing everything we can to relieve the pressure, but we'll need to monitor her progress. Hopefully, surgery won't be necessary."

Felicity nearly buckled. Travis reached out for her, but she collapsed into Mr. Harris who wrapped an arm around her body, hugging Felicity to him. "Don't worry. She's in good hands."

Travis thought Mr. Harris sounded like he was in some kind of daze. He seemed distant, detached. Was he in shock? Had he mentally checked out?

"You're welcome to wait here," the doctor told Felicity. "But like I was telling your father, it could be some time before we know anything."

"He's not my father," Felicity murmured abruptly.

"I'm her stepfather," Nick corrected, a sweep of concern coalescing in his gaze. Was he bothered by Felicity's hasty clarification?

The doctor seemed to take it in stride. "I see. Either way, you're welcome to stay. I'll let the staff know you're here."

"Can I see her?" Felicity asked.

"Of course. I'll ask the nurse to let you know when she's settled. Though I want to caution you—she won't be able to respond but she might be able to hear you and understand what you're saying."

Nodding, Felicity tightened her hold on Mr. Harris.

"I understand this is the result of a fire." Lines rippled across his forehead as he instructed, "I wouldn't make any mention of the fire while in her presence. Do not discuss the events of the evening. Her stress should be kept to a minimum."

Because she could hear them, Travis mused, unsettled by the notion. And it would upset her. As the doctor left, Mr. Harris and Felicity walked to the waiting room. There was no goodbye, no acknowledgement of his presence. They simply walked away from him like two zombies. "Felicity, wait."

They turned but Felicity didn't make a move toward him. She stood clinging to Mr. Harris like some kind of lifeline.

Mr. Harris let go of his hold. "Take your time," he told her, his voice devoid of emotion. "I'll let you know if anything changes."

Felicity's gaze trailed him inside as though she longed to be with him. Returning her focus to Travis, she crossed her arms and looked at him expectantly. Her hair was a spray of frizzy curls around her face, her cheeks and forehead shone with baked-in perspiration. Both of them smelled foul, the sterile environment no match for the rank scent of smoke. But worse than her looks was the cutting edge in her gaze.

"Felicity, I'm sorry about your mom. I'm sorry about the fire, but I'm glad you and Blue are okay." Visibly struggling against tears, Felicity zipped her mouth tightly closed. Travis scraped a hand through his hair, frustration filing through him. "Felicity, what's wrong? What's going on?"

"What do you think is wrong?" she asked, anger wrenching her delicate features, rendering her freckles an angry red. "My mother is lying in a hospital bed, Travis. Horses have been injured, property has been destroyed."

"I get all that, but you seem to not want me around. What the heck did I do?"

Felicity grew rigid, her green eyes suddenly glittering beneath the fluorescent lighting. "Why didn't you come back for me?"

"What are you talking about?"

"In the stables, after you carried my mom out. Why didn't you come back for me?"

"I did come back for you. I searched all over for you!"

"Not in the stables. You never came back in to help me and Blue."

"Felicity, I was helping your *mom*. I told you to get out. I went back but they told me you weren't inside."

"You expected me to leave my horse? Did you seriously think I was going to listen to you?"

"You should never have gone inside in the first place. It was a stupid risk.

Felicity's expression morphed into such a hideous rejection he almost expected a fire-breathing dragon to leap out and scorch him. "You call saving Blue from burning alive a stupid risk?"

"You know what I mean." Thankfully the corridor was empty. Travis was glad no one was here to witness the hostility between them. "There were other people there who could have helped. Some of the staff had returned. They could have saved your horse without you endangering yourself."

"Why? Because they're men, or because you didn't see fit to save her so they had to finish the job?"

"Felicity. I was trying to help your mom. I knew Troy was in there. He could get Blue."

She glared at him. "Don't you think he had his hands full? I mean—he was busy trying to save *all* the horses, not just mine. But he did. He saw you desert me and he saved me *and* Blue."

"Desert you?" Travis bit back his next response. Felicity was making Troy into some kind of hero and totally ignoring the heroic act *he* performed. "The stables are his *job*. He works with those animals. Of course he's going to go in after them. You didn't have to go in. You should've stayed outside where it was safe."

"Safe. *Safe*, while my horse's life is threatened? Not a chance. I can't believe you would even suggest such a thing."

And Travis couldn't believe she was flying out of control like this. What had gotten into her? Why was she being so irrational? Clearing his throat, the bitter taste of smoke an ever present reminder of the chaotic evening, he tried to remain calm. "Listen, I don't want anything to happen to you, is that so bad?"

"You're treating me like I'm some kind of helpless baby." Felicity unwound her arms and said, "Well, I'm *not*. I'm a grown woman who can take care of myself, and I'm sick and tired of you coddling me like I'm some kind of child who needs protecting."

Genuinely shocked, his eyes went to the small heart-shaped pendant at her collarbone, the one he'd given her the summer before college. It had been a gesture of his love, his undying love and devotion to her, and that included wanting to protect her. "Felicity, since when is wanting you to be safe a bad thing?"

"When it means you don't think I'm strong and capable of taking care of myself."

If she called running into a burning building to save her horse and nearly meeting the same demise as her mother strong and capable, she needed to hear otherwise. Her mother was lying in a hospital bed because she hadn't thought about what she was doing. She totally missed the falling beam and if it hadn't been for *him*, she'd be dead right now!

If it hadn't been for Troy, Felicity could have met with the same fate. What part of that didn't she get?

"If you'll excuse me," she said nastily, "I'm going to be with my mother. If you want to make yourself useful, why don't you track down my father and see if he has an alibi. I'll bet he *doesn't*."

Travis returned to the hotel. With Felicity camped out at the hospital for the foreseeable future and uninterested in his whereabouts, he decided to pursue the person or persons responsible for the fire. Felicity clearly thought her father was responsible for setting the blaze, but Travis believed otherwise. His lighter outside the stables had most likely been lost during his attack on her mother. He had no motive to be there otherwise. Jack Foster was pursuing his revenge in the court room.

Unlike Jeremiah Ladd. It was no coincidence bad things started happening upon his return to town. It was only a matter of proving his connection to them—a matter Travis hoped Mr. Ward could assist him with. At the moment, Mr. Harris was walking around in a stupefied haze and would be of no help, which led Travis to his partner. Once he learned what Travis had discovered, Mr. Ward might be able to take it a step further.

Pulling into the parking lot, Travis was surprised by the number of police cars. There were half a dozen pulled up near the hotel entrance, a few more were parked on the grass along the gravelly drive, their lights actively flashing an insistent creepy red glow against the green trees. Milling alongside the cars were policemen. Tons of them. How many cops did it take to gather evidence?

One of the officers eyed him suspiciously as Travis slowed his truck to enter. Raising a hand, he ordered Travis to stop.

Rolling to a stop, Travis lowered his window and waited for the man to make his way over. Flames were no longer visible uphill, but the evidence of fire hung heavily in the humid air. It filled his nostrils, sank into his heart, plastering his mind with flashbacks from the fire, the hospital, Felicity's withdrawal from him.

"Is there something I can help you with, son?"

Securing the officer within his focus, Travis stated, "I'm here to see the manager."

"Do you have business with him?"

"Yes." Simple, straightforward it wasn't a lie. He didn't have an appointment, but he was certain Mr. Ward would want to hear from him.

"At this hour on a Sunday evening?" the officer questioned.

"Yes, sir. It's personal in nature."

"What's your name?"

"Travis Parker."

The police officer jotted down the information. Glancing up the hill, he said, "This isn't a good time. There's been a fire on the property and the management has asked us to keep activity to a minimum. You'll have to come back another time."

About to tell him he was here to discuss the fire, Travis thought better of it. No reason to raise any more suspicion than a late night Sunday visit already had. "Sure, no problem."

Shifting the gear into reverse, Travis backed out and drove up the road toward town. He should have said he was here to pick up his brother or help with the horses. Lying would have ensured an easier access. Instead, he went with the truth, which drew the attention of the police.

Driving out of sight, Travis circled back and returned to the hotel, keeping a wary eye out for the officer who'd stopped him. Passing the main lot, he continued on to the employee lot which was lined with cars from those called back to work, but Travis noted a narrow space available on the end. Slipping in, he decided he'd trek up to the stables under the cover of forest by taking the employee route up. Shoving his truck keys into his pocket, he pulled out his cell phone and used the light to illuminate his way. Slinking through the black of forest didn't make him a criminal.

Only made him feel like one. A feeling he didn't care for. But it wasn't like he was breaking the law. Only doing what he had to do to set things right.

Chapter Sixteen

Marching up the narrow passage, the light from Travis' cell phone illuminated the path, pine-needles blanketing the forest floor, a slew of rocks and roots poking up from beneath. Unaccustomed to taking the employee route up to the stables, he hadn't committed this trail to memory. Thoughts of the years he'd spent walking this land, these trails, brought the magnitude of the events home. Whoever set the fire intended to do serious damage. Not only had they shown total disregard for the safety and well-being of the horses, they obviously had little regard for the land. Travis might not own Ladd Springs, but burning any natural preserve went against his grain. He'd grown up in these woods. His family lived up the street, their property connected by forest. If the group of them hadn't been nearby for the Serenity Scape performance, who knows how far the fire could have spread, how many animals could have perished.

Wildfires didn't discriminate. They only destroyed.

Exiting the trail, Travis gazed up the hill. The sight of the stables half burned to the ground cut raw. The flames might be gone, but the smoke had managed to permeate the entire mountainside, hanging in layers. The stench angered him. Fire engines emitted a steady flash of red light over the stables and paddocks, white walls barely recognizable as most of the building had collapsed into a massive heap of charred wood and bent metal, ribbons of smoke twirling upward as they vanished into the black of night. In contrast to the dead rubble of devastation, the area was a hive of activity. Horses had been collected, were being attended to by stable staff. Troy would be there overseeing the animals, ensuring their safety, keeping them calm. Despite their differences of late, Travis recognized Troy had a talent when it came to the animals. When they were growing up, horses had always been a part of their lives. They rode every day, worked them, took care of them. Neither used saddles. They weren't necessary. The feel of a horse beneath their bodies was as natural as a pair of jeans and boots. But Troy had always demonstrated an emotional connection with the horses that Travis did not. It was like he spoke their language, understood what they thought. Travis couldn't attest to that level of expertise, but according to Miss Delaney, Troy was as good as they came.

Hiking the remaining distance, Travis redirected his thoughts to the "who" and the "why." Whoever did this was sick. Twisted. And he would pay.

Skirting the fire trucks, Travis strode the vicinity of the building, scanning the myriad faces in search of Mr. Ward. With Mr. Harris tied up at the hospital and going nowhere fast, Travis needed to find Mr. Ward and tell him what he'd learned about Jeremiah's debt, his meeting with the strangers in town. It was possible that Mr. Ward had done his own research, and between the two of them, they could put their minds together and solve this crime. Distracted by the blackened rubble, inundated by the sour scent, his heart caught at the sight of scorched stall gates. A few hung open, dangling from their hinges, looking like they could break at any second. Felicity had tried to get Blue. Her mom had tried to save them all. Fixing his gaze on a row of leather tack scarred by flame, Travis thought about all they had nearly lost. Miss Delaney was in the hospital. Troy and a horse had been burned, but it could have been worse.

Travis glanced from roof to walls to ground. This fire had not only been devastating to the animals, it would cost a fortune for Mr. Harris to rebuild and re-outfit. The horses had lost their home. They could live outdoors, but many were new to the stables. Heck, the stables were new to Ladd Springs! Allowing his gaze to drift toward the animals gathered in the open night air, he thought they appeared calm, normal after their traumatic evening. With the stables burned to a crisp, where would the horses stay?

"Travis." He turned at the sound of the masculine voice coming from behind him. "Have you been to see Delaney?"

Malcolm Ward appeared out of nowhere like a gift from Heaven. Despite the destruction around him, he looked clean and fresh. Must be the white head of hair. Against the dark and desolate scene surrounding them, his hair jumped out as though he had averted disaster. Which he hadn't. The dirt stains on the knees of his pressed khaki slacks told a different story. He had been there with Delaney when the ambulance arrived.

Travis coughed, slung the long bangs from his eyes. "Not exactly. I went to the hospital with Felicity but they were doing tests. The results weren't good. She's in a coma."

Malcolm dropped his head forward. Running a hand over his head, he heaved a sigh. "I'm sorry to hear that. I assume Felicity is still at the hospital?"

Travis nodded. "She's with Nick."

The fact registered in Malcolm's expression. Nick was his partner, his friend. The fact that he was suffering struck deep, like he shared in their tragedy. "The two will need each other to get through this."

"Yes," Travis murmured in reply. His girlfriend needed Nick, not him. Travis attributed her reaction tonight to stress. Her horse's safety had been jeopardized for the second time in less than a week, and it was taking its toll on her. Emotions ran high and tight. That much he understood. But her reaction to him was a different story. It felt more like rejection than stress.

"Are you here to see Troy?" Malcolm asked.

Caught on the chin, Travis realized it was the obvious question. If he wasn't at the hospital with Felicity, what was he doing here? Shifting his weight, he set hands to his hips. "Actually, I'm here to see you."

"Me?"

"Yes, sir." Checking the immediate vicinity for anyone who might overhear, he said, "I've been doing some digging and I've learned that Jeremiah Ladd's marker was paid via a local bank here in town."

Malcolm raised his brow.

"I was able to trace the wire but there was no name attached to the transaction. Apparently it was paid in cash."

"Good work," Malcolm commended, his demeanor easing a degree. "I like a man who understands the value of detective work."

Travis straightened. "Thank you, sir. But that's not all."

Malcolm tipped his head. "I'm listening."

"I followed Jeremiah Ladd downtown. He went to a house in a pretty bad section of town and met with some guy. I saw him when he came out but didn't recognize him."

"Did he look like a local?" Malcolm asked.

"Could've been." He shrugged. "I have no idea. But I did take a picture." Travis pulled the cell phone from his back pocket and searched through his photo album. Locating the photo, he handed the phone to Malcolm. "That's the guy."

Malcolm peered at the image, zooming in for a better look. While his features had relaxed, his gaze was consumed in deliberation. "I've never seen him before."

"I don't know if he's from here or not."

"Doesn't look like a man who could pay fifty thousand dollars on behalf of Jeremiah."

"Agreed. It's possible he's just an old friend or something, but I thought it significant."

Malcolm returned the phone. "Good work. I say we head down to the hotel and show Cal. See if he recognizes the man."

"Okay."

If the man thought that would help, fine. Travis didn't have anything else to do at the moment.

Walking in silence down to the lobby of Hotel Ladd, the two men were content with the privacy of their thoughts. It had been a long night yet it wasn't getting any shorter. Not surprisingly, a few guests milled about, driven by morbid curiosity. Whispers had spread quick as the fire. There had been an explosion. The stables had been burned to the ground. Ambulances had carried away the owner's wife. Police were on scene to investigate. Travis understood it was human nature to gawk and question, but it didn't prevent him from wishing the people had vacated the premises. For him, this blow had been personal.

Malcolm opened the glass-paned lobby door, directing Travis in ahead of him. A single female clerk manned the front desk. Not particularly unusual for a Sunday evening, especially considering half the hotel was up the hill, checking out the damage to the stables, but Travis found it disquieting. The mood was pensive, the ambiance unnerved. Hearing the gurgle of fountain water didn't help, only serving to underscore the aberration of events.

Malcolm strode over to the desk, ushering a smile as he said, "Good evening, Patty."

"Hi, Mr. Ward."

"Is Cal around?"

"Yes, sir. He's in the office."

"Thanks."

Waving for Travis to follow, Malcolm made his way behind the check-in desk as Mr. Foster emerged from the office. "Did I hear my name called?"

"You did," Malcolm replied. "Travis and I wanted to speak with you. Do you have a second?"

Cal glanced between the two, a heightened curiosity nipping at his gaze. "Of course. In the office?"

The three men walked into the small office and Cal closed the door behind them. Without enough chairs for them all to sit, they remained standing. "What's up?" Cal asked.

"Travis has been doing some research into Jeremiah's debt situation and discovered his marker was paid from a local bank here in town." Cal glanced at Malcolm with an odd mix of confusion and curiosity but said nothing. Malcolm smiled. "It seems he's also taken it upon himself to do a bit of investigating work."

Cal centered on Travis. "What kind of investigative work?"

Travis looked to Malcolm who gave him the nod. *Go ahead and show him*. Pulling his phone from his pocket, he brought the photo onto the screen and handed it to Cal. "I followed him to a shanty house downtown where he met with these guys. We were wondering if maybe you recognized one them."

Cal examined the imaged, zoomed in as Malcolm had, scrolling through the few photos Travis had taken. "I don't know... The one looks familiar but the shot was taken too far away. It's possible I've seen him around town, even here at the hotel, though by the looks of him, I doubt the latter." Looking up, he said, "You know, Troy mentioned he saw Jeremiah in the woods with two men."

"He did?" Travis asked. "When?"

"When he was out looking for Spirit. Jeremiah was looking to grab some of the gold, but there was none to be grabbed. According to Troy, he and his cohorts weren't too happy."

Travis felt a warm rise in his cheeks. Why hadn't Troy mentioned it to *him*?

"It's possible Ladd has hooked up with some old friends while in town," Malcolm said, "engaging in a bit of freelancing on the side."

"Maybe. I think we should show this picture to Troy," Cal said. "See if he recognizes the fellow as one of two in the forest with Jeremiah.

Malcolm prompted, "I find the beard interesting, don't you?"

The question snapped Cal to attention. "*Yes*. I do. Should we call Becky in?"

"If you don't think she'll mind coming into work on a Sunday evening, I do." Malcolm grinned. "The police are already on site, which would make it convenient to take her statement."

Cal handed the camera phone back to Travis and picked up the phone from his desk. Travis didn't understand exactly what was happening, but dutifully followed as Malcolm walked out of the office. "What was that about?" Travis asked, unable to stem his curiosity.

Passing the desk clerk, Malcolm took him aside by the fountain. Lowering his voice, he explained, "The gift shop was robbed the other night."

"*Robbed*?"

"We've tried to keep it under wraps so as not to alarm the guests, but the man responsible had a beard."

Comprehension sank through him like stone. "You think this might be the guy?"

Malcolm nodded. "Seems likely. He fits the general description."

"I told Felicity I didn't think it was a coincidence that Jeremiah was back in town and things started happening," Travis said, the notion gaining steam. "She thinks it's her father who's responsible. She thinks he's behind all the trouble."

"I'm not ruling out Jack Foster."

"You're not?"

Malcolm shook his head. "He could have easily paid the marker for Jeremiah. You said the money came from here. He's here."

"But why would he help Jeremiah?"

Malcolm stared at him. "He doesn't care for Delaney? He knows their history? Seems to me now is not the time to pull any chips from the table."

Travis stood stunned. *Felicity could be right*?

Chapter Seventeen

Travis tagged along as Malcolm and Cal made the trek back up to the stables. The police officer who had stopped him earlier noticed Travis and narrowed his gaze, his expression sour as he trailed the three men walking past him. *Yes, I'm with them.* The man made a move toward him until a couple of guests walked up to the officer, distracting the evil eye he had trained on Travis.

Tamping down a rush of nerves, he thought, *whatever.* Tugging the shirt from his body, he did what he had to do. These men had to know what he knew, though unlike Mr. Ward, Travis maintained his belief Jeremiah seemed the most likely culprit. While Jack Foster might have it in for Felicity's mom, he didn't have any grudge against the hotel. Other than the fact Troy worked for Hotel Ladd, but Travis thought that connection was a stretch. The sticky point was the money. Mr. Foster definitely had the money to help Jeremiah get out of jail. His daddy owned the biggest bank in town making it easy enough for him to wire the money without leaving a footprint. But still...

Travis wasn't ready to give up on his theory quite yet. His gut wouldn't let him. Climbing the hillside with little effort, he listened as the men conversed.

"Where's Jillian tonight?" Malcolm asked Cal. "Any idea if she's in house?"

"I don't know. I haven't seen her since I came down from the bonfire."

"Hm."

"If she had anything to do with this, so help me God, I'll make her wish she never set foot on this property."

"You're not alone in that sentiment," Malcolm said.

"How's Delaney?" Cal asked.

Malcolm tossed a glance over his shoulder at Travis before replying, "Not good. She's in a coma."

"A coma?" Cal swore under his breath. "Gosh, I'm sorry to hear that. I assume Nick is with her."

"He is."

Cal ground his jaw, muscles jumping beneath his skin. Travis understood the emotions churning through him. They were the same ones he was experiencing, although his were compounded by a sense of betrayal. Why didn't Troy share his news about Jeremiah with him? Differences aside, they were brothers who cared about the same people. They helped track down the missing horses, helped handle the blaze. Why couldn't they be a team? Didn't Troy understand they were working toward the same goal?

Arriving at the stables, Travis noted firemen were loading up their truck. Flames no longer leapt into the night sky, the fire nothing but a smoldering mess of destruction. Several guests hovered about the edge of the bright yellow crime scene tape. A lone group of men walked the perimeter of the paddocks. Horses looked normal. Travis didn't see Troy anywhere.

As an older staff member walked past, Cal asked him, "Is Troy still around?"

The man nodded. "He's in the barn." He hooked a thumb over his shoulder. "They're making room for the horses."

"Thanks," Cal replied and headed over.

They didn't have to walk far. Troy was on his way back to the paddocks. When he spotted them, he picked up his pace. His arm was bandaged in white, a stark contrast to his soot-covered skin and the black of his T-shirt. Malcolm said he'd been burned. He'd suffered the injury while saving the horses. Travis' lungs constricted. Saving Felicity's horse.

"Hello, Mr. Foster." Troy tipped his head. "Mr. Ward."

"How's it coming with the move?" Cal asked.

"Fine. I think they'll be all right in there temporarily. I've moved the carriages out back, and dependin' on the weather, most of the animals can stay outside during the day."

Cal added, "How's Spirit?"

His brother's dark eyes turned inky black, a menacing spark lighting them as he replied, "Not good. The fire spooked him bad. I think he must have been near where it started 'cause it looks like he tried to bust clear out of his stall."

"Is he okay?"

At the upheaval in his brother's eyes, Travis knew the answer before Troy said, "He's hurt. The vet is here taking a look at him, but he scraped himself up pretty badly."

Malcolm placed a hand to Troy's shoulder. "We'll take care of him, Troy. If there's anything that can be done, we'll do it."

Troy mumbled, "Yes, sir."

His brother appeared on the verge of tears, which meant this must be the horse Felicity had told him about, the one Troy and only Troy seemed to be able to handle. Memories of an injured horse put down during his childhood overcame Travis, hitting harder than he expected. God help Troy if he had to put down this horse. Travis prayed the injuries were only superficial and wouldn't warrant such a drastic measure. Ending an animal's life was tough. Too tough.

"I hate to take you away from your business," Cal said, knowing full well Troy had no "business" here. He was here as a volunteer, no longer an official employee on duty. At least until his name was cleared at trial.

"No, sir. That's fine." Troy glanced at Mr. Ward. "What's on your mind?"

No concern in his voice, rather Troy seemed heartened by the distraction.

"Travis has some information regarding Jeremiah that we want to ask you about."

Troy looked at him. "What?"

Blunt, challenging, he went straight to the source, Travis mused. Pushing his shoulders back, he said, "Mr. Foster said you saw some guys in the forest with Jeremiah Ladd," inflecting a *"why didn't you tell me"* into his tone.

"I did."

"Well, I followed him downtown where I saw him meet with some guys."

"We want to know if the men are the ones you saw in the woods," Cal said. Troy shot a questioning glance to Travis. "He has a picture," Cal said, prodding Travis to share it with Troy.

Pulling the phone from his pocket, he displayed the photo depicting Jeremiah and the taller man on the screen. "Is this one of the guys you saw?"

Troy examined the picture for a second and said, "Yep. That's one of 'em." Focusing on Travis, he said, "Where did you see him?"

"Downtown, over by Pine Street."

Anger funneled into his gaze. "He's up to no good." As though mentally connecting the dots, he asked, "Do you think he had something to do with this fire?"

"We don't know," Malcolm answered. "He could have, but we don't want to rule anyone out at this point."

"What about that Jillian woman?" Troy asked boldly. "She was together with Mr. Foster at a motel in town. Do you think they had something to do with it?"

Travis gaped at him. "Jillian was with Felicity's dad?" Disbelief coursed through him. What else didn't he know?

Troy flashed a look of disdain but duly revealed, "She told me the other day. Said she saw them the afternoon we found the horses."

And she didn't tell me? Travis grumbled silently.

Cal and Malcolm shared an unsettling glance, before Malcolm turned his lens on Travis and Troy. "Now that we're putting our cards on the table, is there anything else you boys think we should know?"

Travis was spent. He had nothing more. He looked to his brother. Did Troy?

He shook his head and scowled. "That's all I know, except whoever did this is gonna pay."

"Troy," Cal cautioned, "think about what you're saying. With the trial coming up, don't give Jack any more ammunition to use against you."

Troy grunted his displeasure but Travis thought it good advice. Troy didn't need any more trouble than he already had. Especially trouble that was preventable.

"Okay," Malcolm said. "Do me a favor and keep it to yourselves. I don't want anyone getting ahead of us on this one."

Chapter Eighteen

The knock on Jeremiah's motel door sounded like a jackhammer to his skull. Lying prostrate across his bed, he was nursing a hangover of epic proportions and wanted no visitors. None. "Go away!" he yelled

"We ain't going anywhere until you give us our money!" came the angry reply through the cheap metal door, followed by another round of pounding.

Jeremiah groaned. Gripping his forehead, he squeezed his temples to ward off the noise. He was in no mood for a confrontation. Not after a night of drinking at Bucky's. Running into one of his old pals at the cell phone store, they'd gone over to the bar for a few drinks, a few drinks that turned into a night full. The last thing he wanted to do was get up and answer the door.

The incessant pounding continued, followed by, "You'd better answer this door 'fore I kick it in, Jeremiah!"

"Dammit!" Jeremiah exclaimed, rolling halfway off the cheap mattress. He glanced at the digital clock. Eleven-thirty. Oh, *jeez*. He'd only slept six hours? His head throbbed. His stomach felt like rot-gut. The room rolled and tipped.

"Hurry up! I ain't waitin' all day!"

Pushing to a standing position, Jeremiah swayed a bit, his brain a soupy mess of pain. Suddenly, he felt the need to hit the toilet. Unfortunately, the physiological detour might send his dimwitted cohorts over the edge causing them to knock in the door!

Idiots. Shuffling toward the door, Jeremiah fought the stabbing pain in his head and unlocked the door. Within seconds the brothers pushed their way in, a blinding flood of sunlight spilling in behind them. "Why ain't you answering our calls?"

"I lost my phone," Jeremiah replied, squinting against the invasion of daylight as he headed for the bathroom.

"You don't expect me to fall for that lame excuse, do you?"

"Yeah," the second one pitched in. "Sure you lost it all right." He pointed to the nightstand with a sneer. "What's that over there? A walkie-talkie?"

Ignoring them, he unzipped his jeans and relieved himself.

"We want our money," Rob warned in a gravelly voice.

"So you said," Jeremiah replied through the open door.

"We want it now."

Zipping his fly closed, Jeremiah flushed the toilet and walked back into the room. The air smelled like stale cigarettes, much like his clothes. Outside the confines of a bar, the scent grated on him. Made him sick, actually. Fighting a tide of nausea, he pulled the brothers into focus. Drawn with lines of displeasure, Rob's face was tanned, his long hair greasy and thin, his chin hair a scruffy excuse for a beard. His brother was no different, only rounder, chubbier, his hair line receding before that of his older brother's. Both wore jeans and T-shirts, the grubby status-quo since they'd been here. Jeremiah doubted they did laundry. Too much effort.

"Well?" Rob demanded.

Irritation curdled in his stomach. "I told you I'd get it to you."

"Yeah, and I ain't seen none of it."

"What about them pendants?" the younger asked.

"I gave you half of them," Jeremiah exclaimed. "What more do you want?"

"We want all of them."

Jeremiah glared at the older brother. Greedy bastard. If he thought Jeremiah was gonna hand over the entire heist he was crazy. Wasn't gonna happen. The goods were staying with him. But Jeremiah knew better than to ignite the man's temper by revealing as much. The guy was crazy as a coon dog on the hunt and nastier than a rattler. It was a lesson he'd learned the hard way back in high school and had the scars to prove it. But that didn't mean he couldn't outsmart him. "I've made a plan to get more."

"There ain't no more."

"There's always more money," Jeremiah snickered.

"What plan you talkin' about?"

"Hotel Ladd has a safe and where there's a safe, there's more money."

"I already checked that last night and there ain't no gold in it. Nothin' but a pistol."

The younger's eyes lit up. "A right nice one, too!"

"You stole it?" Jeremiah asked incredulously.

"Yep! They had a fire over there and made it real easy to get in and out," he said, fanning his feathers like a peacock.

Jeremiah smacked a hand to his head before he realized the painful effect. Groaning loudly, he wanted to slug him. "Why didn't you leave it be? Guns are easy to get around here!"

The fool brightened. "So was this one," he said, pulling it from the waist of his dirty jeans.

Flat and black, the weapon snared his complete attention. Steal a firearm and you've entered a new level of criminal charges. "Great. Just great."

"What are you worried about?"

"My connection to you, moron. They find you, they find me!"

"But you didn't take it," the younger added, wondering what all the fuss was about.

Jeremiah fired into him, "It's called 'accessory to the crime', you idiot. You stole the pendants—pendants I have in my possession." Something that was going to have to change and quick. He was going to have to pawn them sooner rather than later, which would drive down his price. Any pawn shop owner worth his salt could sniff out desperation.

"So what's that got to do with the gun?"

"It has everything to do with it, you imbecile!" Jeremiah wanted to crawl out of his skin, he was so itchin' mad.

"Hey, watch who you're talkin' to." Rob stepped in. "Forget the gun. We helped you. Now it's time for you to help us. We want our money. You got twenty-four hours to deliver."

Giving a shove to his younger brother, he directed him out the door.

Watching them walk out of his motel room, Jeremiah slammed the door closed, instantly regretting the motion as his head swelled with pain. His two allies had just changed sides. Now what was he going to do?

Malcolm paused at the doorway of the private room. The sight of Delaney's unconscious body lying in a hospital body cut deep. This was a woman who never stopped, never slowed down, ran on eight cylinders at a hundred miles an hour. To see her incapacitated was unnatural, much like the tubes connected to her body, the monitors lit up overhead, their red lights blinking, blue lights glowing. Looking at her was almost as bad as the sight of his best friend sitting vigil at her bedside. Nick Harris was a dynamic figure, imposing in both vigor and strength. This was a guy who powered through life. He didn't doubt his own ability. He didn't accept no for answer. *Can't* wasn't a word in his vocabulary. He moved like a freight train, steamrolling over obstacles. He didn't get derailed by trouble. Actually, he usually caused it. To see Nick Harris rendered helpless was unsettling.

Understandable but unsettling.

Rapping lightly at the open door, Malcolm waited for Nick to acknowledge him. Slowly, he turned. It was a jolt to the system. Black eyes were gouged of life, underscored by dark circles. The lines in his face were carved deep, his expression that of a walking waxed man.

"Hey."

At the single utterance, Malcolm second-guessed his decision to discuss business. Nick was in no shape for it. But since he was here, the least he could do was pay his respects. "Hey," Malcolm returned quietly. "How is she?"

"No change."

"No change has its positives," Malcolm offered, walking into the room. If the swelling didn't worsen, he thought, that was a good thing, right?

"Any word on the cause of the fire?"

Malcolm sighed. Straight to the point despite the circumstances. "No, nothing yet. The forensic people were back this morning combing over the site. Hopefully we'll know something soon."

Nick nodded, returned his focus to Delaney. "Did you locate Jillian?"

"She strolled into the restaurant this morning. Cal asked her about her whereabouts last night and she says she has an alibi."

Nick stared at his wife and said, "She's behind it. I'm sure of it."

"Then we'll be able to prove it. Until then..." Malcolm ventured a peek at the monitors. Picking up on an increase in rhythm, he finished reluctantly, "we wait for the investigators." Aware that coma patients could hear what was being said around them, he didn't want to upset Delaney's recovery by discussing the fire that sent her here. Debating whether or not to reveal what he'd learned from Travis, Malcolm lingered near the foot of Delaney's bed. They could always discuss matters in the hall.

"What is it?" Nick asked, staring at him as though seeing him for the first time. "What aren't you telling me?"

Casting a wary gaze toward Delaney, Malcolm hitched his head toward the door.

Nick was up instantly. Patting Delaney's hand, he told her, "I'll be right back, sweetheart." With a kiss to her forehead, he joined Malcolm out in the hallway. "What's up?"

Malcolm took a deep breath, glanced in either direction and said, "Travis came to me last night with some information. Seems he's been digging into Jeremiah's situation and learned the same thing we learned, the money came from here."

"So?"

"So, he followed Jeremiah to a house downtown and caught him meeting with two men. The same two men Troy saw in the forest with Jeremiah."

Visibly turning the information over in his mind, Nick looked to Malcolm for explanation. "What's the connection?"

"One of the men he met with is responsible for our gift shop robbery."

"Well, we suspected that much."

"What I didn't tell Travis is that our office was broken into last night."

"*What*? When?"

"During the commotion after the fire. Someone snuck in somehow and broke into the safe."

Nick raked a hand through his hair, the lines in his face deepening. Tunneling in on Malcolm's eyes, he asked, "They took the gun?"

Malcolm nodded.

"*Damn* it, things keep turning for the worse."

"But there's good news." Nick froze and locked onto Malcolm as he said, "They found fingerprints. They're running them now."

"Good. It'll be our first take-down, followed by Jillian and Jeremiah."

"There's another twist," Malcolm added calmly.

"What?"

"Jack and Jillian seem to have hooked up."

"You're kidding me."

"Wish I were. Felicity saw the two of them together outside his hotel. Apparently there was no mistaking the relationship." Malcolm wondered if he should have revealed the fact sooner but didn't think it important at the time. Nick had seen them together the last time she was in town. Would he care they were back at it?

Nick swung his head away, muttering, "Now what has she got up her sleeve?"

"I don't know, but as to the fire, I'm not entirely sure it was her."

"It was her," Nick smacked back. "It's her specialty."

"Except for the fact that Cal ran into Jeremiah at a gas station yesterday and said he had several gas cans in the back of his pickup truck."

Nick's gaze sharpened to a laser fine point. "You think he's in on it with her?"

"Or with his two friends." Malcolm wasn't sure. "How'd they know to hit the hotel safe while the fire took everyone's attention?"

"Dumb luck?"

"Maybe. Jeremiah's debt was paid anonymously and in cash from a local bank. The two he's running with could have paid it," he said, despite the fact they didn't look like they had a nickel between them. "Besides, if Jillian was involved, she had to have a local connection, someone who could be tracked." Malcolm planned to discuss the issue with Cal.

"Keep checking," Nick said as he glanced through the open doorway. "I still think Jillian is behind this, but whoever put Delaney in this hospital bed is going to answer to me."

Malcolm turned to go, startled to see Felicity standing in the hallway. "You think Jillian had something to do with this?"

"We don't know anything," Malcolm returned, backing off quickly. "It's too soon. But you can be sure we're checking all avenues. We'll find out who's responsible, don't worry."

Felicity cleared her throat. "Yes, please do." Checking with Nick, she asked, "Any change?"

He shook his head, a sadness seeping into his gaze. "I'm afraid not. Would you like to sit with her?"

She nodded and Malcolm took the opportunity to excuse himself. "I'll talk to you later."

Felicity edged into the room, overcome by the sight of her mother's inert figure. It was weird seeing her like this, the woman who was always on the go. At home, her mom rarely sat down. She was always busy, occupied. From caring for her horses, the stables, to caring for Felicity and Nick, her mom was always in motion which made her present condition all the more intolerable. It wasn't right. "Do you think it's possible that Jillian had something to do with the fire?"

Nick settled a brooding gaze on her mother. "It's possible."

"Do you think my father was involved?"

He turned to Felicity and his expression changed. It was as though he knew something but didn't want to tell her. "I don't know." Pausing, he said, "Malcolm told me you saw the two of them together."

Felicity bit down on her lip, a flurry of nerves swarming her breast. "I did. Outside the hotel where he's staying." Nick waited, as though he expected her to say more. "I think they're together," she spit out quickly. "I think they have a *thing*, or something."

"Jillian uses people. That's her thing."

To set fires? Felicity wondered. Is that what Nick meant? Taking in her mother's body, images of the fire burned hot in Felicity's mind. Travis had pushed her mom out of danger, then carried her out to safety. The doctor said she suffered a blunt force trauma to the head, and that's why she was in a coma. Had Travis caused it when he tackled her to the ground?

Felicity shuddered. She didn't know anything about comas or trauma, but she did know about her father. He had it in for her mother. His lighter was found outside the stables. He was seen with Jillian Devane, a woman Nick and Malcolm apparently believed capable of arson. If he was capable of lying in court to send Troy to jail for something he didn't do, why wouldn't it be plausible for him to team up with her mother's arch enemy?

"Will you call me if anything changes?" She stood abruptly.

Nick's surprise made Felicity feel like a heel, like she didn't care enough to sit with her mother, but at the moment she had something more important to do.

He placed a hand over her mother's. "Sure. I'll call you the minute something changes."

"Thanks," she mumbled and hurried out of the room. Her father was responsible for the fire. But she needed to find something more than his lighter, something that linked him to the fire, maybe to Jillian. If she could, it might be exactly what was needed to prevent him from going to court against Troy—because he'd be in jail where he belonged.

Chapter Nineteen

Malcolm walked the distance from hotel to stables, the ease of his stride a sure sign his physical condition was improving. A fairly steep incline, the mountainside trail that led guests up to the stables was graded for their comfort but taxing on the muscles. Only the physically fit would enjoy the climb. The others would opt for a ride up, courtesy of the hotel. Inhaling the blue sky above, the line of evergreens and oaks that created the horizon, he recalled it wasn't that long ago he was chasing Lacy around these mountains and having a bear of a time keeping up with her. A bear of a time. Malcolm chuckled at the direction his terminology had taken. His first visit to the mountains had been little over a year ago—a visit he'd expected to take weeks had lasted months. Years, really, considering he and Lacy planned to make Tennessee their home.

Home base, he corrected. While Malcolm might enjoy the pure country air and layers of hills, his heart yearned for travel. Born and raised in Los Angeles, Malcolm's desire had been bred into him. From summer jaunts to Europe to sea excursions through the islands, Malcolm was no stranger to an airport or the jet-set lifestyle. Not only his personal life but his career had taken him coast to coast. In fact, it had been during a stint in New York City that he'd met Nick. Malcolm had been head of the marketing department for a restaurant in the city when Nick arrived on scene and tried to woo their head chef away to one of his exotic destinations. Malcolm's boss had a fit, sending Malcolm's cooler head in to prevail. Unfortunately, Nick could be a smooth operator when he wanted to be and talked not only the chef into a new job but Malcolm as well!

Laughing at the memory, Malcolm was glad for the decision. He and Nick worked well together, both personally and professionally. Their styles were a perfect complement to one another, and it wasn't long before Nick offered Malcolm a partnership stake in the business. Said if he was going to grow, he'd need more time and to spread out across the globe and the knowledge he had a man he could trust at his back. It was a proposition Malcolm couldn't refuse. Harris Hotels offered him not only the chance to exercise his management and marketing capabilities, but the eco-friendly aspect challenged his creative side, as well making for a career that held his interest year after year.

He paused at the top of the hill, anger shredding his pleasurable feelings as he took in the sight of formerly white walls charred black, many collapsed in on themselves. Burnt out horse stalls and scorched leather tack reminded him of the animals that had been hurt. A putrid scent lingered in the air, inciting a desire for revenge. Malcolm had never considered himself a violent man. He wasn't outwardly physical like Nick, didn't swagger or hurl threats, but the sight of Hotel Ladd's stables in ruin roused an ugly need. It was visceral, demanding. Someone had deliberately destroyed an integral part of their property, and that someone was going to pay.

The sooner the better, he mused, and headed to the nearest police officer on hand. The forensics team was on hand to determine the cause of the blaze, a cause that would lead Malcolm directly to the culpable party. He moved toward an older man, the grim lines in his face suggesting he was a senior officer, one who was probably all too familiar with senseless criminal acts. "Officer..." Malcolm spied the name on his tag. "...Griffin. Have you learned anything about the fire?"

"And you are?" he shot back with a surly glower, his ruddy cheeks plump and covered by a glistening sheen of perspiration. The uniform he wore groaned at the seams, suggesting a man who liked good-cooking.

"Malcolm Ward. I'm one of the hotel owners."

The officer's hostility slackened. "Yes, we think so. It was an IED set off by remote control."

"IED?"

"Improvised explosive device."

Malcolm knew what it meant but couldn't believe that was the cause. "Someone set off a bomb in our stables?"

"Sort of." Officer Griffin called out to one of his detectives, "Randy! Bring me that device, will ya?" Turning back to Malcolm, he explained, "Know anyone missing a cell phone?"

"Cell phone? No," Malcolm replied, confused by the question.

"Forensics is still working to confirm, but we think the fire started in the back corner of the building on account of the concentration of char patterns in that location. We think the bomb was detonated remotely using a cell phone."

The younger officer jogged up and handed a gnarled piece of metal to his superior.

"Thanks," the man said briskly.

Malcolm barely acknowledged the junior police officer, engrossed by the sight of the fire's cause. It was so small. "That's it?"

"Yeah. We don't see too many of these around here, but one of the guys out of Chattanooga used to work in the military and he nailed it on the spot. Basically what we're dealing with is a makeshift fire bomb set off a by cell phone." Malcolm gaped at him. Taking the hotelier's silence as a cue to continue, the officer explained, "All you need is a few well-placed electrical wires, a fuse, a power source attached to a can of gasoline and you have yourself an explosive device."

Staring at the piece of black metal in the man's hand, Malcolm was amazed by the amount of information they had been able to gather. There must be more to it. "I don't understand. How can a cell phone set off a bomb?" he asked, wanting the information to be that easy but needing it to be accurate beyond a reasonable doubt.

"When the phone is called, it activates the ringer which makes the connection between the components and kicks off the signal to detonate. The idea is to create a signal between the positive and negative circuit which then sets off the fuse."

None of it made any sense to Malcolm. This was not his area of expertise.

"Now that we've located the device and cause, we can track down cell signals in the area around the time of the explosion. Based on witness accounts, we have a good idea when that occurred."

"And that would lead you to the person responsible?"

"It will get us closer. I expect whoever managed to rig this device isn't stupid." Turning the metal cover plate in his hand, he said, "It's likely they used a phone solely for this purpose. My guess is it's attached to phony account."

"Of course," Malcolm said, disappointed by the realization he was no closer to finding out who did this than before. He wanted to give the officer a few suggestions on where to begin and who to question but thought it unwise at this time. Let the police take the lead. There was time later to assist, if needed. "Which makes it all the more difficult to discover who's responsible."

The man brightened. "On the contrary. The method of operation and the means used to set off the device can tell us a lot. How they set up the fuse, the material used... If they've done this before, we can connect the pieces used at this bomb site to others done in a similar way. By analyzing the data, you'd be surprised at what we can track down in terms of the parties responsible. Sometimes even tracing the tape used in this explosion can lead us to a particular manufacturer, a point of sale, possible DNA..." He shook his head, adding, "It's not time to give up hope yet."

Malcolm thought he must look as gloomy as he felt for the weathered old police officer to act as a cheerleader for hope. But, dammit, he couldn't help it. Casting a weary gaze over the debris, add the dislocated animals and their injuries, the problems this created for his business and Malcolm couldn't help but feel down. Trace the manufacturer of a scrap of half-blown away tape? That was his big hope? Malcolm sighed. "Thank you, Officer. I appreciate your efforts."

"No problem. I'll let you know when we have something more definitive."

"Yes, please do."

Suddenly drained of energy, Malcolm ambled toward the barn. He needed to make another check on the animals, clarify their health and ability to accommodate guests. He and Cal had decided against cancelling the trail rides, aiming to get back to normal as soon as possible but at this rate, they might have to. No one was going to want to walk by this mess, nor did he want them to. It was a sledgehammer to the mood and exactly the opposite of what a "serenity stay" meant. Heaving a heavy breath, he walked by a pen where several horses idled about, a single male staff member among them. The stable hand was standing between horses, holding blue nylon rope leads close. Not sure what he was doing, Malcolm neared. A black cowboy hat popped up, the man's face becoming fully visible over the animal's body. Realizing it was Troy, Malcolm detoured over.

"Troy."

The young man turned, a sudden guilt gripping his features. "Mr. Ward."

"What's going on?"

Concern tightened in his dark eyes. "I was walkin' the horses, checking them out. I'm sorry about spending so much time on the property, Mr. Ward, but I've got to be here. I know I'm not official or anything but I can't sit home and do nothin'."

"I understand. How's it going?"

"Not good. The horses are still a bit spooked, Spirit especially."

"That's the one you've been working?"

"Yes, sir. The men told me you and Mr. Foster haven't cancelled the trail rides for this afternoon but I'd have to advise you to cancel."

"You would?"

"I would. These animals have been through a lot. They've lost their home, their peace of mind. I think I'd give them a while. I know it's not good for business," he added quickly, "But that's just my feelin' on the subject."

Malcolm paused, settling on Troy. The kid had a sixth sense when it came to the animals. If he didn't think they were ready, that's all Malcolm needed. "Then we'll cancel the trail rides."

"Sir?"

"I trust your judgment."

Like an eraser, Malcolm's show of confidence removed all doubt from Troy's expression. "Thank you, sir."

Glancing about the immediate vicinity, Malcolm dropped his voice and said, "Listen, there's something I want to discuss with you."

Troy walked closer, horses in tow, closing the space to a mere fence line. The horses stood idle but their eyes were keen on Malcolm. Once again, the severity of the incident hit hard.

"Yes, sir?"

"We need to discuss your trial. It's set for next week, but we need to look into a continuance."

"A continuance? What for?"

"On account of your star witness is lying in a coma."

"Oh no..." Troy absorbed the significance. It was the instant vulnerability of a child who'd just learned the worst. "She isn't gettin' any better?"

"Not yet, and the doctors can't give us any more detail other than she has swelling in her brain and it's serious. They might have to take her to surgery." Troy looked away, clearly pained by the news. "I'm sorry, Troy. I know you two are close."

"She's like a momma to me," he murmured, refusing to make eye contact.

She was also the key to his freedom in his case against Jack Foster. "I'll keep you posted on her condition, but I wanted you to be aware of what was going on with your case."

"Thank you, sir." Troy hauled his gaze back to Malcolm, his eyes glistening beneath the shadow of his black hat. "I appreciate everything you and Mr. Harris are doing on my behalf."

"Wouldn't think of doing anything less." Malcolm was only sorry Troy's parents hadn't been more supportive in the beginning, but now that he and Nick had hired the big guns, the Parkers were fully vested. Not that Malcolm could blame them. Of modest means, they couldn't afford to hire the kind of legal team he and Nick could, but more, they were caught in the middle of small town family feud. Delaney had given him a rundown of the players and positions. The Parkers were friends with the Ladds, but they were also friendly with the Shores. The Shores were friends and allies with the Fosters, their son, Officer Gavin, the tool being used as a wedge between Jack and Delaney. While Delaney and Gavin went way back, he held a grudge against Nick and Malcolm for not revealing Jeremiah's gambling troubles. Gavin could have rounded him up but instead had to receive the order from his commanding officer. His ego had taken a hit.

Across the board, loyalties were being tested, morality was being fought, and all for public consumption. If Jack Foster didn't drop his charges against Troy, the Fosters would have to own up to the ugly behavior of their son, Jack. The Shores would be caught in the middle, but either way Troy could end up in jail. "He said-she said" didn't sell well in a courtroom stacked against you.

Overwhelmed by the slate of negativity, Malcolm brushed it from his mind. Right about now he needed a dose of positivity, and there was no better place for that than at home with his wife, Lacy. He swore her spirit was loaded up with enough to cleanse the whole town of this rotten business! "Anyway, I wanted you to know. Once Delaney's out of the hospital, we can go forward."

In Troy's gaze Malcolm felt the brunt of what was left unsaid. If Delaney didn't make it, Troy could be going to jail for a very long time.

Chapter Twenty

Felicity stood outside the hotel room, riddled with doubt. The air around her was mired in a mix of heat, warm rubber, exhaust fumes and dead calm, making the seconds drag by as she waited. His truck was here. He was here. Would he answer the door?

Biting her lower lip, she wondered about this encounter as she stared at the tan-painted metal door, the peep hole he might very well be staring through this minute. What if he didn't let her in? What if he didn't fall for the ruse? He could get mean. He could take it out on her. Felicity's heart thwacked with an irregular kick. But he wouldn't hurt her—she was his daughter, his own flesh and blood. Spouses had issues that parents and children didn't. He wouldn't do anything to harm *her*. After all, he's the one who championed the value of family, of blood kin. He was the one who insisted she should meet with her grandparents and rebuild their relationship. Why would he doubt her now?

He had no idea what she knew. He'd regard her as an innocent. So long as she acted innocent. Her spirits drooped. But it looked as though she'd never get the opportunity to find out. As she turned away, the door swung open and a look of shock burst into Jack Foster's eyes. He searched up and down the sidewalk, his brown eyes registering her presence with obvious uncertainty. "Felicity. What are you doing here?"

Swallowing hard, she was overcome by a waft of his cologne. Rich and expensive, it underscored the slacks and tailored button-down he wore, the tan color glimmering like satin cream in the sun. "I came to see you," she replied softly, her voice overwhelmed by the engine of a passing truck.

Breaking into a friendly smile, he welcomed her heartily, "I'm glad you're here, but I wished you would have called. We could have met somewhere...more suitable."

"No—this is fine," she said.

A hint of suspicion moved between them, and Felicity wished she hadn't spoken so quickly.

Eyeing her a bit more guardedly, he offered, "I guess I should ask you to come in."

"Thanks." Hesitating, she reprimanded herself to come across more sincerely. This was never going to work if she didn't watch her every word!

Walking in, Felicity remained very aware of his nearness. This was his space. His personal space, cramped and transitory as it was. Beds were made, but littered with her father's belongings. A suitcase sat open on a luggage rack in the closet. Papers lay strewn over the guest room desk, a black computer bag sat off to one side of his open laptop. Felicity gulped. Was he researching his case against Troy?

Nonchalantly as she could, she sniffed the air for the scent of smoke. His clothes would have reeked from the blaze. Hers had.

"Something wrong?"

"What?" She tried to dish out a smile. "No. I just thought I smelled something."

"Something in particular?" he asked.

"No, of course not." A flutter of doubt flitted through her heart. Was he taunting her? Did he know that she knew?

"So tell me," he asked, a trace of humor in his voice, "what really brings you by?"

"Well," she began, trying to begin as she rehearsed on the way over. "I've been thinking a lot about the importance of family and what you said about us being close."

Dark eyes dancing, he arched a brow but said nothing.

"I know you and my mom have had your problems, but that shouldn't prevent us from trying to have a relationship."

"That's what I was trying to tell you before," he said with a healthy dose of skepticism in his gaze.

"I know." She gave a few quick nods of her head, brushed her hair behind an ear. Hugging arms to her body, she reminded herself to remember this was a man familiar with the seedy side of people. He was street smart and savvy. If she didn't keep her story as close to the truth as possible, he'd see right through her. "I don't think I really understood what you meant until my mom wound up in the hospital."

"Your mom is in the hospital?"

Struck by the tone of his reaction, Felicity almost believed his surprise was genuine. "Y-yes," she stumbled, trying to read his response. "She got hurt in the fire last night."

"What fire?"

"The one at the stables."

"What happened? Someone drop a match in a hay bale?"

Try lighter, she mused bitterly, irritated by the continuation of his act. Of course he knew. The least he could do was pretend to be upset for show!

Chuckling softly, he said, "Can't be too careful about who you hire these days."

She wanted to slap the smirk clear off his face. His callous disregard for her mother's well-being was unbelievable. Unconscionable! But seriously, had she expected anything less? If the man was willing to attack his ex-wife, set the stables on fire, potentially harming the horses, compassion for others would be last on his list. But Felicity refused to be put off from her mission. She was here for a reason. A reason that included pinning *him* with the responsibility he deserved. "Yes, well, it was horrible. She got hurt when one of the beams fell down."

"Sorry to hear that," he said, strolling to the opposite side of the far double bed.

Looking around the room for clues—his clothes from yesterday, something, anything—she continued cautiously, watching for signs of his acceptance of her lead. "Like I said, it makes you realize the importance of family. I guess it got me to thinking about you and Troy and..." Unsettled by the rigid edge that had entered his stance, Felicity persisted in her ruse. There was no going back now. "Well, I've been think-ing how unfortunate the situation is."

"Your friend is a punk and I intend to teach him a les-son."

Felicity steeled her emotions against the insult. *He* was the punk, not Troy.

"And listen, about your mother," he said, not breaking stride. "I hate to be the one to tell you, but he might have something going on with her."

Felicity gaped at him. "What?"

A glimmer lit up his dark eyes as he smiled. "He was with her that night in the stables. It's why he shot me, to pre-vent me from talking. Did she tell you? Did he?"

Troy and her mother? That was ludicrous—he was in love with Casey!

The pounding at the door stopped Felicity's heart. *Was that Jillian?*

Jack slid a wary gaze to the door then back to Felicity. "Expecting someone?"

"Me? No, of course not," she snapped. Heart-pounding, she walled off her eyes from seeking the door.

"Funny. Neither am I," he said and strode across the room.

Felicity suddenly felt trapped, like this had been a mis-take. It never occurred to her that Jillian Devane might walk in while she was here. No telling what she'd do if she found Delaney Wilkins' daughter outside the protective shield of her mother—not to mention Felicity would lose all hope of finding evidence.

Jack opened the door.

Ohmigod, ohmigod, ohmigod. What had she been think-ing?

"*Felicity,*" Travis expelled breathlessly.

Jack flashed back to her. "If this is your idea of a game, I'm not amused."

Travis stepped in between them. "What are you doing here?" he asked her.

Jack glowered at him and demanded, "Thought you could put your girlfriend up to conning me out of putting your brother away?" Brown eyes glinted. "Bad move. He's going away for a long time, leaving you on my radar." He snickered. "Which means I'd be careful if I were you."

Reeling from the unexpected sight of her boyfriend, she cried out, "Travis didn't know anything about this! I came here on my own. *Honest.*"

Her father cocked his head. "Nice try." Grabbing the door knob, he said, "But if you'll excuse me, I have more important things to do."

Standing with a hand to the door, his dismissal was clear. Stuck in time, Felicity hung in place. Should she leave? Try and stay? How did he know where to find her? Why had he barged in on them?

"I'm not messing around," Jack said, directing his animosity to her.

Swallowing against the rock in her throat, she slinked by him, avoiding his heated gaze as she passed. There was no way she could salvage her case now. He wouldn't believe another word she said!

Travis followed her out and the door slammed closed. "What the hell were you thinking, coming to see your father?"

Anger flared hot in her breast. "I was here looking for evidence! Until you barged in, that is. What are you doing here, anyway?"

"What evidence?"

"Setting the fire?" Hello? Had he been knocked stupid? "Malcolm and Nick think Jillian had something to do with the fire and that my father is hooked up with her. Makes sense he had something to do with it, don't you think?"

"No I don't 'think' and neither should you." Travis whipped a gaze to the closed door. "You don't know what you're doing coming here like this. Your father doesn't mess around."

"He's not going to hurt me," she asserted, not fully convinced of what she was saying but angry that Travis didn't trust her. All he cared about was telling her how *wrong* she was to have tried—which she wasn't. "If he had something to do with the fire, his clothes would smell of smoke. There might have been evidence in his room, evidence I was in the middle of looking for until you stopped by."

Travis groaned aloud, then whirled on her. Running a hand through his hair, he grabbed hold of a clump, exclaiming, "You're insane! You can't do this, don't you get that? Have you forgotten what he did to your mother?"

"I'm his daughter." She locked arms across her chest. "Ex-wives are different."

"Not if he thinks you're here to convince him to drop charges against Troy, they aren't!"

"That was my diversion tactic so he wouldn't be suspicious."

"What?" Travis closed his eyes, shook his head. "Felicity, please. You can't do this. You're messing with the wrong man."

"No. My mother is lying in a hospital bed and my father is responsible. I'm doing for her what she can't do for herself."

"Let the police handle it."

"He's got half the police force in his pocket! They're not going to get anywhere with him."

"And neither are you."

Resentment split her in two. "At least I'm willing to try. I'm not going to sit on hands and wait idle while you *men* go around and try to figure everything out. If you hadn't interfered, I could have learned something."

Travis looked into her eyes, and for the first time Felicity felt the condemnation Casey and Troy must have felt all these months. Raw and cutting, there was no doubt what Travis thought of her. He disapproved. Worse, he thought she was incompetent. "I'm not a helpless, stupid child. This is my mother and my battle," she said, jabbing a finger to her chest.

"I have my own mind and my own plan and if you disagree with it, *tough*. I'm finished with your protection routine."

Like a punch to the gut, Travis sputtered, "Felicity."

"By the way, how did you know I was here?" she demanded.

"I saw your car."

"Really? Next time you see it somewhere, don't stop." Felicity turned on her heel and left him. "I don't need your kind of interference on my behalf."

Felicity yanked open the door to Fran's Diner, the clang of bells reverberating in her chest. Travis made her so mad. Why did he have to butt into her business? Now she'd never get close enough to her father to get the information she needed, and it was his fault. All his fault. Sure, she might have been feeling a bit uncertain at the moment he barged in, but she could have recovered. Now, she would never know. Her mother was still in a coma, her father was still walking free and she was helpless to do anything about it.

It wasn't fair. None of it was fair.

The scent of fried chicken broke through her anger. The lunch crowd was scarce but she could see the cooks were busy preparing for the dinner rush. From the back of the restaurant, Fran Jones spotted Felicity immediately and waved her over. She was talking with Ashley Fulmer, probably about her mother. Ashley was as close to family as someone could get without actually being blood. She'd been Felicity's grandmother's best friend. "Two seeds in a melon," Ashley always said, using one of her many garden analogies. "Your grandmother Susannah and me were close as sisters." Felicity's mom claimed Ashley had been like a mother to her, filling in the void after Susannah Ladd died. Felicity had only been six at the time and didn't remember much but she knew one thing: Ashley Fulmer was the first to raise her hand when help was needed.

Standing behind the counter, Fran folded the top of a paper bag and pushed it toward Ashley, absently tucking stray red curls beneath her hair net. Next to Ashley's pop of spring blue clothing, Fran's white uniform seemed sterile. Unfriendly. It reminded Felicity of the white coats the doctors wore as they walked the halls, delivering the bad news to families and friends.

Heading over, Felicity wondered if it was more food for Albert. With her mom in the hospital, Ashley would be the sole caretaker for Uncle Albert. He still lived on the property though Felicity didn't see him much anymore, not like she used to when Uncle Ernie was alive. He used to insist she visit every night and play her flute for them. Albert listened and seemed to enjoy the music, but he never asked for her after Ernie passed. It seemed when Ernie died, so did Albert's desire for music. Her mom said he was becoming one of those odd recluse types, refusing her invitations to dinner and bonfire gatherings, claiming he didn't have the energy for it. Felicity feared that Albert could wither away and die without anyone knowing about it.

Thank goodness her mom and Ashley checked up on him.

"How's your momma?" Fran asked, her heavily-lined brown eyes sharp with concern.

"Has there been any word?" Ashley echoed.

"Same," Felicity replied dully.

Ashley's big blue eyes recoiled. "Isn't there anything the doctors can do?"

Felicity shrugged, sinking a hip into the counter. "They say they can't. Not yet, anyway. If mom doesn't get better on her own, they might have to take her to surgery."

"Surgery?"

"That's what they say. Nick's with her now but I'm on my way over. I wanted to pick up some food for her, maybe get her to smell what she's missing out on and wake up."

The bittersweet compliment drew a smile from Fran. "That's good thinkin', child. How about I send some biscuits and cornbread with you, maybe some fried chicken? Delaney never could resist the smell of fried chicken, and I have fresh batch coming out right now."

"Sounds good. If nothing else, Nick can eat it." Felicity hadn't seen him eat a bite a food since he'd been at the hospital, but she knew he had to be putting something in his stomach or else he'd starve. Might as well be Fran's cooking.

Fran drew a hand under Felicity's chin and cupped it. "I'll go put together a bag for you right now." She kissed her cheek then went straight to work, leaving a heavy drift of her perfume behind.

"Thanks."

Ashley rubbed a hand up and down Felicity's arm, gathering Felicity in her gaze. "Oh, darlin'. I'm sorry you're having to go through this. It's a shame what's happened to your momma. Is there anything I can do?"

"Not really. Helping with Albert is probably the biggest thing."

"You know I will. That poor man wouldn't survive otherwise." Curling a finger to dry a tear at the corner of her thickly mascaraed eye, her glitter-coated bangles sparkled pink and green at her wrist, rivaling the sparkle-outlined cat image on the front of her aqua T-shirt. Ashley didn't have any cats on account of the foxes might nab them, but she loved the furry felines all the same. Like Ladd Springs, her property was surrounded by forest and wildlife was part of the deal.

"Now tell me," Ashley went on. "What about the stables? Are the horses all right?"

"Troy's been helping to get them settled. One was burned."

Ashley clasped a hand over her mouth. "Oh, no! It wasn't Blue or Sadie, was it?"

"No. A horse by the name of Lola, but the vet says she'll be okay."

"I *swear*, the only good thing about Delaney's condition is that she doesn't know anything about what happened to her stables. If she did, she'd go plumb crazy."

"Nick agrees. He said when she awakens that I'm not supposed to mention it."

Moisture shone in Ashley's eyes, catching in her lashes. "That Nick is a smart man and sweet as pie. I saw him at the hospital this morning, and the nurse told me he hasn't left Delaney's side, not for one second."

"He hasn't," Felicity said, warding off a slap of guilt because *she* had. But she left for good cause. A cause Travis had ruined. "Anyway, I figured he could use the food."

Stroking the lengths of Felicity's hair, Ashley smiled affectionately. "You're precious, you know that? A gift from Heaven." Felicity slumped, crossing her arms. She didn't feel precious. She felt mad, worn out. She felt inadequate. "You tell your momma I'm comin' to see her this afternoon and she'd better be awake when I get there."

Felicity smiled at the obvious tease. "I will."

Ashley rose, planting a kiss on Felicity's cheek. "Tell Fran I had to run, will you?" Lifting her bag of food she paused. "It's all going to work out, darlin' you'll see. The Good Lord won't take our Delaney from us. Not yet. You don't give up hope, you hear?"

Willing it to be true, Felicity nodded. She wasn't sure that prayers could be filled as reliably as orders from Fran.

Chapter Twenty-One

"Jeremiah Ladd?"

"Who's looking?" Jeremiah wheeled around toward the gruff voice and froze. It was a police officer dressed in full uniform. Biting back a curse, he straightened on the barstool. "What can I do for you, Officer?"

"I'd like to have a word with you." He flicked a glance toward the front door of Bucky's. "Outside."

Jeremiah knew that could only mean one thing. He was here to arrest him for something. "Is there a problem?"

"Nothing that a few questions can't solve."

Resignedly, Jeremiah pushed up from his seat. Resisting arrest wasn't smart. It would only add to whatever charges the man had in store for him—charges he could weasel out of if he had to. Wanting nothing more than to throw back the half glass of whiskey sitting before him on the wooden bar top, he thought better of it. Better a clear mind when evading police interrogation than a blurred one. "Sure thing."

As the men walked out into the sunshine, the bright light felt like running into a wall. Adjusting his vision, Jeremiah considered the numerous offenses he'd committed since being in town. The man could be here to question him about any number of things. Tugging at his shirt collar, Jeremiah decided to play it cool. Whatever the officer wanted to discuss, he had no proof. Jeremiah had made sure of it. Coming to a stop several feet from the entrance, he turned and asked innocently, "How can I help you?"

"I'd like to know your whereabouts around seven-thirty last evening."

"Last evening?" Jeremiah asked, squinting against the glare. "Why, I was here, drinking with a few of my buddies."

"Can anyone vouch for you?"

"Sure can," he said, suppressing a chuckle. After all, it was true. He'd been here with the boys going over Plan B.

"What do you know about the fire at Hotel Ladd?"

"Fire?" he asked. "What fire?"

"The fire deliberately set in the stables. We have it on good authority you could be involved."

"Sorry, Officer, but it wasn't me. Whoever is feeding you the information is wrong."

"Do you own a cell phone?"

"Of course. Who doesn't?"

"We'd like access to your records."

Hell, no, he wasn't giving them access to his records! What—did this guy take him for a fool? "I think you need a warrant for that," he responded, zipping a rise of nerves. Getting nailed for arson was serious business. The fact they were interrogating him so quickly was not a coincidence.

The man cocked a brow. "Is there a problem?"

"No, sir. Just an average Joe American who believes in his right to privacy, that's all. If you have evidence to support a warrant, then I guess I'll have to open my private life up to scrutiny. Until then, I don't."

The man nodded his reply, marking Jeremiah as obviously guilty. "How about we check out your alibi first."

"By all means." And then I'm going to make whoever tossed my name up for grabs *pay* for their mistake.

Jillian Devane waltzed into the lobby like she didn't have a care in the world. Cal tracked her every step to the coffee machine, her every move as she made herself a cup of steaming black coffee. Set up outside the gift shop, the coffee station was replete with organic creamers and herbal sweeteners but she used none of them. Retrieving a copy of the local newspaper from the wire stack nearby, she strolled over to one of the overstuffed chairs by the fountain and made herself comfortable. Most guests enjoyed their coffee outside, at one of several bistro tables situated between here and the spa pleasantly shaded by trees. But not Jillian. She was here to taunt. *Well, make yourself at home, sweetheart. The police are on their over to speak with you.*

The officer in charge of the investigation had asked Cal if he knew of anyone who might want to do harm to the hotel or Delaney Harris. "Darn right I do," he replied and rattled off three names. Jeremiah Ladd, Jillian Devane and Jack Foster, the last being the most difficult. But if he was going to be fair, Cal had to include his brother. His lighter had been found outside the stables. He did have a grudge against Delaney and the hotel. If he was innocent, the police would learn as much. But this one, he mused, marveling at Jillian's deliberately drawn-out movements, her conscious avoidance of his direct gaze—she was a different story.

Jillian knew he was watching her. He wasn't making it a secret. He was watching her and would continue to watch her until he watched her walk out of here in handcuffs. Burning a building was one thing. Burning one filled with live animals was completely another. The images from last night were seared into his mind. The stench, the wild cries from the horses...

Cal forced the visions from his thoughts, tightened his stomach against the pitch of nausea. Jillian was responsible. Perhaps her and Jeremiah together, but definitely her. If she could spark a blaze on a competitor's land in South America as payback for a perceived wrong, then there was no reason to think she wouldn't do so again. Only this time she wasn't going to get away with it. He would make sure of it.

The front lobby door opened, the flash of movement catching his eye. Officer Griffin had arrived. Cal cast a glance toward Jillian and exhaled a stream of tension from his lungs. Hopefully this wouldn't take long.

"Mr. Foster," the heavyset police officer summoned him over.

"Yes?"

"We're here about questioning one of your guests, Jillian Devane." From his peripheral vision, Cal could see she had cued in at the mention of her name. "Can you contact her room for us?"

Cal smiled. "That won't be necessary." He held a hand out. "Ms. Devane is sitting over there."

Surprised, the older man turned. A heightened curiosity entered his gaze, as happened when a man locked in on a beautiful woman. "Thank you."

Cal nodded, savoring a private victory. *Have fun.*

Jillian looked up as the stocky police officer made his way toward her. Sizing him up in seconds, she determined he was a career officer grown stale from too many years in a small town, where his most thrilling detective work was rescuing a cat from an electrical high wire. Petty theft and public drunkenness were undoubtedly the more popular offenses around these parts. By the looks of his bored yet surly expression, combined with his age, she estimated he held high rank in the department.

Jillian smiled. If he thought his sour expression was going to unnerve her, he was mistaken. "Ms. Devane?"

Casually flipping through the pages of the dribble of an excuse they called a newspaper, she hummed, "Yes?"

"May I have a minute of your time?"

She paused, but only briefly, continuing her leisurely perusal. "What for?"

"I have some questions I'd like to ask you."

About to decline, her standard insult to male ego, she pretended to think about it. Why not reel him in a bit, make him think she would be cooperative? Submissive. Drawing her lips into a slow practiced smile, she purred, "What kind of questions?"

"About the fire last night."

She rounded her lips into an "O" shape and uttered, "It was horrible, *no*? Such awful devastation."

"Yes," he said. "It started last night, around seven-thirty. Did you happen to be around at that time?"

She knitted her brow and feigned contemplation. Pushing out her lips, she subtly smacked them together, amused by his involuntary glance to her mouth. "Hm, I don't think so."

"Don't think so?"

"I don't like to watch the clock when I'm on vacation."

As if he understood she was purposefully dodging him, his voice coarsened, "Where did you happen to be last night, Ms. Devane?"

"I was in the company of a male suitor," she teased, winking conspiratorially.

"Happen to have a name?"

She shook her head and smirked. "Wasn't important at the time."

Jillian took pleasure in the man's discomfort. A seasoned police officer, yet the line of questioning was clearly growing uncomfortable for him. How hard would he push?

"I'll need an alibi for your whereabouts last evening."

"What for—am I under arrest?"

"No, ma'am, but as part of our investigation we need to confirm the whereabouts of anyone possibly connected—"

She emitted a gasp. "You think I'm connected?"

Her immediate objection gave him pause. "Well, er, we were given your name as a possible suspect and—"

"Let me guess." She cut him off and rose sharply from her seat. In heels, she stood eye-to-eye with the man. Arching her back, she pushed her chest toward him. "My ex-*lover*, Nick Harris is trying to throw my name in as a person of interest, isn't he?"

"Well, I can't reveal exactly where I received the tip from, but it's my job to follow every lead," he replied, openly avoiding a peek at her chest but clearly unable to manage the feat.

"Love can be so *cruel,* Detective." Jillian knew her perfume would be filtering through the man's senses right about now, knew the close proximity of her bare cleavage would distract him momentarily as she whispered, "Have you ever been in love? Deeply passionate love? Do you know what hungry desire can do to a man? " Jillian paused, allowing images of her naked body to form in his mind. "It can drive him to do horrible, mean things." Thrusting out her lower lip, she dropped her gaze to his mouth. "It's so sad when love goes wrong." Inching closer, so close she could hear his breathing, Jillian murmured, "It can make a woman *crazy* for the touch of another." The man blinked and dodged her pointed gaze. Jillian counted the reaction as a minor win and retreated with a soft reply, "I'll call my lawyer and he will provide you with *any* information you need about my whereabouts last evening."

The officer took a step back, cleared his throat. "Thank you, ma'am. I would appreciate it."

Sliding a knowing gaze toward Cal, Jillian winked. *Game on, sweetheart.*

Catching sight of Jack Foster through the glass front door, Jillian excused herself. "If you don't mind, Officer? My date has arrived."

The man turned and his jaw slackened. "Jack Foster?"

Taking satisfaction in his surprise, she asked, "Do you know him?"

"Yes." With a glance toward Cal, he said, "I do."

Jack breezed over and kissed her cheek. "Hello, Jillian."

"Jack," she replied, his name rolling out with ease.

The police officer gave Jack a once-over, acknowledging him with a mere nod, then to Jillian, "Appreciate your time. I'll be expecting a call from your lawyer by morning."

"On second thought," she said. "A call to Whiskey Joe's lounge should be all you need. Ask for the bartender on duty last night. He'll vouch for me."

Her statement garnered a questioning look from the officer. "Thanks."

Yes, she mused. *Go ahead and wonder how the two men fit together*. Abandoning her untouched coffee, Jillian slipped a hand around Jack's arm. "Shall we?"

"You bet." Sliding a hand around her narrow waist, he said, "Have a good day, Officer."

Officer Griffin grumbled under his breath, "Good day."

Chapter Twenty-Two

Cal sat rigid in his seat while he and Malcolm waited for Officer Griffin to give them a rundown on the police department's progress in their investigation. Gathered in the manager's office, the two were dressed identical in pale blue shirts and khakis, their eyes pasted on the detective. Malcolm said Nick was convinced it was Jillian's doing, but Cal wasn't so sure. Jeremiah and his cohorts could have easily rigged the explosive. All they needed was a few minutes perusing the Internet and they'd have all the information needed to produce the crude construct. The callous disregard for life and property came naturally.

Officer Griffin flipped through pages in a yellow note pad, locating his notes for their case. "Fingerprints from the safe proved to be mostly partials," he began, "looks like the guy might actually have removed some of his fingerprint. My guess it was done to thwart any database match."

"What?" Malcolm glanced at Cal and asked, "How does someone remove their fingerprint?"

Aging gray eyes etched by cynicism met him directly. "Easy. Sandpaper, super glue. I heard of some crazies using acid to do the trick. The idea is to remove enough of the ridges to prevent a hundred percent match."

Malcolm sat back in his chair. "So we have nothing?"

"I wouldn't say nothing. We picked up a strand of hair and sent it to the crime lab for a DNA analysis."

"But that takes a while," Cal said.

"We can get it back in a week or so," he replied. "But I have good news for you on the arson. Both alibis checked out, but we managed to track down the number of the cell phone used to detonate. Forensics managed to get an ID on the cell phone used in the blast and as we suspected, it was a phony account. The number that called it was legit."

"And?"

"Belongs to Jeremiah Ladd."

"I knew it!" Cal exclaimed, relieved, angry and exhilarated all at the same time. "I knew he had to be involved somehow."

Malcolm asked the officer, "How sure are you?"

"Hundred percent. We matched the time of call with the time of explosion set by witnesses. It's a match."

"So you're going to pick him up?"

"Not yet."

"Not yet? What are you waiting for?"

"The call came from his phone. We have to prove he made it."

Stunned, Cal asked, "Who else would have made it?"

Malcolm's blue gaze flattened. "I can think of a couple of people."

"No way," Cal objected. "Doesn't make sense."

"He says he lost it Saturday night," the officer said.

"And you believe him?"

"My job is to work the evidence I have. He went out and purchased another phone over the weekend."

"So he could use the old one as a bomb detonator." Cal supplied the obvious.

"Phone call doesn't render a phone inoperable," Malcolm posed.

"But it would render it hot. Jeremiah would want to dispose of it and quick."

"Have you located the cell phone in question?" Malcolm asked. "Maybe it would provide fingerprints of a third party."

Cal gaped at Malcolm. *What was wrong with him*? Had he forgotten what Jeremiah did to their wives? He took Lacy and Annie against their will, threatened their lives with a deadly weapon. Why was Malcolm fighting the fact that Jeremiah was a bad man and likely responsible for the fire in the stables?

Rising from his seat, Officer Griffin seemed to wonder the same thing. "Maybe. We're still checking. If anything new develops, I'll let you know."

Malcolm stood and extended a hand. "Thanks."

Cal did likewise. "Appreciate your help, Officer Griffin." In the meantime, Cal decided he'd do a bit of checking on his own.

Jeremiah drove downtown and stormed up to the front door of the dump of a house the guys had rented. Heedless to the snap of a hinge as he wrenched it open, Jeremiah called out as he entered, "Robby!" He stopped short, finding the brothers sprawled out on the couch watching television, empty beer cans scattered about them on the table. A few others lay on the floor half-smashed. Inhaling a whiff of cheap beer, he said, "We got trouble."

Rob slung his gaze toward Jeremiah. "What's new?"

"I'm serious. There's been a fire at Hotel Ladd and they're trying to pin it on us."

"Did we do it?" the younger asked, looking between Jeremiah and his brother.

Rob rolled his head sideways. "Does it matter? The police looking for us ain't never a good thing."

"Well, I didn't burn no hotel!" the younger cried, bolting upright.

"It doesn't matter," Jeremiah said, "They're coming for me. And if they get to me, you two won't be far behind."

"What are you saying?" Dark eyes grew cold and black beneath Rob's shaggy brow. "You talkin' about givin' us up?"

"I'm talking about there's a short line between you two and me," Jeremiah said, cautious of coming across too unsympathetic to their position. He couldn't give a rat's hide about what happened to these two but letting on to that fact could cause him serious injury. They didn't want a return to jail any more than he did. But staring into the familiar eyes of a hardened criminal with nothing to lose, he knew Rob was dangerous in his sheer lack of concern for Jeremiah's welfare. There was a time to press and a time to draw down. "All I'm saying is we need a distraction."

A heavy silence permeated the stale, dank confines of the living room. "What kind of distraction?"

"The kind that gets people's attention."

"I'm listening."

If Clem could kidnap Delaney, Jeremiah could do one better. The fool had snagged her with the intention of dumping her in the woods so he could steal the gold on Ladd Springs, but her boyfriend stepped in, hunting them down, putting an end to their plan. Jeremiah would grab Delaney's daughter without a worry. She didn't have anyone watching out for her and with Nick Harris at the hospital with his wife, the girl would be easy to snatch. It was the first glimmer of hope he'd felt since the local blue paid him a visit. Delaney might think she could pin this fire on him and threaten his freedom, but he was going to threaten her kid.

Hurrying through the empty house, Felicity jogged down the steps to her car. Nick had yet to come home except for one brief grab of clothing and a quick shower, preferring to wait it out bedside with her mother. He believed she would come to any minute, and he wanted to be the first thing she saw when she awoke from her coma.

Felicity appreciated his devotion, but she couldn't share in his inactivity. She needed to do something. She needed to get to the bottom of who did this to her mother. For the first time in her life, she understood how her mother felt when it came to protecting those she loved. It was fierce, demanding. It was all-consuming. Felicity would stop at nothing until the person responsible for this crime was brought to justice.

And that person was her father, Jack. His nonchalant re-action yesterday sealed it for her. He couldn't have cared less that her mother lay helpless in a hospital bed. She was fighting for her life against an invisible swelling in her brain, yet all he could do was laugh and blame it on the help. He was disgusting. The sooner he was put in jail for his crimes the better. Right now, she had bigger things to worry about. Nick had called this morning and said to come quick—the doctors were taking her mom into surgery for a craniotomy, a fancy term for poking a hole in her skull to relieve the building pressure.

Because the medication they tried wasn't working.

Felicity shuddered as she jumped into her car and gunned the engine to life. With surgery came risk. If it didn't go well, her mom could have permanent brain damage. If they didn't perform the procedure, her mother could have permanent brain damage. It was an awful choice, and all because she'd been trying to save her horses from burning alive. Memories from the evening flooded in. Horse shrieks mixed with the scent of burning wood. Gray-brown smoke billowing through stalls, licks of bright orange flames crawling up and over everything in sight. Felicity shut her mind to the images, jamming her foot to the accelerator, yet she couldn't escape the sounds and sights from the stables. The horrific trauma caused to the animals, the complete and total devastation of the stables.

Those stables had been her mother's passion. She lived and breathed her horses, spent sun-up to sundown with them... Felicity hated that someone had taken that from her. She hated that someone had been so cold-hearted with regard to the horses, the property.

Her mother's life was in danger. Yet her father hadn't broken stride yesterday when she told him about the fire, about her mom's condition. He didn't give a crap about either one of them. It was all about him, and what he wanted. Always had been.

As she peeled out of the drive of her home, the sight of a black truck similar to the one Travis owned reminded her of another man who cared only about himself. Travis didn't trust her. He didn't believe in her. He thought he knew best and she didn't.

Well, he was wrong. She was taking the reins of her life, and like her mother before her, Felicity would take care of herself. A squiggle of nerves zipped through her as she thought about the gun stowed away in her bedroom. In the wake of Jeremiah Ladd's last visit, her mom had taught her to shoot. She wasn't old enough to get a concealed weapons permit yet, but she knew how to handle a gun now, knew how to hit a moving target. The knowledge gave her a sense of power, like she could defend herself if trouble came calling. Felicity had surprised herself with her accuracy. Her mom, too. Recalling the pride in her mom's face the day she nailed the center bull's eye tugged a small smile from her lips.

Travis drove the country mile to Hotel Ladd, more dazed than focused on the road. Felicity hadn't returned any of his calls. After leaving him standing outside her father's hotel like a fool with his heart in a handbag, she'd refused to speak with him. She was angry. Angry because he cared about her, was concerned for her welfare. Angry because he tried to help.

What had gotten into her lately? She was like a different person. Ever since Troy and Casey got back together, it was like Felicity had turned on him. She'd taken up with them, defending Troy at every turn, hanging out with Casey and the baby instead of going riding with him. Travis didn't get it. What had he done wrong?

Nothing. For the millionth time he reassured himself he'd done nothing wrong. She was stressed out because of the thing with her father. She wasn't acting in her right mind. She'd nearly lost her horse—twice. Her mom was in the hospital, the hotel was in a shambles over the fire. Travis understood that stress could throw people out of whack, and despite her claims to the contrary, Felicity needed him. This was her time of need and Felicity needed *him*—whether she knew it or not. He was going to surprise her with an early visit. One way or another, he had to get her to see more clearly.

Chapter Twenty-Three

Running on auto-pilot, Felicity drove the tree-lined road, consumed with thoughts of her mother and what the day held. Would she get a chance to talk to her before they took her back? Would Nick make them wait? What if she didn't make it? What if Felicity missed seeing her mom before they wheeled her into the operating room? Would they wait?

They had to. Felicity grabbed her cell phone. Nick had to make them wait. Keeping one eye on the road and the other on her touchpad, she scrolled through her contact directory. She'd tell Nick she was en route and to please make them wait. *Don't let them take her back without me getting a chance to say goodbye.*

Good luck, she corrected in a rush. Not goodbye but good luck! Locating the number, Felicity barely registered the red truck passing her on the left until it swerved in front of her. At the flash of red tail lights, she cried out, "Oh!"

Instinctively she slammed a foot to her brake. Her phone went flying as she jerked the steering wheel hard to the right. Her small car skidded roughly over the side of the road, narrowly missing a rear end collision. Adrenaline sprayed across her chest and arms. Her heart pounded, a cloud of dust billowed around her vehicle. Two men jumped out of the truck, one in grubby jeans and T-shirt, one in a lime green button-down and jeans. Alarm fired in her brain. *Jeremiah Ladd*!

She hurried to lock her door as the dark-haired bearded man charged toward her. But she was too late. He yanked it open, scary black eyes boring into her.

"Stop!" she screeched, heartbeats pounding in her throat. *What were they doing*?

Ignoring her, the stranger hauled her from the vehicle. Felicity fought his iron grip, shouting. "Leave me alone! Let me go!"

Leering at her, Jeremiah held the door open as the man shoved her inside. Another bearded man inside reached for her arm.

Travis' heart kicked at the sight of the stopped truck, the strawberry blonde head of hair ducking inside. Felicity! Instinct took over, propelling Travis' vehicle hard and fast straight for them. Jeremiah Ladd spun around and froze. In a split second, he jumped into his truck, but Travis rammed into him, throwing his body forward and back upon impact. The man by Felicity's side was jettisoned from the truck.

Travis leapt out and ran toward them. "Felicity!"

Their eyes locked. "Travis!"

Jeremiah shoved from his truck in a rage. "Back off, Parker!"

"Let her go!" Travis returned.

"Get lost." Jeremiah pulled a gun and leveled it at Travis.

The pistol drew Travis' full attention.

Felicity clambered free from the back seat, her thoughts splintering. "Stop!"

Travis lunged. "Felicity—no!"

The weapon discharged.

Felicity screamed. Travis felt a punch to his chest. An engine sounded. Felicity raced toward him, her pulse battering wildly. "Oh no—*Travis!*" Blood oozed from the wound, forming a pool of red beneath the blue-gray plaid of his shirt.

Behind her, Jeremiah bellowed, "Let's get out of here!"

Felicity heard the skid of wheels as the truck lurched backward, then forward, speeding past her. A beat-up farm truck traveling in the opposite direction slowed. Inside, an elderly man looked down at her in shock. "Call 9-1-1!" she shrieked. Panic clawed at her chest. "Call 9-1-1!"

Felicity didn't remember anything about the ambulance ride. She didn't remember anything about the man who called for help. She could only remember the grotesque blend of red and blue and gray as Travis' shirt became soaked in blood. Too much blood. It was on her hands, her blouse. She'd pressed her palms against the bullet wound to stem the bleeding, but it seemed futile. The blood kept coming. Watching them load him into the ambulance, she'd placed a hand to her mouth. The metallic taste of it stayed with her.

Following the paramedics into the Emergency Room like a robot, she remembered only the blood. "Is he going to be all right?" she mumbled, transfixed by the sight of his open shirt, the white square of gauze, the tubes running from his arms.

"We're taking him to surgery," a medic replied briskly. "You can wait upstairs in the waiting room."

Surgery. Waiting room. *Her mother*. Felicity felt faint.

"Miss." Someone grabbed her by the arm. "Are you okay?"

Okay? She looked around, the room felt like a swirl of images. Was she okay?

No. Her head felt like it was spinning. Her stomach was empty and raw. Pressure built in her lungs. She wasn't okay. Travis wasn't okay. Her mother wasn't okay.

"Get her a wheelchair," a voice shouted.

Felicity panicked as they rolled Travis from her sight. "Wait!"

"Honey, calm down." A slender hand pulled her down into a seat. "Everything's under control."

"No—you don't understand. I need to see him. That's my boyfriend," she cried, watching Travis and the medical team disappear into an elevator. "I need to be with him."

"I've got you. I'll take you up."

Felicity glanced up. The woman hovering over her had kind eyes. Friendly. Safe. "Okay. *Okay*."

The nurse wheeled Felicity to an elevator, took her up to another floor. The ride felt like she was floating. *Ding*. Metal doors slid open and the woman pushed Felicity out and down a wide corridor. It was a hall of doors with a shiny floor. Felicity's gaze drifted to the end, landing on a set of double doors. The nurse turned just shy of them. "Here you go, honey. You can wait in here for word about your boyfriend."

"Felicity."

Nick's voice cut through her haze like a steel knife. Grasping onto Nick's imposing figure, she mouthed his name.

Crossing the small room in seconds, he demanded, "What happened? Why is she in a wheelchair?"

The woman replied evenly, "Her boyfriend's been taken to surgery. She's—overwhelmed," the woman said, settling on a kind description of Felicity's state of utter shock and collapse.

Nick fired his gaze into Felicity. "Travis?"

She nodded, the acknowledgement drawing tears. Travis was in surgery. He'd been shot—by Jeremiah. Focusing on Nick, she murmured, "How's mom?"

"They just took her back. I told the doctors to wait, but..." He dropped to a knee and finished, "They decided against it."

The guilt in his eyes was misplaced. It wasn't his fault. It was her fault for not being here by her mother's side like him. Twenty-four seven, Nick had been here for his wife. Felicity reached out for him. Her mother was lucky to have him. Hot tears fell. She hadn't been here and might not ever be able to tell her mother she loved her.

Or Travis. A hard knot formed in her throat. If anything happened to him after the way she'd been treating him...Felicity didn't know if she could ever forgive herself. The two most important people in her life were on the verge of losing theirs and she hadn't been able to tell either of them she loved them. *I love you.* Tears blurred her vision. *If only I could have told you.*

The nurse left the room as Nick wheeled her chair to the space where he had been sitting. It made her feel like a heel.

She should get up and walk, march herself right over there and be strong—for him, for her mom. For Travis. If she could have moved the first muscle in her body, she would have. But every shred of muscle, every ounce of energy had been sapped. The reality of what happened on the roadside was sinking in. Jeremiah and his friends had tried to kidnap her. They had forced her into their truck. If it hadn't been for Travis, Felicity would have been who knew where right now in unthinkable danger. Instead, she sat nestled in the safety of Nick's protective watch. She closed her eyes as guilt poured into her. Travis was lying on a bed in an operating room because he tried to protect her. Without any regard to his own safety, Travis charged Jeremiah and been shot because of it.

"Can you tell me what happened?" Nick asked, his voice a slip of velvet. Warm, soothing, his presence enveloped her.

"Jeremiah shot him."

"*What*?"

"Jeremiah shot Travis. From ten feet away, he pulled the trigger and shot him straight in the chest."

As he stared at her in silence, Felicity could feel something change inside him. The line of his jaw hardened, his gaze lost its compassion. It was flinty and cold. Dead. It was like the soul had left him, leaving icy hatred in its place. He didn't ask another question. He didn't say another word. Nick simply took her hand in his and cradled it with a tenderness unimaginable. He would take care of her, of them. With Nick, all things were possible. They were lucky to have him.

A fresh wave of fear blindsided her. She was lucky to have Travis.

Hopefully it wasn't too late to let him know.

Chapter Twenty-Four

Nick rose the minute he saw Malcolm and Lacy walk into the waiting room. Cutting the distance in seconds, he said, "Thanks for coming."

"We would have been here sooner but with everything going on—"

Nick silenced him with a hand. "Understood." Glancing down at Lacy and the baby, he felt a pang of guilt. "Don't feel like you have to stay if the baby needs to go," he said. "Ashley said she'd come once she got Albert settled. Said it shouldn't be too long." Albert had a doctor's appointment this morning, and she was shuffling him back and forth between there and home and planned to come as quick as she could to be here for Felicity.

"Oh, poo," Lacy said, dishing out a mock frown. "Ashley can come if she wants but I'm staying put for the duration."

Nick smiled. Leave it to Lacy's spitfire personality to ease his mind. Malcolm had married an EF5 tornado packed into a beautiful, petite package. Shiny black hair, ivory skin and big blue eyes, the woman rivaled any Southern California beauty. Leaning down, he kissed her cheek. "Thanks."

He'd been running out of options. Casey was helping her mom with Emily, while Cal tried to work between visitation with his daughter and the investigation going on at the hotel. Troy was occupied with the business of getting the horses right. From what Malcolm said, the fire had caused horrific trauma to the animals, and if it weren't for Troy, they might have lost a few. Considering the brothers hadn't been getting along of late, it wasn't a complete surprise to learn Troy chose the horses over sitting vigil for Travis. His parents were here. That was enough.

Lacy's big blue eyes latched onto Felicity. Sitting in a chair, the girl continued to stare numbly at the wall as she had for the last few hours. She barely spoke to Travis' parents. The couple sat two seats over, their hands locked together, yet neither party spoke a word. "How's she holding up?" Lacy asked.

Nick followed her gaze. "As expected, she's pretty stressed. At least we got some good news on her mother. Turning away from Felicity, he said, "Doctor came out a little while ago with an update. The procedure was a success and they're taking her to recovery but Travis..." Nick's voice drifted. "He's not so good."

"You said the bullet hit him in the chest?" Malcolm asked.

"Missed his heart by four inches."

Lacy flung a hand over her mouth, her eyes widening in horror. "You said Jeremiah did this?"

Nick nodded, uncertain how much of his animosity to release, considering it was Lacy who ran off with the man to Atlanta. According to Malcolm, they'd never been intimate but still... If she'd been willing to run off and live with the man in a strange city, she must have had feelings for him. "Yes, and he had two men with him."

"Does she know who they are?"

"No. But we have photos. Travis took them of Jeremiah and the men downtown. They're in his camera."

"Do you know where that is?" Malcolm asked.

"No. Could be with his personal belongings here at the hospital. Could be in his truck."

"That was towed from the scene," Malcolm said. "We saw it on our way over."

"We'll get it," Nick said. "As it stands, I hold Jeremiah responsible for the shooting. He pulled the trigger."

Malcolm nodded.

"If the boy dies, I'm going to see that Jeremiah meets the same fate."

"Nick!" Lacy hissed, swiping a glance toward Felicity and the Parkers.

"I still believe in an eye for an eye," he said, avoiding the reproach in her gaze. "Not to mention it's the law." Shaking the darkness that was beginning to fill him, Nick shrugged it off. "Travis is going to be in there for a while." And he needed to go. Nick wanted to stay with Felicity, see her through this crisis, but at the same time he felt compelled to do something. He couldn't sit idle any longer while the people who did this roamed free. With Delaney stowed away in ICU, he needed to get productive. "I have to get back to the hotel."

"I don't think that's a good idea," Malcolm cautioned. "Jillian has an alibi. The phone belonged to Jeremiah. Let the police handle it."

"I don't care about her alibi," Nick growled under his breath. "There's a young man lying in there fighting for his life. Delaney, too. Jeremiah might be responsible for Travis, but I know damn well Jillian had something to do with the fire."

"You're forgetting about Jeremiah's two accomplices."

"No." He ground his jaw. "I'm prioritizing. I'll see to *them* after I take care of the viper and the vixen."

Malcolm stared at him, hard. Nick understood. Malcolm would prefer he handle the situation through the proper channels, but he couldn't. He couldn't stand by and watch Jillian and Jeremiah walk away scot-free because the police believed their bogus alibis. They were guilty and he needed to prove it. "I can't let it go."

Malcolm placed his arm around Lacy's shoulders and nodded, reluctance pulling in his pale blue eyes. "I know. Be careful, will you?" He glanced over at Felicity, adding quietly, "I don't want to come back here for a visit to your bedside, next."

"Don't worry. You won't."

Jeremiah whipped open the front door to the boys' rental house, inflamed by the turn of events. Anger pulsed through his brain as his mind wrapped around the situation with a white-knuckled grip. They had failed. A simple straightforward kidnapping of a teenage girl and they'd botched it. Because her stupid boyfriend had bad timing. Unbelievably horrible bad timing and now Jeremiah might have to answer for a dead body. Already on the police radar for a cell phone call in connection to arson, the addition of a murder charge would send him away for life. "Damn it!" he yelled, slamming a fist against the wall as he passed into the living room. There was no way he was going back to jail. No way he was taking the fall for shooting that kid. It was self-defense. He had two witnesses. It was his word against hers.

Swiping a bottle of whiskey from the kitchen counter, Jeremiah opened it and slugged back a long swallow, cringing against the burning sensation. Licking his lips, he took another. He should have shot the girl. He should have shot her cold. *Leave no witnesses.* Wasn't that the deal? Leave no witnesses, erase all connection and make a clean getaway. Smacking the bottle to the Formica, Jeremiah looked around the rat hole of a kitchen as he soaked in the gradual numbing sensation spreading through his limbs. The alcohol was working its way through him, the effect slow and gradual.

There was no way he was going to jail. He wasn't *ever* going back to jail. Taking another swig, Jeremiah stalked back into the living room. Both brothers stood in the center of the room.

"Hey, gimme that!" the younger hollered at him. "Don't you go drinkin' all my liquor!"

Jeremiah's first instinct was to whack the guy over the head with the bottle, easing the tension riddling his body. But darting a glance to the elder, Jeremiah thought better of it. Rob didn't need an excuse for a fight—a diversion Jeremiah didn't need at the moment. Setting the bottle on a dining table, he needed to plan, not fight.

Rob looked at him, sullen and brooding. "Now what?"

"Now I'm thinking," Jeremiah shot back.

"Don't take too long. The cops are gonna be out lookin' for you."

"Me?"

Rob didn't look away but instead iced his gaze. "The girl don't know me from Adam." Tapping a brief gaze to his brother, he said, "We pack up and leave, we're gone. Disappeared."

Fury wound deeply through Jeremiah as the significance of the statement sunk in. *Son of a bitch.* Rob was gonna hang *him* with crime? He was the one who yanked the girl from her vehicle! Jeremiah never touched her! Visions of Clem Sweeney swam in his mind, another dirtbag from his past. Jeremiah recalled he was sitting in jail for the very same crime. Fool had used two idiots to help kidnap Delaney, and look where it got him. Jeremiah glanced between the brothers. Two bumbling idiots, kinda like these two.

Except Rob. He might not be the sharpest tool in the shed but he was meaner than a rabid possum. What he lacked in brain-power he made up for in temperament. Turning from them, he stuffed his anger away. He wasn't going down for this one. Clem might be rotting in jail but not *him*. Jeremiah was a hell of a lot smarter than old Clem and planned to stay one step ahead of the law *and* everyone else—including these two. Rob was wrong. At the moment time was on his side. Jeremiah couldn't be sure, but he'd made a clean shot to the chest, up close and personal. If the Parker punk wasn't already dead, he'd be in surgery for hours—if the blood loss didn't wipe him out first. A thought that would have brought a smile to Jeremiah's face if he weren't so damned mad. "We've got to do something."

"Like get out of town?" posed the younger of his cohorts.

Jeremiah wheeled. "No, you *idiot*. I'm not walking away from here without making it hurt." Someone was going to pay for his loss. The gold was gone. The safe had been fruitless. Sure, the pendants brought in twenty grand, but split three ways it amounted to nothing. Squat. "I'm talking about giving them a little token of our appreciation."

The brothers stared at him, not a clue between them. Jeremiah scowled. Fools. What the hell did they know—it wasn't their property that had been stolen. It hadn't been their father's name on the deed. It had been *his*. Ernie Ladd had owned this property and he alone. As his only child, the entire tract of land should have reverted to Jeremiah when the bastard died, but it didn't. It went to Delaney and her daughter because they conned a bitter old man into giving it to them. They played on his senility and conned him into believing they deserved it and Jeremiah didn't. What they *deserved* was to suffer. Vengeance snaked through his heart. Delaney didn't understand what it felt like to live in rot-gut conditions, to get by on the power of your cunning and wit. She'd never been abused by her parent, tossed out to the curb without a care as to how she'd provide for herself.

No. Aunt Susannah had been the only bright spot in Jeremiah's life. Delaney's mom had soft smiles and kind words for him and everyone around her, while his father met him at the door with a belt and a beating. It wasn't fair that Delaney lived in a loving home while Jeremiah had to endure a hellhole.

Resentment cut him raw. Jeremiah despised his father. Ernie Ladd was nothing more than an animal, a sorry excuse for a human being, his brother Albert no better. As he honed in on the brothers, something shifted in his gut. Ladd Springs belonged to him. Jeremiah deserved the property as payback for all those years he'd had to endure living under the same roof as his old man. Delaney might think she had taken it from him, tied her life up into a nice pretty package with a big fancy bow, a new husband, new hotel and probably a brand new home, same as Annie. Wicked pleasure licked at him as he imagined Delaney's world going up in flames around her. "I know what we're going to do. We're going to burn the place to the ground."

"Excuse me?"

"You heard me," he said coolly, the idea gaining steam. "We're going to burn the whole damned place to the ground."

"I ain't going to jail for your vendetta," Rob told him. "I want my money, plain and simple."

"The money? There is no money!" What part of an empty mine site did he not understand?

"Maybe not here, but that ain't my problem. It's yours."

Staring into the cold eyes of a stony-faced criminal, a man he'd known all his life, Jeremiah wanted to spit. Rob understood what was at stake. He'd been where Jeremiah had been. They'd endured the worst and survived. These people didn't deserve to be rich and happy. They didn't earn it. They didn't suffer for it. Not a bit. "Scared?" Jeremiah taunted.

"I ain't interested in burning no hotel down!" the younger brother cried out.

Rob flicked a glance to him. The effect was silence. Then to Jeremiah, he said, "I ain't in no mood for games."

"Who's playing games?" Jeremiah questioned. "And why the pussy foot around? You know they deserve it."

Returning a humorless gaze, Rob approached, kicking Jeremiah's pulse into overdrive. Sticking a grimy finger in his face, he said, "I done told you I'm here for my money, nothin' more and nothin' less. I told you so from the get-go."

"You know I don't have it," Jeremiah said, trying to calm the battering in his chest.

"Get it." Grabbing the bottle of whiskey from the table, Rob tossed back a swallow. Glistening lips spewed a sour breath into Jeremiah's face. "No games, no fire, just money."

Jeremiah fumed inwardly. And let them walk away scot-free while he was picked up for murder and arson? Not a chance in hell. "Fine. I'll get your money. But I'm leaving a mark, just the same."

Chapter Twenty-Five

After a quick bite of lunch in the hotel café, Annie, Emily, and Cal gathered in the hotel lobby with Casey and her infant child snug within her arms while she spoke to Troy on her cell phone. The way Casey handled the baby, Cassidy Jo seemed more an appendage than a separate entity. But that was Casey's style of parenting. Where she went, Cassidy Jo went.

Casey ended her call and slipped the cell phone into a back pocket of her jeans. "Troy said we could go up and take some of the hotel horses," Casey said. "He thinks it would do them good to get out of the barn and out into the forest."

Cal was glad to hear it. He was anxious to get back to normal operation but wasn't about to push. Troy knew the horses. If the okay came from him, he was good with it. "Now that's the best news I've heard all day."

"Are you sure you can't come, Daddy?"

Staring down into the eager eyes of his daughter, every fiber of Cal's being wanted to join them. He wanted nothing more than to ride through the hills, sharing tales of the land and forest with her, but with Malcolm still at the hospital with Nick and Felicity, he was on manager's duty. With the investigation in full swing, they wanted to remain available to the police department should they require any assistance. His ride with his daughter would have to wait for another day. "I'm sure. But I plan to be free by supper time, so will you save me a seat?"

She smiled. "Of course."

"We're going to Fran's," Annie told him.

"Good idea. I've been hankering for a plate of fried cabbage and Fran makes some of the best."

Emily scrunched her nose. "That doesn't even sound good."

"I realize some of our dishes take a bit of getting used to..."

"Like those boiled peanuts?" Emily didn't miss a beat. "Those things are *awful*."

Cal gave her a teasing glare. "Now don't go disparagin' my favorite snack food, young lady. I'll have you know that's the greatest food on the planet. Healthy too."

"They are?"

"Yes, ma'am. Packed with protein and full of antioxidants!"

Nick Harris walked in the front door, his presence sucking in Cal's complete attention. Annie and Casey turned. The determination in Nick's step as he walked over shouted the man meant business. Had he heard something?

"Cal."

"Nick."

"Hello, Annie. Casey."

"Hello," they replied in unison.

"So you must be Emily Foster," Nick said, his tone easy and relaxed with a smile to match.

Which couldn't be easy for him, Cal mused. Nick was under an inordinate amount of stress at the moment, and Cal appreciated the gesture. "That she is," he said, then introduced, "Emily, this is Nick Harris. He's the owner of Hotel Ladd."

"Really? Wow, it's so beautiful..."

"Thank you. I hope the fire hasn't ruined your ability to enjoy yourself." He glanced at Cal and said, "It's normally a very tranquil place."

Shadows entered her gaze. "No. I'm only sorry it happened to you and the horses."

"Me, too. But we've got the best hands working the situation and they'll be back to normal in no time."

"We're going to see Troy and the horses," Annie said, ushering forth a small smile. "See if any would like to get out of the barn for a while."

"Sounds like a great idea." Placing a hand to Casey's shoulder, Nick said, "Give Troy my sincerest thanks, will you? I know he's done a lot for the animals, and I can't tell you how important that is to me."

Casey nodded. "He loves those animals."

"I know he does. It shows in everything he does."

As though uncertain whether or not to broach the subject, Casey ventured softly, "How's Travis?""Still in surgery."

"Lacy called," Annie said. "She said Delaney is out and doing well?"

"So far it looks that way," he continued. "Only time will tell, but I've got all the confidence in the world in her. Delaney's a fighter. She'll pull through."

Annie released a tight sigh. "Oh, good. We're planning on stopping by the hospital on our way to Fran's later."

"I know she'll appreciate it. Felicity, too." Clearing his throat, Nick switched gears. "Cal, can I have a word with you before you?"

"Sure." Leaning down, he kissed the top of Emily's head. "Listen, you girls go take good care of those horses. I'll meet up with you later."

Annie nodded, steering Emily toward the door with Casey in tow.

"You riding with the baby?" Nick asked, a hint of amusement in his voice.

"No. I'm going up to visit with Troy before he takes them out on the trails."

"Sounds like a good idea."

"Have fun." Cal waved them off. Waiting until the women were out the door, he asked, "What's up?"

"I want to know where Jillian is."

"I don't know. Haven't seen her since yesterday when the police came to question her."

"Do we know if she's still here?"

"No."

"Can we check her room?"

The mounting urgency Cal heard bothered him. Nick sounded like he was ready to check for himself. "I can ask housekeeping if they've been to her room today."

"How about I do one better? What room is she in?"

"*You're going to her room*?"

"You have a better idea?"

Better than infringing on the privacy of one of their guests? Jillian or not, the idea of Nick barging in unannounced could not bode well. "How about we call up to her room?"

Nick visibly bridled, clearly on the verge of refusal, but said, "Fine. Call her."

Cal went for the house phone by the fountain and dialed Jillian's room. He knew the number by heart. It had been ingrained on his psyche since she checked in, as he prepared himself for potential trouble. It was ringing. "No answer."

"Doesn't mean a thing."

"You can't go up there, Nick. I mean, think about what you're doing." Cal was beginning to feel like Malcolm. Nick was clearly not in a state-of-mind where he should be confronting Jillian. "What are you after? Do you think she's going to confess to you?"

"No. But I will be able to detect the lie in her eyes."

"And then what? You going to drag her down the stairs and take her outside for a whooping?" Cal hated to overstep his boundaries with his boss, but the hotel was under enough duress at the moment. Images of Nick and Jillian in a screaming match on the third floor would only incite the situation.

The blunt question seemed to shake the cobwebs from Nick's brain. "She's guilty. The police need to arrest her before she leaves town."

Cal hadn't thought about her skipping town. She seemed pretty comfortable around Officer Griffin yesterday when he was questioning her. Then Jack waltzed in and the two were nothing but a cozy couple. Jillian appeared to be flying above the fray on this one. "The police are doing everything they can. Forensics is tying the evidence together, and if Jillian is guilty, they'll be able to prove it."

"They said the call came from Jeremiah's phone."

"That's what they said," Cal said, realizing Nick didn't buy it.

"Do we know if the police have picked him up yet?"

"For what? The shooting?"

"I called Malcolm and told him to make the report."

Cal had been here for the conversation. "He called but I haven't heard anything since."

"Damn it," Nick burst out. "Don't they get that these people can skip town? Are they even competent at their jobs?"

The pace of rural living did not keep up with a man used to getting his way and getting it on demand. It had only been two days since the fire, two hours since the shooting. Cal wasn't going to fault the police department for taking their time and getting it right. "Listen, I hear what you're saying. If I see Jillian, I'll let you know." Cal understood a man's need to do something, but sometimes action did more harm than good.

"I'm going up to the stables," Nick said. "Call me if you hear anything." Without waiting for a response, he headed for the door.

Cal watched him go, debating whether or not a return to the scene where Nick's wife nearly lost her life was such a good idea. It seemed the stables were the last place Nick should be. But Cal turned, and walked back to his office. It was Nick's hotel. He could go wherever he wanted.

Nick made it to the top of the hill, disturbed by images of blackened walls and yellow police tape. As he paused, a sickening nausea rolled in his gut. He hadn't seen the place in the daylight. He'd only seen the swell of orange-red flame as it raged against a night sky. In the clarity of day, the sight of collapsed walls and sunken metal roof broke his heart. This was Delaney's second home. This was where she lived and breathed and wanted to be. Nick didn't doubt her love for him but he understood and accepted that her heart dwelled here.

Steering clear of the investigation area, he was mindful of the professionals sifting through the embers in search of clues. Nick knew from experience they would find their clues, isolate the point of origin, piece together the blaze and follow it straight back to the culprit responsible. Nick would love to save them the time and energy and deliver Jillian Devane to them on a silver platter, but Cal was right. It was better to let the authorities handle the details. If Jillian ran, he'd follow her. He'd hunt her down to her home in South America or wherever she decided to flee. She might have gotten away with setting a blaze to burn out her competition in Brazil, but she wouldn't do so here. This was his jurisdiction. The U.S. was Nick's territory and he would drag her back kicking and screaming to face the charges she deserved.

In the distance he could see several of the horses gathered outside the barn. Nick imagined Troy was saddling them for his family's trail ride. Visions of the kid running into the burning stables to save the horses burned deep in Nick's heart. He owed Troy. He didn't even think about the animals. The second he saw Delaney lying on the ground, everything else vanished. A sharp pain wrenched his heart. His first thought had been: she was dead. Her body had been lifeless. Her stables were on fire and she lay on the ground. Only death would keep her from her horses.

Nick kicked himself to move. Extinguishing the images from his mind, he warned himself to get away from the building. Move. There would be time to rehash the fire and chain of events once he knew Delaney was safely on the road to recovery. Until then, Nick would flatten anything that stood in his way between here and justice.

Chapter Twenty-Six

Malcolm checked his watch again, the silver hands on the navy dial warning it was growing late. He didn't want Felicity to feel like he was counting the minutes but in fact he was. He needed to get back to the hotel. Cal should be with his family. He should enjoy his daughter's first visit to Tennessee, not stand around and hold the fort for his boss while he sat doing nothing at the hospital. Lacy and Emma Jane could stay with Felicity. Malcolm glanced over at his wife as she held their daughter. Emma Jane was sound asleep in Lacy's arms, her long black lashes a standout against her creamy white skin. The child was a beauty. Reaching over, he caressed the butter soft skin of her tiny hand. Everyone thought their babies were beautiful but Emma Jane truly was. From her ruby-pink lips to her full head of jet-black hair, the girl was perfection. Like her mother, he thought, moving his gaze from baby to woman.

Emma Jane was going to grow up and look just like Lacy, their coloring identical. He hoped so, anyway. Lacy was beautiful, inside and out. The layers of black hair had grown out from her pixie cut, the ends textured into points around her ivory-skinned neck. Despite living in a small town, Lacy kept her appearance stylish, on the cutting edge of fashion. The fitted royal blue halter dress and black strappy heels were the bounty gained from a few quick trips to New York and Los Angeles. But Lacy would look good in anything. Petite and curvy, she was more beautiful than any glamorous model yet maintained her country girl charm. And that's what Lacy was, he mused. A country girl, through and through. When family called, she answered. When the going got rough, she dug in her heels and picked up a shovel. Lacy was youthful, vivacious, yet strong as an ox and not afraid to get dirty. Malcolm still couldn't keep up with her when they hiked up the mountain, but he enjoyed trying. Staring at her now, Malcolm didn't think anything would slow her down, not even baby number two. Excitement rippled through him. *"What about our travel?"* he'd asked her when she broached the subject of a second child. She merely laughed. *"Don't think any babies are going to slow* me *down!"*

He chuckled. Nothing slowed Lacy down.

Glancing over at Felicity and Travis' parents, Lacy whispered, "What's so funny?"

"Nothing." This wasn't the time or place to be running through the positives in his life. Not when Nick and Felicity were hurting so deeply. "I'm sorry, it was just a fleeting thought I was entertaining. Listen..." He leaned close, momentarily distracted by the rich perfume she wore. Decadent, a supple blend of violet and suede, it was a sophisticated woodsy floral and his absolute favorite. As he kissed her near the ear, wisps of hair tickled his nose. "I need to get back to the hotel. Will you be all right by yourself?" Ashley hadn't made it on account of Albert's appointment running long.

"Of course." She shooed him off. "You go on. I'll stay with Felicity."

"You don't think she'll mind?" Malcolm asked.

Lacy summoned a quick smile and patted his hand. "I don't think she even knows you're here. She won't miss you but I will."

She winked and he pecked her cheek. "Thanks."

A nurse entered the room and Malcolm rose, instantly wondering if they had news on Travis.

"Mrs. Parker?" she asked the room at large.

Travis' mother raised her hand. "That's me."

"I have your son's things," she informed her and walked over, handing Mrs. Parker a white plastic bag imprinted with the hospital's logo.

"Thank you." Mrs. Parker set the bag in the chair beside her.

Felicity registered the delivery but didn't utter a word. In the center of silence and grief, Malcolm had a sinking feeling. Had Travis died? Is that why they were returning his possessions? When the nurse exited the room, Malcolm hurried out after her. "Miss?" he asked, despite her obvious forty-plus years of age. "Do you have any word on Travis?"

Her eyes filled with the detached compassion of a professional. "No, sir. His mother simply asked for his things."

"Oh." Relief floated in. "Thanks."

She smiled and continued down the well-lit corridor, her rubber-soled shoes noiseless on the spotless Linoleum flooring. Returning to the room, Malcolm wondered at the contents of the bag. Was Travis' phone inside? The photos he'd taken were the only solid proof they had as to the identity of Jeremiah's cohorts. Malcolm wanted to run the images by Felicity for a positive identification before taking them to the police, and while he was sensitive to the timing, Malcolm knew the police would need any and all evidence they had to make charges against Jeremiah stick.

Approaching tentatively, Malcolm called out softly, "Mrs. Parker?"

She looked up at him and the pain in her gaze took a gash out of his heart. But Malcolm was on a mission that would ultimately serve her son. The rationalization alleviated the stab of guilt he felt at asking, "May I see if Travis' cell phone is in the bag?"

Mrs. Parker stared up at Malcolm while her husband asked, "Why?"

"I think there might be evidence in the way of photos." Darting a peek toward Felicity, he said, "Travis used his phone to snap some pictures of Jeremiah. There were two men with him. I'd like Felicity to take a look and see if the men are the same two that were with him this morning."

Giving a silent okay, Mr. Parker nudged his wife to check. She rifled through the bag and pulled out a cell phone. "Here." Mrs. Parker glanced over at Felicity and Malcolm felt a strange tension pull. Then it occurred to him. Mrs. Parker wasn't blaming Felicity for what happened, was she?

Shaking the absurd thought, Malcolm took the phone from her and said, "Thank you." It was insane for him to even think it. Taking a seat by Felicity, he asked gently, "Do you mind?"

She shook her head. Malcolm searched Travis' phone, scrolling through his photo album. When he located the photos, he handed the phone to Felicity. "Were these the men with Jeremiah?"

Peering at the image, she said, "Yes, it looks like them."

"Can you zoom in on them, just to be sure?" She'd only glanced at the photo and Malcolm needed her to be sure. He wasn't going to mention it to the police if she wasn't absolutely positive that these were the same men.

As though surprised by his request, Felicity did as he asked. Nodding, she said, "Yes, that's them."

Lacy craned her head to look as Felicity handed the phone back to Malcolm. "Thank you. I'm sorry to ask, but this will help the police locate them."

"Let me see them," Lacy said.

Malcolm hesitated. Lacy was beautiful and wonderful but she was also nosy.

"C'mon, now." She jabbed out an open palm. "You never know if I might know them."

Doubtful, considering she'd spent most of her adult life living in Atlanta. But resigning himself to the inevitable, he handed the phone to her. Why not? She was spending her day sitting in a room doing nothing. Might as well give her something to look at.

Lacy peered at the image, her blue eyes those of an eagle honing in on its prey. Awkwardly she tried to zoom in, but cradling Emma Jane in her arms was proving an encumbrance. "Let me help you." Reaching over, Malcolm took his daughter from her mother's arms.

Lacy released her child without looking up, riveted to the small cell phone screen. "I've seen these men before."

Malcolm's antennae shot up. "What?" Hugging Emma Jane to his chest, he peered over her shoulder. "What do you mean you've seen them before?"

"Yes, yes." Pressing her lips together, she zoomed in on each man's face as closely as she could. She gnawed on her lower lip as if she thought staring hard enough would force the recollection. "Yes!" she cried out, nodding vigorously. As she flipped her heart-shaped face to his, Malcolm's heart took a leap. "I *thought* I saw Robby Ladd the other day."

Malcolm gaped at her. "What are you talking about?"

"At the gas station, the other day. I wasn't sure at first. He looks so different with his beard and mustache. But I remember having a funny feeling, like I knew him from somewhere." She glanced back at the image and nodded. "But looking at it now, I'm sure of it. That's Albert's oldest boy, Robby."

Beside him, Felicity came to life. "Uncle Albert's sons?" The Parkers had tuned in as well.

"Yes," Lacy announced, "but they've been gone for years. Word was, they robbed a gas station and Billy was sent to juvie for it, but Robby ran out of town." She fixed her gaze on Malcolm and a pang of remorse swept into her gaze. "It was around the same time I left town with Jeremiah."

Malcolm stiffened. "Jeremiah and these guys were in trouble together back then?"

She nodded, darting a guilty glance toward Felicity and the Parkers. "It was never proven and Jeremiah denied it, but that was the story. He helped them with the robbery and then left town. I wonder what they're doing back?"

Wonder? Malcolm wanted to explode. They were back in town on account of Jeremiah! "How do we find them?" he asked her quickly. "Any idea?"

"Oh, heaven's no." She feathered a hand to her breast. "I haven't heard or seen either one of them since my move to Atlanta."

"They have any other common friends?" Malcolm prompted, eager for any lead he could get. "Men that Jeremiah and the Ladd brothers would know and connect with?"

"Not that I'm aware of. I can ask Annie. Maybe she'd know, but as far as I can remember, the boys were loners."

"Do you think Albert would know?" Felicity asked, suddenly engaged in the conversation.

Malcolm turned to her, a sleeping Emma Jane rousing at his neck. "I doubt they'd contact their father, especially if they've hooked up with Jeremiah." Delicately prying Emma Jane's grip from his collar, he exchanged Emma Jane for the camera. Energized by the new information, Malcolm stood. "I need to get this to the police." Now that he had a positive ID, it would be possible for the police to draw a straight line between the Ladd boys and the hair sample and prints they collected from his office. Pecking Lacy's head with a kiss, he said, "Thanks, sweetheart. You might have busted the case wide open."

She beamed, her blue eyes glittering with happiness. "Oh, good!"

"Call me when you know something about Travis, will you?"

"Of course," she exclaimed and wriggled her fingers. "Toodles!"

Malcolm strolled into the office, a new vigor sweeping in with him. "We've got our first lead."

Cal glanced up from a letter in hand, briskly re-folding it as he asked, "We do?"

"Lacy positively identified the two men Jeremiah has been meeting with."

"Who are they?"

"Robby and Billy Ladd."

Cal's mouth fell open. "Albert's boys?"

"One and the same."

Tiny photo images mixed with a slew of memories and Cal pieced the information together in his mind. He recalled feeling like he'd seen the dark-haired men in beards before, an uncanny sense that he knew them from somewhere. Turns out he did. From twenty years ago. "Is she sure?"

Malcolm grinned. "Seems to be."

"Well, I'll be... Robby and Billy." A thought struck. "Does Albert know?"

"I doubt it. According to Lacy, the boys were estranged from their father. She said Jeremiah used to tell her stories about how Albert took a belt to them when they were kids and there was no love-loss between them. When she left town with Jeremiah, Robby took off while Billy ended up in jail."

"I think I remember hearing something along those lines." But Cal had never been close with the Ladd brothers. He knew who they were to see them around school, but that had been the extent of it. "How did they hook back up with Jeremiah?"

Malcolm shrugged. "That's a piece of the puzzle yet to be solved. I've alerted the authorities to their identity and approximate whereabouts. They should have them picked up for questioning by sundown."

Relieved, Cal said, "That's good to hear."

"Why don't you go ahead and get out of here," Malcolm prodded. "You've got a daughter in town who I imagine is anxious to see you."

Cal smiled. "Thanks." Collecting his personal items, he slid the aged letter back into its envelope and placed it in a slim leather portfolio. "If you need anything—"

"I know where to find you," Malcolm finished for him. Coming around behind the desk, he swapped places with Cal, asking, "By the way, have you seen Nick?"

"Yes. He was here earlier." Concern swamped his thoughts as he revealed, "He was looking for Jillian."

"Figured as much." Malcolm's solemn gaze mirrored the emotion coursing through Cal. "She's not here."

"No?" Cal asked, wondering how Malcolm knew.

He shook his head. "I saw her in a truck with Jack after I left the hospital."

Jack. Cal tightened his grip on his leather case. He hoped his brother wasn't mixed up with Jillian other than for kicks. That Jack had nothing to do with the fire. His brother was in enough trouble as it was. "Okay. Call me if you need anything."

"Enjoy the time with your daughter."

"Will do," he said and walked out of the office. Right after a brief pit stop at his parent's home. Nerves skirted through his chest. Cal planned to make one last appeal to his mother before she helped Jack steal the freedom of an innocent young man.

Chapter Twenty-Seven

"Felicity Wilkins?"

She glanced up at a man standing in the open doorway of the waiting room. Dressed in a white coat, she presumed him to be a doctor. "Yes?"

He approached with a solemn face. Electricity cracked through her veins. Had something happened to Travis? Pulse thumping, she darted a glance to the Parkers. Their eyes were glued to the man but neither said a word. Did they feel it too?

The doctor folded his hands together before him, a small smile creeping onto his lips. "Your mother would like to see you."

Felicity gripped the wooden arms of her chair. "*What*?"

"Your mother wants to see you." His smile broadened. "She's awake."

Felicity fired up from her seat. Was he kidding? She shot a glance to the Parkers. Was this a dream?

The man stood waiting.

"Where? Where is she?"

With a hesitant glance toward the Parkers, he instructed, "Follow me."

Felicity followed him down the hallway, her legs a boneless mess of automated movement. Her mother was awake. She was asking for her. Felicity could hardly believe it. She stumbled into an elevator behind him, and they ascended to a floor crowded with staff and beds and machines. Trembling in the chilled air, Felicity covered her nose, warding off a horrible stench. The place smelled like a mix of cleaning sprays and vomit. One man coughed like the contents of his lungs were about to spew free. Pasting her gaze to the doctor's white coat, she avoided eye contact with the patients as she passed their beds, the space open and completely lacking in privacy. *I'm here to see my mother. I'm here to see my mother.*

"She's here," the doctor stated, pausing by the foot of a bed.

Felicity slid a reluctant gaze toward the head. Butterflies swarmed her belly. Lying immobile, her mother was covered by thin white blankets, her light blue patient gown loosely tied around her chest and shoulders. Felicity couldn't breathe. The doctor left, leaving Felicity to stare dumbly at her mother's pale figure. Gone was her vibrant tan, replaced by chalky skin and a gauze-like head cover. There were no signs of her mother's blonde waves. In a rush, Felicity realized they must have shaved it. She looked dead.

Her mom's eyes fluttered open and a small smile erupted onto her lips. Tears sprang to Felicity's eyes. *Mom.*

Heart beats pounded within her chest. "Mom," she mouthed.

Delaney's smile remained intact, but she didn't speak, only curled a finger to come closer.

Felicity's body responded before her mind could calculate what transpired. Her mom was awake. She was alive. She was communicating and conscious! "Mom," Felicity uttered again, this time with more breath, powered by a flood of relief. It swept the angst clean, leaving only an open hopeful heart in its place. For a moment, Felicity felt lighter, freer. "Mom, you're okay."

The reply was a bare nod of her head.

Felicity reached for her mom's hand, careful to avoid the tubes taped to her arm. "Hi."

"Hi," she whispered.

Could she not talk? Was her voice gone? "How do you feel?"

"Good."

Her voice was strained, coarse, but she could talk. Relieved, Felicity squeezed her mom's hand. That's all that mattered. Her mom knew she was here.

"How are the horses?"

The utterance struck like an iron pan. Felicity didn't want to tell her. She didn't want to divulge all that had happened—was still happening—because it might interfere with her mom's recovery. Hadn't the doctors said as much before?

"They're fine," Felicity said quickly. "Everyone's good," she lied, thinking how Travis was on another floor, his chest split open as they tried to save his life, Troy's arm was bandaged, a horse had been burned, another bruised in the stampede to escape.

Her mother's gaze crackled with questions.

Felicity's pulse tripped. Tears filled her lids. Could her mom sense the truth? That her horses had suffered? Did she know all was not well and that her daughter was lying? "Troy is with them," she said, grappling for something to fill the balloon of doubt growing before her very eyes. "He's been with them the whole time." Felicity's emotion burst open like a dam unleashed, and she clung to the slender hand within hers. Hot tears spilled onto her cheeks. "I love you. I'm so glad you're okay. *I love you.*"

A mix of joy and sadness mingled in her mother's dark eyes but her smile faded. As if she knew...

Without hearing the words, her mom could tell things were not good.

"I'm going to call Nick," Felicity said at once. "I'm going to let him know you're awake." Guilt washed over her as she brushed the tears away.

He should have been here. He was the one who'd been sitting by her bedside this entire time. It wasn't fair that he was gone the moment her mother came to, and she was here.

Nick stalked Jeremiah as he hiked through the woods, a barely controlled rage streaming through his veins with each and every step. On his way down from the stables, Nick caught sight of Jeremiah entering the trails. Clouds had shrouded a setting sun, burying the landscape in hazy gray hues, but it didn't prevent him from spotting Jeremiah across the meadow. He'd been walking along the edge of forest that bordered the trails leading up to Zack's Falls, darting into the woods at the trailhead. Jeremiah kept his head down, wearing a dark cowboy hat to conceal his identity, but Nick recognized the pop of color in his shirt. It stood out like a bright green lizard on a brown tree. Around these parts, Jeremiah Ladd was the only man with the audacity to wear bright lime green stripes that couldn't be hidden, not against the dusky green tree line or beneath the black backpack he wore on his back.

There was only one reason Jeremiah would be slinking around the property at sunset. He was here to cause trouble under the cover of darkness—trouble Nick was going to prevent.

Tracking Jeremiah like a hunted prey, he maintained his distance while managing to keep him in sight. They moved through the older section of property, passed the original Ladd homestead, nothing but a mound of decaying lumber and a tumbledown of a chimney. Next they came upon the dilapidated stables, the structure Delaney used to house her horses before they built the new stables. Traversing with a purposeful stride, Jeremiah made his way up the hill and behind the main hotel. It was harder to see him now, the last of their filtered light all but gone, but Nick wasn't about to lose him, closing the distance as the trees and foliage grew denser. Trails were narrow but navigable, a wall of mountain rising to his right.

Jeremiah paused and Nick did likewise. Squatting on his hunches in what appeared to be a patch of clearing, Jeremiah removed his hat, tossing it aside, then slid the pack from his back. Unzipping it, he began removing items. Nick angled his body behind a tree, unable to make out the contents from here, but what troubled him more was the fact that they were within sight of the hotel. Down below, a screened porch was clearly visible. It ran the length of the hotel's rear side, overlooking the creek that meandered between here and Ernie's old cabin, now the History Hut. The faint trickle of stream could be heard, the occasional katydid winding up for the night's performance. Not far beyond their current location lay the property line, providing Jeremiah the perfect location to do something sinister and disappear off site without being seen.

Unless someone was watching him while he did it. Anger burned in Nick's heart. He could kill Jeremiah with his bare hands. Right here, right now, he could twist the man's neck and listen to it crack like a twig without a shred of remorse. As he watched and waited with nothing but the sound of his own breath, it became increasingly clear with each passing minute that Jeremiah was here with criminal intent. The only bright spot in the pursuit had been Felicity's text. *Mom is awake.* There was no mention of Travis, only that Delaney was awake. Nick had responded, informing Felicity to hang in there, he'd get back as soon as he could.

First, he needed to tie up loose ends here.

Assembling something in his hands, Jeremiah glanced around the forest, scanning the area for signs of detection. Nick kept a low profile, concealing himself behind the wide tree trunk. He couldn't have planned his attire better if he'd tried. Hunter green, his shirt provided excellent camouflage, especially at this hour of the day. Forty, maybe fifty feet away, he could see Jeremiah without revealing his position. Perfect for surveillance. Judging the scope of space between them, the narrow but relatively clear path, Nick figured he could close the distance in seconds.

Jeremiah stood. Nick's pulse bolted. He held his breath as he watched Jeremiah inch closer toward the hotel. Creeping toward him, Nick would have liked to snap a photo of what Jeremiah was doing as evidence but feared the flash would give him away. Wasn't worth it. He'd grab the evidence when he grabbed the man. A flare of light snagged Nick's attention and his heart caught. Jeremiah was lighting something! He wound his arm back and Nick charged.

"Jeremiah!" he yelled.

Whipping his head toward Nick, Jeremiah froze. Nick sprinted down the trail. Branches lashed at his face but he ignored them, drilling his focus into his target, the glow of flame within his hands. Jeremiah turned and chucked the bottle toward the hotel.

The bottle smashed against a tree. Flame fell to the ground. Jeremiah took off, running straight. Nick took off after him, cursing as his boot snagged a root. He tripped. "Jeremiah!" Nick shouted, pushing up from the tangle of roots and rocks.

Flames were crawling up and around the dead branches and leaves. Jeremiah was getting away. "You're finished!" Nick yelled, lunging down the hillside, more a skid over mountain brush and debris than run. He couldn't ignore a fire but he couldn't let Jeremiah escape.

Jeremiah stumbled, but regaining balance, hurled himself over a fallen tree, hitting the ground running. Nick's cell phone rang. Delaney's face flashed before him. Could it be trouble with her recovery? Word on Travis?

Heart hammering the breath from his lungs, rage lit into him. Jeremiah was going to suffer for what he'd done. He was going to rue the day he ever returned.

"Fire!"

Somewhere in the background Nick heard the warning cry but he was fueled by vengeance. He drove forward, fighting branches, rocks and bushes. Several yards ahead of him, Jeremiah was held up by a massive clump of trees. Nick took a nosedive. Jeremiah tried to dodge him but making solid contact, their bodies hit the ground in motion, branches cracking beneath them as they tumbled. Jeremiah cried out as they hit a stump, the impact breaking their momentum. The blunt force nearly knocked the wind from him.

"Fire!"

Nick wrenched an arm around Jeremiah's neck and raised a fist, burying it in his jaw. He shot Travis. His men robbed the hotel. He probably helped Jillian set the stables ablaze. Sinking another fist, Nick drove Jeremiah's head into the ground as he struggled beneath him.

Shouts pierced the forest like spears but he ignored them, wrapping his hands around Jeremiah's neck. Nick could feel his pulse within the heat of his palms and knew he could squeeze it cold. Fury surged. Sweat trickled into Nick's eyes. Hatred burned. With steely precision, he knew he could squeeze him dead. Building, swelling, the desire seemed to take over.

"Help! There's a fire!"

A distant male voice. People shouting from the hotel. A reminder of time and place. Eyes locked in sync, they were two men, one vendetta. The edge belonged to Nick.

"It's burning up the tree!"

In a roar of anger, Nick pushed up from Jeremiah's body and yelled out, "Call the police!" Shrieks of response were scattered as Nick dialed into the situation. Through the dim light he saw bodies dash in and out of the screened porch. Several guests stood by the stone patio downstairs. There was a hose. They could use it to curb the flames. Nick slung his gaze uphill. Flames were growing. "Grab the hoses!"

Instinctively Nick grabbed his phone and called Malcolm. His partner answered the first ring. "What the hell's going on?"

"There's a fire. Behind the hotel. Get all staff on hoses," Nick barked, urgency ramping his tone. "Call the police. I've got Jeremiah." Ending the call, he drove his boot into a squirming Jeremiah. "You're not going anywhere."

"Hell I'm not!" From out of nowhere, Jeremiah pulled a gun.

Staring down the barrel, Nick jumped backward.

A gunshot rang out.

Screams sounded from the hotel.

Jeremiah scrambled to his feet but Nick sprang for him. Another shot pierced the forest. Nick felt the metal barrel of a gun slam into the side of his head as they collided, plunging over a small cliff. Sailing over bushes, they crashed onto solid ground. The pain to his ribs was sharp. Mindlessly Nick struck at Jeremiah. Blow after blow, he connected wherever

he could. Above them, guests shrieked in horror as they witnessed the conflict. Wrestling, branches jabbing, Nick managed to straddle Jeremiah. Pinning his hands, Nick searched
for signs of his weapon.

Anger twisted Jeremiah's bloodied face as he writhed to
break free. "Get off me!"

"Not a chance." Chest heaving, Nick stared down at him.
The man was garbage. He had no respect for others, for life
or property. He'd taken a shot at him! Honing in on the puls-
ing vein in Jeremiah's sweaty neck, Nick flipped his hold
from hands to throat. Squeezing the last breath from his lungs
would bring immense pleasure. Jeremiah seemed to understand the same. Fear scored his light brown eyes. He tried to
tear Nick's hands from his throat.

He didn't stand a chance. Nick's grip was a steel clamp.
"Nick!"

Malcolm's voice cut through the chaos. With unerring
accuracy, it locked onto the vise-grip around Jeremiah's neck.
Riveted by the cold eyes of a killer, Nick lingered in his desire, the feel of Jeremiah's bony throat in his hands. Seconds
passed until both men understood the moment was gone.
Nick wouldn't kill Jeremiah in cold blood. He wasn't that
animal. Jeremiah's lips twitched, then turned up in pleasure.
Jeremiah *was*.

Nick shoved Jeremiah's head into the ground, nailing it
against a rock then pushed up from him with a kick to the
ribs. Jeremiah grabbed his side, crying out in pain. "It's
over," Nick muttered. "It's over."

Several male staff members were climbing the hill, aiming a hose high into the air. A few others manned fire extin-
guishers but none of it made a dent as flames fanned the
brush, lighting the air to a smoky gold. The scent of burning
wood conjured up images of Delaney and the stables, snapping Nick back into action. Hauling Jeremiah from the
ground, he dragged him to the hotel and thrust him toward the
stone patio. White beams were flung up tree trunks around
him as people converged on scene with the flashlights. Draw-

ing the gun from his waistband, Nick handed it to the nearest fellow and clipped, "Watch him."

The man didn't hesitate, as though he inherently understood Jeremiah was responsible for the fire. Nick locked gazes with Malcolm. A glow of flame hung between them, casting solemn expressions in crystal clear clarity. Another fire. Another blow. Nick vowed it would be the last.

Running up hill, he pointed toward the porch where several guests had gathered to watch. "Get those people out of there!" Distant sirens whistled through the cooling night air, chilling the hair on his neck. *Please don't let this reach the building.*

Chapter Twenty-Eight

Felicity stood at the end of Travis' bed. She gazed at his inert figure, her emotions wrung out like an old dishrag. She couldn't get near him. A mask was taped to his face, tubes secured to his arms. He looked like he'd been hog-tied in place so he couldn't jump up and run away. A patient in the next bed lay mouth agape, his lips dried and cracked. Felicity shuddered, hugging arms to her body. These were the lucky ones. From what the nurse said, Travis was lucky to be alive. The bullet hit an artery. The damage had been severe. Felicity remembered the blood, remembered being frightened by the enormous soaking into his shirt.

Her instincts had been correct. Doctors said the blood loss had almost killed him.

Struggling not to crumble as doctors and nurses moved around the intensive care unit, she swallowed over the painful rock in her throat. Travis wasn't safe yet. They said the next twenty-four hours would be crucial. It could go either way. They said she could see him but he wouldn't know she was here. Tears surged and her lips quivered. *Please, get better.* Digging her hands into her bare arms, she willed him to heal. There was so much she wanted to say, so much she wanted him to know.

She never even thanked him for saving her mother.

Standing like a heel, a stump, she stared at him. His parents had been here first. They spent almost an hour with him doing God knows what. There was nothing to do! She'd waited for them to leave, counted the seconds but, now, wondered why. There was nothing they could do. He wasn't Travis. He was a body, one more patient lying in intensive care. Pushing herself closer, she wanted to touch him, hold him. Wanted to connect.

"Travis," she whispered. "Travis, can you hear me?"

Monitors bleeped. A machine swelled and hissed. She knew it was foolish, but she wanted him to know she was here. They'd said her mom could hear her. Deep in a coma, her mind had still been able to compute her presence. Could Travis?

Felicity touched her fingers to his arm, heartened by its warmth. Exhaling a ragged breath, a well of relief poured into her. "You're going to be all right. The doctors say you did great." A flutter in her chest betrayed her claim, but he didn't know. He couldn't feel the pound of her heart, the flock of nerves in her breast. Steadying her voice, she said, "You're strong and healthy and you're going to pull through this. They don't know it's because you think you can do anything." A nervous laugh erupted as tears spilled free. "They don't know how strong-minded you are, how determined. That's why you're going to be okay. That's why," she said, her voice breaking. "Because you have to. *You have to*, Travis."

"Felicity."

She whirled, startled to see Troy standing behind her. No hat, no smile, he stood rigid, seemingly uncaring to anyone who didn't know him. But she did. Hot, fluid, his dark eyes were steeped in pain. Troy was hurting.

Felicity went to him quickly. Throwing herself against him, she wrapped her arms around his neck and pressed her face in his shoulder. "I don't know, Troy. I don't know if he's going to be okay."

Hugging her to him, he hooked his cheek to hers. "He's got to be, Felicity. He can't die."

Troy's words gave life to the fear she'd hidden away deep inside. Die. Death. Surrendering to the strength and warmth of her closest friend, Felicity let go. She unlatched the lock on her heart. Released the fear, the doubts. Tears flowed and she let them. Troy understood. He was the one person in this world who understood her pain. Friends since childhood, the three of them had been inseparable. They loved the same things, lived the same life. Troy was like family. He knew her heart. Despite his differences with Travis, their bond held strong. They were brothers. Twins. Troy loved his brother. He loved her.

Breathing in the scent of him, the round of his muscle, she cried softly into the dampened T-shirt, "He won't leave us, Troy. He *can't*."

Cal stood on the threshold of his parent's' home, staring into the impassive gaze of his mother. Brightly lit lamps reflected in her eyes, light brown eyes that held no affection. He could smell the roasting scent of chicken from within, knew he'd called her from supper. Idly, he wondered after his father. Was he here? Was he waiting for her? Did he wonder at the interruption?

It was short-lived. Cal was here with a purpose. Fiddling with the ends of the envelope in his hand, he found it painful to look into his momma's eyes and not see an invitation to come in, or the love he'd grown up with, known all his life. Love, happiness. It was all he wanted, really. Hers. His. It wasn't his fault that life dealt her a cruel blow putting Susannah Ladd in Daddy's life before her, his wife, the mother of his children. It wasn't Cal's fault his parents shared a painful past. But it was his purpose to ease her pain.

Her grief, he'd realized. After sharing the letters with Annie, Cal had come to realize what was truly eating at his mother after all these years. His wife had explained it as simple as a man could understand. Women live for love. They give it, nurture it, create new life because of it. For a woman love was the purest form of communication. It sustained them, strengthened them. It was their currency, Cal realized, but Annie explained it went further. Love was the mortar between the bricks. It built the home, provided the shelter. It was the gravity that kept a family grounded, the dreams that kept the clouds floating and the sun shining. If Victoria felt her love had been weakened, damaged, her world would feel like it was crumbling beneath her.

It was a hefty burden, but one he assumed came with the package of living.

"What do you want?" Unwilling to welcome him inside, Victoria Foster held the door half-closed, her elegantly-dressed figure a mere slice of view between door edge and frame.

"I have something for you," he replied softly.

"You've already demonstrated your disdain for this family. What would I want from you now?"

"It's not from me." Cal offered up the letter he'd been holding. "It's from Daddy."

Startled, she looked down at the aged yellow envelope in his hands, but suspicion instantly bucked the surprise from her gaze. "What is that? Is this some kind of ruse he's playing on your behalf?"

Cal shook his head, tamping back a swell of sadness. "He doesn't know I'm giving it to you." In fact, his daddy might be angry about him sharing the letters with Momma, but something had to give and Cal decided it had to be the past.

Victoria took the envelope, a sudden interest taking over. "What's in it?"

Cal didn't say a word. She tore open the flap and he watched silently as she read, his heart pitching as her expression changed. He noticed a slight tremor in her hand when she looked at him. The color had drained from her face. "Where did you get this?"

"In the attic."

"I don't understand..."

"What's there to understand? He loves you, Momma. He loves you. *You*."

Hazel eyes glistened in the lamplight. Soft and vulnerable, they were the pillows of love he'd known from his childhood. Questions flowed freely but not a single one did she voice. His mother was too proud.

Cal straightened, pulled his collar snug around his neck. His job was done. If she didn't want to listen, if she wanted to overlook the facts because her heart had been injured, there was nothing he could do to prevent it. This was about her and Daddy. This was their life, their struggle. While it might affect the entire family, they were the ones holding the reins. He turned to go.

"Wait." His mother reached out for him. "Don't go."

Pausing, hope funneled into him as his mother held his gaze.

"You said your father doesn't know..."

"He doesn't know I found the letter. He doesn't know I'm sharing it with you." There was no need to reveal the others. They'd only cause harm.

Her mouth broke into a nervous smile. Embarrassed. "So you know about Susannah."

"I only know of her, the rumors, but I believe she's the reason you're taking up for Jack against Delaney."

The accusation buckled his mother's stately image of poise and grace. It found its home, made her look small and petty, because it was true. Cal had pegged her like a bull's eye in her heart. While Cal hated to knock her down, he hoped the truth would serve to pick her up again.

Watching her glance down at the letter, he suspected a confession hovered on her lips. Meeting his gaze directly, she said, "I'm not a perfect person, Cal."

"None of us are, Momma."

"I have my faults."

"We all do."

"I wish I could say I was above petty jealousy but I can't." She blinked, evading him for a moment before returning to look at him head on. "I always knew he wanted to marry her, and would have, but for the simple fact she said no."

Cal couldn't imagine the person who would have revealed such information to his mother. He couldn't imagine how they could be so hateful when his mother had done nothing but follow a man from her hometown to his. Victoria Guthrie had been a young socialite from Chattanooga, an innocent woman who hadn't been privy to the goings-on in their community before her arrival. To fill her in after the fact was downright spiteful. "We've all experienced a young crush, Momma, but that doesn't mean it's 'meant to be.' It's nothing but a first kiss."

Staring at him, she seemed rapt by his words.

"Marriage is for life," he said, overcome by a wisdom he felt undeserved but driven to share. "It's about building a home, a family, continuing a love through the generations. Daddy wanted that life with you. He might have loved Susannah, but he also loved you. Isn't that enough?"

Victoria Foster pressed her lips together and nodded. Tears sprang to her eyes but she nodded, quickly, surely. She nodded, *yes*.

Cal remembered the words penned by his father verbatim.

Susannah, I'm writing to inform you of my engagement. Victoria Guthrie of Chattanooga has accepted my proposal for marriage. She is a beautiful woman who I am sure you would approve. Not only of excellent upbringing and education but she has a heart of pure gold, making my days shine with joy, my heart overflow with love.

I know you and Harry have been married and I wish you nothing but happiness for the years to come. Your friendship has meant the world to me and I hope you will wish the same for me. While we have shared many special moments, it occurs to me that I should tell you I cannot imagine my life going forward without Victoria. You and she will most assuredly cross paths and I wanted you to have this in your heart to hold. I am dedicating my life to Victoria.

Yours truly, Gerald.

Chapter Twenty-Nine

The fire ravaged several acres before firefighters were able to extinguish the last of it. Men in boxy suits hiked heavily up and down the hill, their horizontal reflector stripes flashing iridescently as they crossed walls of light flooding from portable lamps. Nick stood entrenched, watching the progress. He'd wanted to leave hours ago. He wanted to see Delaney, tell her how much he loved her, but his presence had been required here. After scouring the mountainside, retracing his roll down the hill with Jeremiah, he'd managed to locate the gun. The pistol Jeremiah most likely used to shoot Travis, the same one he used to shoot him. It was all the police needed to charge him with attempted murder and haul his butt to jail.

God willing, Travis wouldn't die. According to Felicity it was still touch and go, but he was out of surgery and alive. It was all they could ask for—that and Delaney's recovery. Add the fact the Ladd boys had been picked up on a highway outside of town, and the news was improving all around. Incredibly, Lacy had identified the two with the help of Travis' surveillance photos. Adding a name to the mix enabled the police to identify license plates and send out an alert. Once they matched the hair sample found at the robbery scene, they could tie the men to the hotel burglary and send them away for a long time. Wicked pleasure coursed through him. Stealing a firearm in the process of robbery would chain their jail cell closed.

Unclenching his teeth, Nick massaged his jaw. The bruises on his body were beginning to ache though none of them were too serious. Muscles would heal. Buildings could be rebuilt. Trees would regrow. Nick's only unsettled business remained that of Jillian. Somehow, some way, he had to tie her to the fire. He didn't believe Jeremiah set off the explosive by himself. He wasn't smart enough. But Jillian was. She was smart enough and malicious enough to blow up the stables, including every living animal inside them. She stopped by the stables the day before, which gave her access. She could have easily obtained the know-how to construct a bomb. Motive, she never lacked. Jillian was behind it, he was sure of it.

With the crisis here winding down and under control, his next goal was to connect Jillian to the cell phone. They'd located bits and pieces from the detonating device, but discovering where it was purchased would prove the challenge. Jeremiah's cell phone had been used to call the phone, thereby triggering the explosion, but he claimed he'd lost it. Likely story. More likely he sold it to Jillian for a pretty penny. Of course there remained the business of his bail as well. Someone paid a lot of money to see him go free. Made sense it was a down payment for arson.

Turning away from the disheartening scene, Nick had about all the bad news he was going to tolerate. He strode across the stone-paved patio and up the few steps to the outdoor sidewalk. Malcolm would have some ideas. Between the two of them they could brainstorm their way through any problem.

Malcolm. What would he do without the man? Nick closed his eyes briefly as he walked by floor-to-ceiling windows along the spa. Interior lights were dim, deepening the shadows in and around overstuffed chairs and sofas positioned along the hall of windows. There wasn't a doubt in his mind he would have killed Jeremiah if Malcolm hadn't intervened. He would have locked his hands around Jeremiah's throat and squeezed the life from him. A mild tremor raced through him. It was a death that evoked mixed emotion.

With the spa behind him, Nick wondered briefly as to Cal's whereabouts. Was he at the hospital? Nick hoped not. With his daughter in town, Cal should be spending every last

second with her. Family was precious. Life was short. Hotel
Ladd was his job, not his entire existence.

Shouldn't be Nick's either. He'd been doing a lot of
thinking over the last couple of days, taking stock of his life,
thinking about what mattered. It had been late in his life when
he found the woman of his dreams, and then to have her nearly ripped from his arms had given him pause. He'd planned
on scouting the Asian continent for a new locale next year,
maybe India or one of the islands, but now he wasn't so sure.
His problem wasn't deciding on which exotic locale but con-
vincing his wife to join him. Delaney refused to leave. She
contended the horses needed her, the stable staff needed her.
They weren't ready for her departure, she argued, but Nick
knew the truth. It was Delaney. Rooted deeply in her corner
of the world, the slice of paradise staked out by her family
before her, she wasn't going anywhere. *Maybe someday after
the hotel has been opened for a year or so. Maybe when Felicity is out of college.* But if Nick had learned anything from
the events of late, it was that "maybe" doesn't always come.
Sometimes fate yanks you out of the game before "someday"
arrives.

Swinging open the rear door to the lobby, Nick scanned
the faces mingling about. Most of the guests had gone, leaving only the most curious to probe for information. Taking
stock of his presence, a front desk clerk looked to him expectantly but he waved her off. He wasn't on duty. He was on
his way to the hospital.

Nick walked down the hall to the waiting room for ICU.
He'd called ahead to check on Felicity, wondering how she
was holding up, if she was hungry, if she needed anything.
He could pick something up from Fran's on his way but her
response had been a placid refusal—Ashley had come and
gone with food. Casey was keeping her company at the moment, the baby at home with grandma. While Nick was glad
Felicity had company, he was worried about her. She was

fair-hearted, too young and innocent to be exposed to the uglier side of life.

But after an attempted kidnapping and witnessing her boyfriend's shooting by a lunatic, she could say goodbye to innocence. It had left her at the poker table with a losing hand.

Entering the room, he slowed his pace, treading softly as he took a seat beside Felicity. "Hey."

"Hey," Felicity replied. "Have you seen mom?"

"No. I wanted to see you first." Nick took her hand and held it gently between his own. Warm, slender, it felt fragile, matching the shaky quality in Felicity's gaze. Her eyes were puffy, devoid of cheer. Even the brightly colored floral blouse she wore didn't help to paint a happy picture. Not that he could blame her. Nick was feeling pretty gloomy himself these days.

Casey stood. "I'm gonna go grab some water."

Nick silently acknowledged her departure, then returned his attention to Felicity. He hated that she was hurting, hated that she was hit by two tragedies at once. Giving her a gentle squeeze, he said, "Travis is a strong guy. He'll get through this, you watch and see." She nodded but seemed detached, as though she knew the deal. There were no guarantees. "It was a brave thing he did for you. It's obvious that boy loves you. He'll fight to get back to you, you have to know that. Believe in the power of the spirit, the heart." As he spoke, Nick could feel something churning inside her. There was something she wasn't saying. Alone in the room, he brushed the loose tendrils of hair from her face. "Talk to me. Let me take some of the pain from you."

Red-rimmed eyes peered into his. "Our last words before he was shot...our last conversation...I told him I didn't want him interfering for me."

"What do you mean?"

Tears welled as she averted his gaze. "He stopped by my father's hotel room, he saw my car so he stopped and I told him—"

Alarm bells sounded in his head. "You were at your father's hotel room? What for?"

She blinked, wary yet unapologetic. "I believed he started the fire. I went to confront him about it, and Travis saw my car parked outside."

"*You did what*?" Nick asked, stuck in the part where she said she went to confront her father. Was she out of her mind? Jack Foster was a dangerous man. Nick didn't care that Felicity was his daughter. Jack could strike out at anyone, including her! "Tell me what happened," he demanded, his mild tone barely controlled. "I want to know everything."

Sniffling, she clasped her hands around his and held tight. Staring at their entwined hands, she continued, "Unfortunately, nothing much. I went to his room to see if I could find any clues. I thought maybe if I could smell smoke on his clothing, see something charred..." Her voice fell away, as if she realized how foolish she sounded. But firming her tone, she flipped her gaze to meet his. "I *had* to do something. We found his lighter outside the stables. I know he was involved somehow, and I couldn't just let him walk around—my mom was lying in a hospital bed! You know what that's like—it's awful! *Horrible*." She shook her head. "I had to do something but Travis stepped in. He stopped me before I could learn a thing, and now he's lying in a hospital bed."

Felicity was unraveling. Slowly, before his very eyes, Nick watched her come undone and his heart ached for her. She was voicing the same things he himself had felt only hours before. A loved one is lying helpless in a hospital room. It gives rise to an urge to act, a need to set things right. Nick dropped his gaze and clutched her hands more forcefully. So young and delicate, yet he'd always known Felicity was a strong young woman. Hadn't he told Delaney as much?

Don't sell your daughter short. Felicity is made of strong fiber.

"We need to let the authorities handle the criminals." He was speaking almost as much to himself as he was to Felicity. "We need to step aside and let them do their job."

"He attacked her at the stables and no one listened!" she cried out. "He tried to burn them down—I had to see what I could find out on my own. I figured if I could soften him up, make him think I wanted to reunite, he'd allow me the time to investigate. Then Travis barged in on us. The minute my father laid eyes on him, he accused me of setting him up. I was so angry with Travis... Once we were outside I told him *exactly* what I thought. I told him to mind his own business and stop interfering with me." Suddenly she choked up and sputtered, "I told him 'next time don't stop.' I didn't need his kind of interference on my behalf."

Tears swam into her eyes, cutting him to the quick. If Travis hadn't stopped when he saw her on the side of the road, who knows what could have happened to Felicity.

"Thank goodness he didn't listen to me. It could be me in there instead of him!"

"This isn't your fault, Felicity." Nick pulled her to him and held her close, but she resisted.

"He thinks I hate him! Our last conversation was me *rejecting* him."

"It was a fight. Travis knows you love him."

She shook her head vehemently. "No, I didn't return any of his calls. When he drove up, I hadn't seen him since the fire."

Nick stroked her hair. Satiny, silky, she felt like a child in his arms. Nick had never been a father, never stopped long enough to consider the idea. Truth be known, he never met a woman he'd actually want to father a child with. Not until Delaney.

But, he realized, sobbing at his shoulder was a daughter. Felicity. She was a part of Delaney, a part of the woman he desperately loved. Settling on the notion, the young woman in his arms, Nick felt strength and determination. Misguided as it might be, she tried to do what she thought was right and he respected her for it. Felicity was no longer a child but an adult woman. She was strong and proud and—emotion swept through him, nearly unhinging him—more like Delaney than he ever imagined possible.

As Felicity pressed into him, he could hear a muffled, "If he doesn't make it, I'll never be able to tell him how I feel."

"Shh," he said into her head. "He'll make it. You and Travis will have all the time you need to work through the past."

Nick could only pray it was true. Living with words unspoken could eat away at a person, living inside a heart with no chance for release. Nick closed his eyes and centered on Felicity. He didn't want that for her. She didn't deserve it. She'd only tried to assert her independence, to spread her wings and fly free from the watchful eyes of those who loved her. She shouldn't be punished for it. Whispering a silent prayer, Nick held her until the tears subsided. He couldn't erase the pain but he could ease it. When Casey returned, he excused himself and headed up to Delaney's room. It was time to reconnect with his wife and speak his own words that burned for release.

Nick stood by the open doorway, taking in the sight of her. The head of her bed had been raised slightly, allowing her to read more comfortably beneath the glare of fluorescent light. Her head was wrapped in white bandages, her gown a faded blue. Beneath the sterile lighting, her sun-kissed skin had lost its glow. But none of it prevented him from seeing her beauty. "What are you doing?" he asked, struck by the absurdity of her reading a brochure post brain surgery.

"I'm looking over my instructions for discharge."

"Discharge? And where do you think you're going?"

"Home."

Flat, determined, her response pulled at something inside him. "You're insane, you know that?" Walking into the room, he went to her bedside, removed the pamphlet from her hands and tossed it onto a nearby table. "You're not going anywhere."

"Nick, I'm fine. The doctor said I could go home in a day or so if the swelling subsides."

Nick wanted to shake her. He wanted to strap her to the bed and make sure she didn't leave this hospital until her body was fully recovered. "Your doctor should be fired. What kind of physician allows a patient to go home with a hole in her head?"

She smiled. "It's a tube and he'll remove it before I go."

"Your head has been shaved."

"Only in the back. I have plenty enough everywhere else to make up for it."

Dropping to a seat on the edge of her bed, Nick took her hand in his, savoring the feel of her warm skin within his palm. "What if you're not ready?"

"I am ready. I've been ready since I woke up."

"What if your brain isn't ready?" Staring at her, he wondered what would happen if she had a relapse and they were too far from help?

As though sensing his concern, she gripped his hand firmly. "I'm fine. I'll be fine." Grief slid into her gaze, carving a dent in her ease. "I need to get back to my horses."

"Your horses are fine. Troy has been making sure of it." Delaney smiled, a fondness filling her dark brown eyes. Nick knew the mention of Troy would alleviate her worry. "There's nothing for you to do at the stables. The staff has been working twenty-four-seven, the police are working their investigation. We've suspended trail rides for the interim. Your job is to get well," he said, leaving out the matter of Jeremiah's arson attempt, Travis' gunshot wound. There was no need to undermine what seemed to be a remarkable recovery underway. "Please, stay an extra day or two for me."

"I don't want to, Nick." She expelled a sigh. "I want to go home."

The satiny tone of her voice roused a visceral need. There was nothing he wanted more than to get Delaney back home and into his arms where she belonged but he couldn't jeopardize her recovery. "I'll stay with you here. We'll watch television, play cards… It'll be great." He chuckled at her look of disgust. "What? You afraid I'll beat you in a game of Crazy Eights?"

"Is there something you're not telling me?" she demanded. "Why are you trying to keep me here?"

"Nothing other than I love you." Flooded by a sudden tide of emotion, Nick's heart lurched. He meant it. There was nothing she needed to know other than he loved her. "I want you home. As soon as you're ready to safely come home, trust me, I'll take you. I'll take you home on horseback if it'll make you happy, but not yet. Besides, there's something I want to talk to you about." Delaney's gaze sharpened, as if she *knew* there was something he'd been hiding. Tapping a finger to her nose, he said, "Stop. You're so suspicious. It's nothing bad." Drawing her hand onto his jean-legged thigh, he stroked the length of her fingers, her nails. He wanted to feel and experience every inch of her, reassuring himself she was here and she was okay. Would stay that way. Gazing into her expectant eyes, he teetered on how to begin. "I want to talk to you about where we go from here."

"Where we go?" she asked, appearing confused.

"Yes. I've been doing some thinking, and I'm not sure I want to fly halfway across the world looking at properties."

"What? Why not?"

He shrugged, mildly amused. "You won't come with me…and I want to stay here with you."

"Nick. You can't give up your hotels because of what happened. You *have* to go. You love your job. Shoot, it's not a job, it's your *life*."

She was his life. If he'd learned anything in the last few days it was that. Nick would gladly give up his hotels if it meant keeping Delaney safe, secure. "It's not worth it."

"Nick. I'll go. If this is your way of forcing me to go with you, I'll go."

He laughed softly. "That easy, huh? Forcing you? And what about your stinky horses?"

Delaney screwed her expression. "Leave my stinky horses out of this. If you want me to go with you, I will. I'm your wife, it's what I want."

Nick laughed heartily. "Wow, you're a bad liar!"

And he loved her for it. He loved that she wore her emotions like she wore her ratty jeans. *In your face, I don't care what you think.* Her ferocity was one of the things he liked best about her. "You couldn't stand to be away from Sadie for more than a week. No, make that less than a week," he said, instantly regretting the mention of her mare.

Delaney's fire went out, replaced by longing. "How is Sadie? Is she okay?"

Nick wondered how much Felicity had told her mother. She'd said she kept her report brief and to the point, assuring her mom that all the horses were fine. Did Delaney know that one had been burned? Her stables were in complete ruin? That it would take months to get them back up and running? Shaking the supposition from his mind, he replied, "Sadie's fine. I'm sure she's chomping at the bit for your return."

"And the others?"

"They're fine," he said flatly. "The horses are fine, the hotel is fine. Everyone is fine." Except him. He wasn't fine. He was having odd feelings and desires and he wanted to know if he was alone. "I understand Sadie is your baby and you're worried about her, but maybe you need another one to distract you."

"Why would I get another horse?"

Nick didn't say a word. He simply stared. Delaney stared back. She snapped her mouth closed, an uneasy realization flitting across her sable-soft eyes, erecting a wall in its wake.

"Is it so bad an idea?"

Delaney slapped her glance to the opposite side of the room in a complete dodge. Her hand within his tugged slightly for release.

Nick tightened his hold. "Have you ever thought about it?"

"About a child?" she blurted.

He nodded, pleased to hear her say the words.

"Now who's insane?" she asked, flipping her gaze to the ceiling, then down again to face him. "Do you know I'm almost forty years old?"

"And in excellent shape. Why, you just had brain surgery and you're already chomping at the bit to go home. Don't know many twenty-somethings who could do the same."

"Nick."

"Delaney."

She paled. "You want a baby?"

"I do," he replied, surprised by a sudden rush of warmth flowing through him. Swimming, sweeping, it filled him with a wonderful joy. He didn't realize how much he wanted a child until now. "I want *your* baby."

Plucking her hand from his hold, she crossed her arms over her chest. "Maybe I'd better stay in this hospital bed a few more days after all."

Chapter Thirty

Cal strolled into the hotel lobby, his heart lighter than it had been in days. Jeremiah was in jail. Travis and Delaney were on the mend. The Ladd boys had been picked up and would be charged with the robbery, provided the hair sample belonged to one of them. But Cal didn't have a single doubt they were responsible. The front clerk and gift shop cashier both identified the photos on Travis' phone as the man they'd seen in the hotel. All the police had left to do was connect Jeremiah to the arson and they were finished. Except for the ugly business of Jillian Devane. But she was Nick's problem. Cal's problems were over.

Carrying the cardboard box around the front desk, he nodded good morning to the clerks as he headed for the office. Nine o'clock, he'd already taken his customary stroll around the property, this time with Emily in tow, the two sharing memories of Arizona as they admired the Tennessee landscape. Despite everything that had happened during her stay she was already planning her next trip and he couldn't be more pleased. Rounding into the office, he stopped suddenly. Malcolm and Nick were in the middle of what appeared to be a meeting. "Good morning."

"Good morning," Malcolm returned, his gaze cheerful but curious.

"What's got you so chipper today?" Nick asked, eyeing the box in his hands.

Cal grinned. "Only everything." Setting the box of letters on top of a file cabinet, he blew a breath of air and replied, "Not the least of which being I've solved Troy's legal problems."

"What?" Nick stood in a sweep of motion. "What do you mean, solved them?"

"My mother is dropping her support for Jack, which means he'll drop the charges like a hot potato fry," Cal quipped merrily.

"Explain."

Looking into the eyes of his boss, Cal said, "I convinced my mother her reasons for supporting Jack were misguided and she need no longer continue the charade."

"And she listened to you?"

"What changed?" Malcolm asked, rising from his seat behind the desk.

Cal tapped the box and said, "Let's just say I used a little personal persuasion." Growing more serious, he addressed Nick. "This box is for Delaney. They're love letters between her mother and my father. I have his permission to share them with her," Cal added, amused by their mouth-agape stares. "They tell a beautiful story and I thought she'd like to have them." Cal didn't mention the one he removed for his mother, the one that had changed her heart.

"Where did you get them?"

"My daddy had them in the attic. I went looking for my—things," Cal said, sliding over any explanation as to his guns, his desire for revenge. They were no longer pertinent. Jeremiah was safely stowed away in jail and his family was safe. "I found this box of letters."

"Your dad kept them all these years?" Malcolm asked, stunned by the revelation.

Cal nodded. "He did. Said he forgot they were there when I told him about them." A confession he felt compelled to reveal after his mother's about-face. She would go to her husband and he had to be prepared. Cal had never considered himself a matchmaker before, but getting his parents back together felt good. Real good. Better, it felt right. Theirs was a love that should flourish and prosper. They had a family to think about, a future, and their past had no place in the family portrait.

Nick and Malcolm exchanged a glance, a mutual doubt regarding an old man's memory. Cal shared their skepticism but didn't much care whether his daddy had been pining away all these years or not. So long as he was doing what was right by his momma today was all that mattered. "Is Troy around? I'd like to give him the good news in person."

"I think he's up at the barn," Malcolm said.

"Good." Not scheduled to work today, Cal turned to go

"Cal," Nick stopped him.

"Yes?"

"Thanks."

Clasping Nick's hand in a firm handshake, he grinned, pleasure filling him clear up to the brim. "You're welcome. Give Delaney my best, will you?"

"Sure thing."

"Now if you don't mind, I'm going to deliver the good news."

"Where's Cal?"

Nick, Malcolm and Cal stilled as the familiar voice bellowed through the lobby. A sliver of rancor split Cal's excitement as the anticipated confrontation with his brother Jack loomed front and center. Inhaling a deep breath, he winked. "I'll take this one."

Walking out of the office, Cal settled his gaze squarely on his brother's shoulders across the lobby desk. Jillian Devane hovered by his side, her cat eyes smoldering with carnal pleasure. "What do you need, Jack?" Unwilling to allow any barriers between them, Cal circled out from behind the desk, noting Nick and Malcolm did the same. For the moment they hung behind him.

"What the hell did you do to Momma? She's dropping her support for my case and threatening to pull her money if I don't drop the charges against the Parker kid."

"Wise woman."

Jack stepped toward him and shoved a finger in Cal's face. "You're the cause."

"What? Momma finally came to her senses and you're giving me the credit?" Cal shook his head and knocked Jack's finger from his personal space. "I'm only glad to see she finally tossed you and your lies into the garbage where you belong."

"Don't get cute with me," Jack hissed, bridling on the verge of losing control. "I know you had something to do with it, and I want to know what."

Cal laughed, mocking him openly. "Looks like you've lost your touch, brother. Soon enough, Ms. Devane here will see through your façade as well, though it won't matter much, not with you in jail and all."

"I'm not going to jail," he snarled. "That punk Parker kid is."

"Don't think so. Not with Delaney up and around and ready to testify against you."

Surprise lit up in both Jack and Jillian's expressions.

"That's right," Nick said, flicking an insulting glance toward Jillian. "Delaney is only too ready to put your butt behind bars where it belongs."

Jack didn't back down but he didn't rebut. Jillian did. "Too bad," she said to Nick, pushing out her glossy lips. "She really is a waste on your time and energy."

"Keep it up Jillian," Nick warned. "Keep poking until I bite, because when I do, it's going to hurt. Really hurt." He leaned down and came to within inches of her face. "I know you had something to do with the fire. It has your fingerprints written all over it. And when I figure it out, I won't stop until I see you in prison right along with your boyfriend, here." Straightening to his full six-foot-four stature, Nick taunted, "Oh, wait. There won't be any men where you're going. Only big, mean women who would love to get their hands on the likes of *you*."

A flash of horror graced her face before she revived the nasty beast within, retorting, "You will never have the pleasure, *amorzhino*. I am not going anywhere near a prison."

"Don't be so sure about that. Jeremiah's in custody and will start singing like a canary. Bet your name comes up."

Jack locked onto Jillian. "What's he talking about?"

Ignoring him, she replied smugly, "I have admirers eve-rywhere, you know that. It means nothing."

Jack grew more agitated by the second. Aiming all bar-rels at Jillian he repeated, "What the hell's going on? What's Jeremiah in jail for?"

Cal chuckled under his breath, amused by his brother's complete and total shock. Seems Jack might have been nur-turing a real affection for the woman, a woman who clearly didn't return the sentiment. Nick might be onto something, putting her and Jeremiah together. It was his cell phone they used to detonate the bomb. Fire was her specialty. "Haven't you heard?" Cal asked his brother. "Jeremiah and the Ladd boys have been up to their old tricks."

Jack looked as if he'd been sucker-punched. "The Ladd boys? Robby and Billy?"

"You betcha," Cal replied. At least Jack had been smart enough to avoid getting wrapped up with Jeremiah and those boys, though Jillian made up for the three of them and then some.

"That's right, Jillian," Nick added. "Seems the explosive device was detonated with Jeremiah's phone. Any idea why that might be?"

She tilted up her face. "None."

Nick crossed arms over his chest, staring down at her with a wry smile. "Guess we'll see what the police come up with, huh?" She simply smirked in response. "Oh, and don't go anywhere," he added, his smile gaining steam. "The police will surely want to question you at length."

The lobby door opened and Officer Griffin breezed in, stopping cold. The sight of Jillian Devane had lassoed his complete attention. Kicking into gear, he marched over and said, "Ms. Devane. Glad to see you're still here." She glared at him, all pretense of politeness extinguished as he said, "I'd like to ask you a few questions."

"See." Nick leaned down and murmured close to her ear, "Told you so."

"What do you want, Detective? I believe I've already spoken with you regarding my whereabouts on the night in question."

"Yes, yes you did and your alibi checks out. The boy at the bar said you were with him all evening. Jeremiah said you were with him the next night, and that's when he lost his cell phone."

Jack stepped away from her, drawing an unmistakable line of separation between the two for the officer to take note. Jillian brushed a haughty glance over Jack and replied thinly, "It is not a crime to enjoy the company of men, nor is it a crime to enjoy a *stupid* man."

Officer Griffin cocked his head and pursed his lips. "That might be so, but there's something else. We found scraps of a bag at the site of the explosion. A fancy bag." He looked at the leather purse slung over her shoulder. It was a name brand designer style. "Kinda like the one you're carrying now."

Pulling the bag more snugly against her body, Jillian replied, "That proves nothing. Many people carry a bag exactly like this one."

He smiled, nodded cordially. "Cost a pretty penny from what I understand." Officer Griffin ran his tongue over his teeth, then smacked his lips. "Yep. So expensive, they tag them with serial numbers." He looked Jillian square in the eye and asked, "Did you know that?"

She said nothing, simply stared at him. "Yeah, seems they register the serial numbers at time of purchase. So you know it's not a fake." With a roll of his eyes, he said, "Well, I've never heard of such a thing. You know, we don't have much of a market for those fancy bags around here, but they do in Chattanooga. Seems you recently purchased a purse in a mall over there."

Nick, Malcolm and Cal turned their eye on to Jillian. *Wasn't that interesting?*

"Now why would you do that when you already have a nice purse?"

Jillian laughed. "I have hundreds of purses, Officer. I buy them like you buy your French fries." Touching her gaze to his oversized midsection, she added, "But then we all have our addictions, don't we?"

"So you won't mind going to your room to get the purse in question? It's brown leather material, unlike the black one you're holding there."

She stilled, drawing her black purse close. Amber eyes heated as they sharpened on Officer Griffin. Jillian held him in her gaze, as though she were hypnotizing him into submission, before she replied coolly, "Of course. It is no problem at all."

"Wonder if it's the same purse you were carrying when you paid Delaney that little visit the day before the fire?" Nick posed, his pleasure barely concealed.

Cal fully expected claws to flash from Jillian's fingertips and slash the skin from Nick's face.

"I'm leaving," Jack announced, heading for the door without awaiting a response.

Noting the utter loathing in his brother's gaze as he took stock of the group, Cal chimed in, "I've got a few things I need to do myself."

There was nothing more for him to do here. Nick would see that Jillian followed instructions. Malcolm would manage the hotel, freeing him to seek out Troy and deliver the good news. Good news Cal couldn't wait to share. Catching the door from his brother's exit, he said, "Don't go anywhere, Jack. We plan on pursuing trial as scheduled.

Chapter Thirty-One

Felicity remained a fixture by Travis' bedside. Leaning back in the hard-cushioned chair, she stared at Travis' inert figure outlined beneath the thin white blanket. The breathing apparatus had been removed, but the tubes in his arm remained. A feeding tube. Because Travis wasn't able to eat for himself. He was still considered critical. Stable, but critical. Felicity didn't care much about the terminology of his condition. She only cared that he was alive and going to get better.

Waiting for him to regain consciousness was the hardest. There were so many things she wanted to say to him, so many things she wanted to share. The horse that had been hurt during the stampede was doing well, the one burned in the fire was on the mend. Hotel Ladd's veterinarian had been ministering to the animal since the blaze, asserting his wounds would leave scars, but they'd heal. Anger pricked at her heart. Because a selfish woman had it out for Nick and her mother.

"Felicity?"

The feather voice cut through her reverie. Felicity bolted forward. "Travis?"

His eyes were closed. Long brown lashes fluttered softly against his lightly tanned skin. "Felicity..." he breathed the word. "*Felicity.*"

Tears sprang to her eyes as she reached for his upper arm. "Travis, it's me. I'm here," she replied eagerly.

He offered a subtle nod of his head. Did he know where he was? Did he remember what happened? How close he'd come to dying?

For her. On her behalf. Travis almost lost his life because, once again, he'd stepped in to protect her. "Travis, can you hear me?"

Nodding slightly, he turned his head toward her.

"How do you feel?"

"Hurt."

A lot, she wondered? Was he in severe pain? Did he need medicine? Should she call for someone? Thoughts and fears tumbled over one another as she watched him open his eyes.

"Travis," she murmured, clamping her palm around his arm.

Concentrating on her face, he seemed to struggle to get her in focus. "Felicity. You're okay."

She drew back. *Travis was worried about her*? Did he not know what happened?

"I'm so glad..." Travis closed his eyes and her heart stopped.

She squeezed his arm. "Travis."

He smiled, opened his eyes again. "I was so worried about you," he said drowsily.

"I'm okay. I'm totally okay. How are you?"

Reaching down, she laced her fingers through his, closing her hand over his. "Do you need pain medicine?"

"Nah."

Felicity was disturbed by his slow speech but reassured herself it was normal. He'd been shot, he was worn out from the surgery. The doctor said his recovery would take some time. Patience. But Felicity didn't have any more patience! She wanted him well and she wanted it now. "Have you seen your parents?" she asked, giving him space to regain his strength. She knew they had but wanted to see if he remembered. "They've been here the whole time."

"Yeah... My mom was cryin'."

Of course she was! You can't see yourself. You look awful, horrible. Felicity completely understood why his mother would break down and cry. She couldn't stand to see Travis this way either. His strong body was motionless, draped in a pajama-like gown, his chest beneath covered in gauze. Felicity feared to touch him. A guy who was strong and muscular, yet she feared she'd hurt him somehow. Brushing building tears from her eyes, Felicity forced tears from her eyes. She wanted to be the strong one. She wanted to be brave for Travis like he'd been for her. "Do you remember what happened?"

"Jeremiah shot me."

Felicity gulped. Blunt. Straight to the point. "Yes. Do you remember why?"

The spirit returned to his dark eyes, thrashed within the depths of brown. "He was trying to get you into his truck. He...and those other guys."

Relieved to hear the old Travis rearing up, she nodded. "The Ladd boys. Those men were Albert's sons."

His gaze leapt. "Albert's?"

"Yes. It looks like they're the ones who sent Jeremiah the money to get out of jail."

"Fifty thousand dollars?"

Travis flinched and her heart kicked. She squeezed his hand. "Are you okay?"

"Fine," he murmured willfully. "They traced the wire then?"

"Jeremiah confessed. Said the boys robbed a bank in North Carolina to pay the money. The police are checking into it now."

"Why would they do that?"

"Gold." Felicity slumped at the mention. Finding gold on the property had brought nothing but trouble to them since the day they discovered it. "Jeremiah told the men there was gold on the property and they could share in it. He'd show them where it was so long as they bailed him out."

"And they did it?"

"Guess they're not very bright." That, or greed made people do terrible things. Felicity recalled Clem Sweeney and his attempt on her mother's life over the gold. Jeremiah caused trouble the last time he was in town for the very same reason, including threatening Uncle Ernie's life. Riled by the thoughts, Felicity shoved them aside. Clem was in jail. Jeremiah was in jail. Her mother and Travis were safe.

"What about your father?" Travis asked.

The question stirred mixed feelings. "He's not responsible for the fire," she said, assuming that's what Travis was after. She'd been wrong about him. According to Nick, it had been Jillian all along. Travis thought Jeremiah had had something to do with it but it didn't look like it. His phone had been used, but Nick believed Jillian stole it to make the call and then got rid of it somehow. They were still looking for it in hopes of gathering more evidence against her. Seems she really had it out for Nick and her mom.

Breathing in deeply, Felicity spewed a sigh. Guess they were both wrong. Curling her hands around the fleshy palm of Travis' thumb, she squeezed gently. "Jillian is the one who set off the explosion in the stables that caused the fire. They arrested her at the hotel, but Nick says it's going to be a long-drawn-out battle now that her lawyers have been called in." Lawyers. She rested her gaze on Travis, his boyish face and sweet brown eyes. He was going to be a lawyer someday. A lawyer who fought to protect the innocent and not the guilty—like her father and Jillian. "There is good news where my father's concerned. He's dropped the charges against Troy."

"He did?"

Felicity nodded, disturbed by the sudden increase in rhythm on the monitor above. Darting her gaze between machines and man, she wondered, was she saying too much? But this was good news they were discussing. It couldn't be bad for him, could it?

"Why would he drop the charges?" Travis asked.

"Somehow Cal convinced his mother to stop supporting him in his vendetta, and Nick said without her support, my father has no chance of getting Troy put in jail. Who, by the way, has his job back at the hotel," she added brightly, wondering how Travis would feel about it.

"Good. He deserves it."

Floored by his response, she ventured, "Really? You really mean that?"

Settling on her, Travis slid his gaze down toward their clasped hands. He rubbed the side of his thumb back and forth across her fingers. "Whatever you might think of me, I don't hate my brother. We have our differences...but I don't hate him. He never deserved to go to jail for something he didn't do."

"But you agreed with your parents. You said it was good to teach him a lesson and let him sit in jail."

Travis sighed, taking a minute before saying, "I still do. But Troy's a tough kid. One night in jail wasn't gonna hurt him. It was to give him time to think. Hit the reset button."

Surprised by the revelation, Felicity mulled over his words. She couldn't exactly disagree with him. It was true. Troy was tough. He didn't take crap from anyone, didn't turn away from danger. She recalled how he pulled her and Blue from the stables. The fire was blazing around them yet he didn't hesitate. Troy grabbed her, grabbed her horse and hauled them both outside to safety. Peering at Travis, she realized he'd done the same. He went in after the horses. He'd been on his way to Blue when she called out his name, but then detoured when he saw her mom was in trouble. When a burning rafter fell, almost hitting her, he'd pushed her out of the way and carried her out to safety.

Thinking back, Travis and Troy were more similar than she'd realized. Twins, brothers, they were kindred spirits. Their temperaments varied, as did their style, but their hearts were one and the same. Always had been.

"I never thanked you for saving my mom."

"No need."

His modesty tugged at her heart. They both knew otherwise. Without Travis' heroic efforts, her mom might not be alive today. But that was Travis. Strong and brave. Priceless. "I'm sorry for what I said, the way I acted," she said, the words spilling out of her control. "I didn't mean it. I picked the *right* one. I never wanted Troy over you. I always wanted you."

Hurt washed through his gaze. Had she said too much? The wrong thing? She didn't mean to. She wanted to say everything right, make everything right.

She dropped her head forward. "Travis, I'm sorry for getting mad at you. I was wrong."

For a moment, nothing moved between them. Above, monitors recorded the beat of his heart, machines beeped, fluid dripped from a bag into a tube in his arm. Sitting in silence, Felicity felt trapped by her confession. Humbled by circumstance. She'd never meant to hurt Travis. He'd always been the brother she'd wanted. Since the day the three entered high school, she'd known. He and Troy had fought over her and she enjoyed it. They'd made declaration after declaration, vied for her attention, swore their undying devotion, but Felicity had always known. She'd never loved Troy. Her heart had always belonged to Travis. The heart-shaped pendant at her breast represented that promise. Felicity and Travis. Forever.

It had only been since college that things changed. Only since his rigid ideology stepped between them had she doubted her feelings for him. Travis was so set on his path, so determined that his way of doing things was the right way and everyone else was wrong. When Troy announced he wasn't going to college last summer, Travis came undone. He'd lost it. He'd been mean and it was a side to him she'd never seen before.

Of course Troy followed suit with a slew of his own ugly words, and she found herself torn between them. Then Casey entered the picture and the whole thing blew up in Felicity's face. She'd never been friends with Casey during school, but when it was proven she was family, all that changed. Casey was blood. Her mother had her split the property and encouraged her to start fresh. Felicity did and the two became fast friends. When Casey and Troy became an item, Felicity had sided with them against Travis because of his unyielding stance against them. Strangely, the idea felt shameful to her now. Like she'd dumped Travis and took up for Troy.

Honing in on him, his reserve, Felicity thought it felt shameful because it was. "I'm sorry, Travis. I haven't been a very good girlfriend."

"That's not true," he said and a sadness swamped his gaze. "I was wrong to push. You were right to tell me to back off. Put a cork in it," he added sheepishly.

Shocked by his recall, she remembered the day well. Drifting through the past, she revisited the afternoon. They'd been riding along the river and she wanted him to stop insulting Troy, wanted him to accept his brother's choices, no matter what. But Travis refused, instead comparing Troy to her father. They'd both quit their jobs, made choices by the spit of their temper. Felicity had been trying to see the good in people while Travis was stomping out her sunshine.

She'd been mad. Partly because it was true. Troy hadn't been able to hold down a job. Her father was a skunk. Travis had been right. She'd been wrong.

Well, not totally wrong. Her father was a louse but Troy wasn't. A smile touched her heart. He was a cowboy. Now he was a father and a good one at that.

"Felicity." Travis tugged at her hand, encouraging her to look at him. She obliged, a sharp heartache weaving through years of memories as she clung to his gaze. "I don't blame you for saying the things you did. I can get bull-headed, I know it, but I should have let you have your say, make your own decisions. I haven't been trying to coddle you. Well, not really." He walked the statement back with a small smile. "I just want you to be okay. It doesn't mean I don't think you can take care of yourself. I do. I *know* you can. I just want you to need me." He stilled, brown eyes shining as he asked, "Is that so bad?"

"No, Travis, *no*. It's not bad at all. I do need you. A lot." Images of Jeremiah flashed through her mind's eye, the Ladd brothers... If that didn't prove she needed Travis, Felicity didn't know what did! "I'll always need you but—"

When she hesitated, he asked, "But?"

"Sometimes, maybe the *way* I'll need you will change."

He chuckled, the sound warm and natural. "I get it. Women. Can't live with 'em, can't live without 'em."

She dished out a pout. "Travis."

"I'm *kidding*." Fixing his gaze on their hands, he tugged at their hold. "I just want you to love me."

"I do, Travis. So much," Felicity insisted and meant it, from the very core of her being. She loved Travis, for what he stood for, where he came from...even how he wanted to take charge. It made him strong in her eyes, a man who would make a solid partner in life, like Nick was for her mom. Travis would be that man. And she wanted him to be hers.

"Will you marry me?"

She blinked. A rash of nerves sprinted through her belly. "Marry you?"

He nodded. "When we graduate college, will you marry me?"

Love and adoration toppled through her. He wanted to marry her. *Marry her*. "Yes. Yes, Travis. I'll marry you," she gushed.

He grinned and cocked an eyebrow. "Now listen, this isn't my proposal. For that I'm going to do it right. I just wanted you to promise." Travis angled his head and pinned her with a teasing gaze. "I don't want you running off with some other guy while I'm in law school."

Felicity erupted into a giggle. *Why would she do that*?

There was no other guy in the world for her but Travis. Clutching hold of him, she said, "I love you," pained by words she hadn't uttered often enough. "I love you."

Chapter Thirty-Two

Ashley Fulmer waved them over from across the lawn, a host of jangles sliding down her forearm, a United States Flag emblem glittering in the sun against the blue of her shirt. Standing beside her, Fran Jones grinned, waved wildly, her hair loose and shining a vibrant red in the sunlight of a cloud-less May afternoon. Surrounded by her inner circle--her mom and Nick, Malcolm, Lacy, Emma Jane and Travis—Felicity waved back. Warmed by the sight of the two women, Felicity was glad to see Fran in attendance. It meant Jimmy Sweeney was doing well in his role as Assistant Manager of Fran's Diner.

Taking in the scent of smoky barbecue and live country music, the tangle of final exams cleared from her mind. She was home. Secure in the lap of love and comfort. The last nine months had been tough. After nearly losing her mom in a fire and Travis to a gunshot wound, Felicity struggled to maintain focus on her studies at college. She'd wanted to forego the school year altogether to stay home and help care for the two of them, but her mother wouldn't have it. *You're going to school, period.* Travis echoed the sentiment, insist-ing Felicity needed to stay on course. He'd return to school after a semester of recovery and catch up for lost time by tak-ing extra classes. Felicity had resisted but in the end, Nick convinced her to go. Her mom was in good hands. Travis would be watched twenty-four-seven by his parents.

More importantly, Nick said, Felicity needed to take care of herself and get her life back to normal. Inhaling the sight of her family and friends, a yard filled with people she grew up with, Felicity couldn't disagree with him. Normal was good. Welcome. After what Jeremiah Ladd and Jillian Devane had done to her family, Felicity was grateful to be home without worry or stress. And there was no place like Ashley's annual picnic to lift a girl's spirits and take her mind off her troubles.

"Ashley's been waiting to see you," Delaney said, nudging her forward. "Why don't you go on ahead and we'll get some drinks and join you."

Peering into brown eyes that shone with affection, Felicity hesitated. Her mom's blonde hair was shorter now, cut shoulder-length after her hospital ordeal. With an abundance of long, thick hair, she could have camouflaged the missing section but opted against it. Hair would grow back, she said. She was ready for a change. Not only shorter, there were wisps of long bangs framing her face and Felicity thought the style made her look younger. Nick approved as well, but that was nothing new. He approved of most things her mother did.

Glancing up at him, he looked ever the outdoorsman in his plaid shirt, jeans and boots. Broad shoulders, gentle smile, Felicity felt a pinprick of longing. Nick had been her mother's rock. He never left her side, made sure she followed doctor's orders, didn't return to work too soon. He also rebuilt her stables in less than six months to ensure she had somewhere to go when she was healthy enough. She did, and according to all sources, business was back to normal.

But they were set to travel at the end of the summer, scouting a location for the next Harris Hotel and Felicity would miss her. She was happy for her mom but knowing she wasn't an hour's drive away would be hard. Exhaling heavily, she released the clutch of tension. Felicity understood it was time to let go. She was an adult and needed to grow into her own life. Trouble was, she liked the one she had now.

"C'mon, Felicity," Travis said, placing a hand to the small of her back. "Let's go say hi to Ashley."

Heartbeats peppered her breast. Transported back to high school when Travis' every touch electrified, Felicity shook the gray clouds from her reverie. Strong and steadfast, he was her future—a gorgeous one at that in his red T-shirt, his silky brown hair combed slightly off to the side of his face, dark eyes simmering as they held her close. He'd only arrived home from college yesterday and Felicity was still getting used to having him close. After everything they'd been through together, it felt good to be back together. Really good and she was eager to spend the afternoon by his side. "Let's," she agreed excitedly.

Clasping hands, Travis and Felicity headed for Ashley.

"They've come a long way," Malcolm said, watching them go.

Delaney nodded, overwhelmed with pride and love as a deep ache wound through her heart. Felicity shouldn't have had to overcome anything, yet she had. Strong and bright, she had come through with amazing brilliance. Travis had faced a tougher road, battling a wound infection that nearly took his life, but he overcame the odds and stood firmly entrenched by her daughter's side as though nothing had ever happened. "They certainly have."

Catching Emma Jane's flying hand, Malcolm cupped it within his, wiggling it playfully. "No, hitting."

The chubby baby squealed in delight. "No, Daddy!"

The group laughed as Lacy tapped a finger to the little girl's nose. "Listen to your Daddy," she said, then to the adults, "I think putting the bad guys behind bars helped."

"I think you're right," Delaney agreed. "It gave Felicity the peace of mind she needed to let go." A feat accomplished in no small part because of Lacy. After her initial recognition of the Ladd boys in the cell phone photo, the police were able to track them down and hold them on suspicion of robbery. Once Travis was physically able, he gave a complete statement to the police, and combined with Felicity's account of events, Jeremiah was easily convicted. He was currently trying to appeal the verdict, but his case would go nowhere. He had no grounds. Robby and Billy were in jail too, thanks to the eyewitness testimony of the hotel staff.

"Can't say as I blame her," Nick said. "Knowing Jillian is finally behind bars where she belongs is a nice feeling and all too ironic that it was her penchant for expensive handbags that sealed her fate." He hugged Delaney to his side. "Sure makes traveling a whole lot easier knowing she won't be able to create trouble while we're away."

"Where are ya'll going?" Lacy asked, her big blue eyes latching onto Delaney. "Have you decided, yet?"

Touching her gaze briefly to Lacy's growing midsection, Delaney smiled. "He won't tell me. Only that it's warm and I won't need much in the way of clothing."

Lacy giggled. "Good for you, Nick Harris. It's about time Delaney got out of this town and saw something of the world." Running a hand over the top of her belly, she said, "Malcolm and I have plans to go the Caribbean in January."

Delaney gaped at her. "So soon? What about the baby?"

"Well, why not? John Christopher will be four-months-old by then and plenty ready for travel."

"You want to bring a newborn to the islands? Emma Jane, too?"

"I have children," Lacy snipped. "I'm going to the islands. Where's the problem?"

Malcolm laughed. "Lacy refuses to allow motherhood to stop her from going places." He shook his head, adding, "And I'm not going to argue with her." Bouncing Emma Jane in his arms, he said, "Our trip to California with this princess was a breeze and I have no doubt John Christopher will be just as easy. Besides, Rosalie will be joining us."

Delaney brushed the bangs from her eyes, then tucked her hands into the front pockets of her jeans. "Now it makes sense." Rosalie was their live-in nanny. She'd handle the babies while Malcolm and Lacy enjoyed their trip.

"Does Rosalie have a sister?" Nick asked, circling his arms around Delaney's waist.

"Why?" Lacy asked, then her eyes rounded, locking onto Delaney. "*Are you pregnant*?"

"No," Delaney snapped.

"Not yet," Nick quipped, tightening his grip against Delaney's struggle to get free. "But it's wise to be prepared, don't you think?"

Malcolm's pale blue eyes danced beneath the black of his brow, his tanned skin glowing as youthfully as the ivory-pink cheeks of his daughter. Despite the shock of gray hair, Malcolm looked much younger than his forty-plus years. "I think it's perfect. You and Troy will have those kids on horseback, jumping creeks before they can *walk*."

"Someone call my name?" Troy asked, strolling up behind them with Casey and Cassidy Jo in tow. As usual, he was decked out in black T-shirt and cowboy hat, his dark eyes twinkling mischievously. Casey wore a cute blue sundress and boots, Cassidy Jo dressed nearly identical, plus a matching hat to protect her fair skin. Next to one another, Cassidy Jo and Emma Jane could be sisters, the two boasted the same black hair and blue eyes. That Owens blood line sure was a strong one, Delaney mused.

"We were talking about Delaney's new baby."

Troy and Casey dropped their jaws. "You're pregnant?" he asked.

"No, Troy, I'm not pregnant," she said, breaking away from Nick's grasp. "These men are having fun at my expense."

Casey poked an elbow into his side and he said, "I'm not sayin' it would be a bad thing...just...ya know..." Troy gave up explanation with a sheepish smile.

"Don't worry. I'm not offended. Babies are not what you expect from women my age."

"There's nothing wrong with women your age having babies," Nick said. "Look at Lacy. She's living proof."

Delaney swiped her with a glance and grunted.

"Where's Felicity?" Casey asked, seemingly eager to change subjects.

Delaney pointed. "She and Travis went to say hello to Ashley."

"Oh, good. I'm glad she's here. I wanted to ask her if she and Travis wanted to go riding after the picnic."

"Felicity doesn't need much prodding when it comes to a ride with Blue," Delaney said. "She'd been riding every day since she arrived home last weekend."

Casey beamed. "C'mon, Troy. Let's go."

Cassidy Jo reached her arms out for him and with a wry smile, he tipped his hat and took his daughter from her mother. "Yes, dear. Your wish is my command."

Delaney chuckled. Troy had certainly adapted to married life and did so with obvious pleasure. Because he was happy, she deemed. Now that he had a future to look forward, he focused on his wife and child and never looked back. Jack had not only dropped the charges but left town under the cover of night. Delaney suspected he left the state. Knowing she could press charges against him, Jack would want to be as far away from Tennessee as he could get. A good thing.

"Let's go get those drinks," Nick said.

Following him, the group headed to the food table where pitchers of lemonade and sweet tea sat in tubs of ice. Beside them, crowded on a red and white checkered tablecloth, bowls of collards and green beans competed for space with mashed potatoes and coleslaw alongside platters of fried chicken and biscuits and baskets filled with cornbread. Dessert was on a second table and consisted of pies and cobblers, cookies and jams, just to name a few. The grilled chicken, ribs and burgers would be found over near Ashley's husband, Booker. Faithfully manning the grill, he refused to let his meat sit cold on a table, making guests come to him for their serving.

Nick grabbed four red Solo cups and poured a round of tea for each.

"I'll have water," Lacy said.

Malcolm reached down into a cooler and grabbed her a bottle.

Breaking from a conversation with his brother, Cal and Annie Foster sauntered over. "I was wondering if ya'll would make it," Cal said good-naturedly.

Delaney balked. "Are you kidding? If I missed one of Ashley's Memorial Day picnics, she'd have my hide."

Cal laughed. "True."

"Besides, who'd want to miss this food?" Delaney extended her hand out over the buffet. "It's a feast fit for kings!"

"That it is."

"Casey is so happy to have Felicity home," Annie said, placing a hand over the breast of her frilly white blouse. "She really misses her when she's away."

Delaney nodded, admiring the white diamond-bezel watch on Annie's wrist. She thought it sporty yet feminine and perfectly suited for Cal's wife. She was a woman of means now, and a damn good salon manager. "Has she given any more thought to going to college?"

"The girls have talked about it, but I don't think Casey is ready to leave Troy for even a month at a time, let alone four. She's content to finish out her two-year degree at the community college." Annie shrugged. "We'll see where she goes from there."

"Never too late," Nick pitched in with a wink.

Delaney knew full well he was dually referring to her and motherhood, but she refused to indulge him by acknowledging the same. The mere thought of having a baby unnerved her. A newborn? At her age? Though watching Lacy load a plate with food, she had to admit, the woman pulled it off rather well. Baby number two hadn't made a dent in her lifestyle. Delaney was only a few years older. Would it really be that bad?

"Malcolm tells me your parents are renewing their vows," Nick said, sliding an arm around Delaney's shoulders. "Would they like to have the ceremony at the hotel? It's on me, as a wedding gift."

Cal shook his head. "Appreciate the offer, but I think they're set on doing so at the ranch. They want an intimate ceremony with only family in tow."

"That sounds about right," Nick agreed. "Family is what counts."

Delaney felt a tremor race through her and leaned into the warmth of Nick's body. She was happy for Gerald and Victoria but couldn't shake the thought of what might have been. If Ernie hadn't stepped between them, she had no doubt her mom would have married Gerald. Their love was clearly evident in the words scrawled across the pages she'd read. When Cal had shared them with her, her first reaction had been one of gratitude. But as she read the final word, her heart filled with regret. Delaney couldn't help but feel her mother's pain. In the end, it had been a love lost. Replaced with another, perhaps, but nothing could diminish the emotion held in those envelopes.

Settling her gaze on Cal, Delaney thought about his family. Did he feel it, too? Did he understand what really happened all those years ago?

As though reading her thoughts, Cal's gaze lingered on hers, mellowing as if accepting things neither of them could change. He seemed to look straight into her mind and say, "It wasn't meant to be."

Life was funny that way, taking twists and turns like a mountain trail. Follow it long enough and one can stumble on unexpected beauty, like Zack's Falls. Take risks, explore unchartered territory, and get treated to a panorama vista seen only from the mountaintop.

Inhaling deeply, Delaney took in the people around her, the mountain ridge in the distance, the fields of green dotted with blossoms. This was the heartland. Her home. She'd found gold on this land, in more ways than one. Nick Harris was a gem, more precious to her than a valley full of shimmery metal. Casting her gaze to Felicity, Delaney believed the same held true for her daughter. Travis was a special kid. A keeper. Hands entwined, Felicity and Travis seemed content. Casey and Troy, Annie and Cal, Lacy and Malcolm...they'd all found true love in these hills. They all had bright futures to look forward. Eyes drifting upward, Delaney closed her eyes and thanked God for her good fortune. Life was good in "these parts." She smiled. Better than good.

# # #

The End

Southern Fried Cabbage

1 head of cabbage, cored and sliced into 2 in. square pieces
1 sweet onion, sliced, "half" the rings
4 TBSP butter
pinch of white sugar
salt & pepper to taste

Heat large sauté pan to medium heat and add butter. When butter melts, toss in your cabbage, onions, sugar and season with salt and pepper. Depending on the size of your pan, you might want to add 1/3 cabbage and onions at a time until they soften. Cook until glazed brown.

Serve warm alongside a basket of Delaney's cornbread.

Talk about southern comfort food, this is it! For a truly genuine southern treat, use oil instead of butter and fry a few strips of bacon in the pan, first. Fry them up until they're toasty brown and then break into smaller pieces. Or how about skip the bacon and simply use your bacon fat for frying? Another variation includes substituting squash for cabbage.

About the Author:

Dianne Venetta lives in Central Florida with her husband, two children and part-time Yellow Lab Cody-boy! An avid gardener, she spends her spare time growing organic vegetables, surprised by what she finds there every day. Who knew there were so many amazing similarities between men and plants? Women, life and love and her discoveries along the way provide for never-ending fun on her garden blog: BloominThyme.com.

You can also find her on twitter @DianneVenetta and facebook.com/DianneVenetta. Plus, learn how you can become a member of her street team, Bloomin' Warriors, where you'll be eligible for special discounts, advance excerpts, author swag and unique gift items throughout the year. For full details, be sure to check out her website, DianneVenetta.com.

Other novels by Dianne Venetta:
Romantic Women's Fiction
The Gables Trilogy:
JENNIFER'S GARDEN
LUST ON THE ROCKS
WHISPER PRIVILEGES

Women's Fiction
CONDEMN ME NOT

Mystery/Romance Fiction
Ladd Springs Series:
LADD SPRINGS #1
LADD FORTUNE #2
HOTEL LADD #3
LADD HAVEN #4
LOSING LADD #5